DATE DUE MAY 05

6-16-0			
7/21/5			
GAYLORD			PRINTED IN U.S.A.

TEXAS
MAVERICK

**Center Point
Large Print**

**This Large Print Book carries the
Seal of Approval of N.A.V.H.**

TEXAS MAVERICK

HASCAL GILES

**CENTER POINT PUBLISHING
THORNDIKE, MAINE**

This Center Point Large Print edition
is published in the year 2005 by arrangement with
Golden West Literary Agency.

The text of this Large Print edition is unabridged. In other
aspects, this book may vary from the original edition. Printed in
Thailand. Set in 16-point Times New Roman type.

ISBN 1-58547-554-8

Library of Congress Cataloging-in-Publication Data

Giles, Hascal.
    Texas maverick / Hascal Giles.--Center Point large print ed.
        p. cm.
    ISBN 1-58547-554-8 (lib. bdg. : alk. paper)
    1. Texas--Fiction. 2. Large type books. I. Title.

PS3557.I3443T493 2005
813'.54--dc22

                                                                    2004018836

Chapter One

As his horse topped a timbered ridge where he could look down on the ragged assemblage of weatherbeaten buildings which lined Jackpine's Main Street, Smoke Wylie felt apprehensive, no longer sure he should be there.

He drew his bay gelding to a halt and looked down from the ridge at the traffic moving along the streets of the town, still half a mile away. He hooked a leg around the horn of the saddle and rolled a cigarette, a sun-darkened man with a whimsical twist to his mouth and a shade of worry lurking behind his lead-gray eyes. He puffed the cigarette alive and, in the manner of men who spent much of their time alone on the range, spoke aloud of his growing misgivings.

"This might be the most damn-fool thing I've ever done," he murmured. "Things can't get much worse, though, so I'll do what I came for."

The bay twitched its ears at the sound of Smoke's voice and stamped restlessly. Smoke chuckled. "Not your problem, huh?"

Finishing his cigarette, he crushed the fire out against the saddle horn and tossed the crumbling remains aside. Out of habit he tugged at the buckle of the studded shell belt which held his walnut-handled Colt and started to remove the holstered weapon. His jaw tightened and he dropped his hands away, leaving the gun anchored low on his right thigh.

In that instant he almost decided against pushing his

luck too far. Because of an old quarrel, his father had forbidden him to wear a gun in town, but this was the day, Smoke told himself, that he would take control of his own life.

That was easier said than done, and he might be going about it the wrong way, but he did not know any other way. After a restless night of reflecting on old grudges, he had ridden away from his section of the Pitchfork roundup shortly after breakfast. One of his father's rules was that a member of the family always worked with his men at the start of roundup, and Smoke had broken it. Wearing his gun was another infraction, and it was dangerous to defy Nate Wylie—as risky for one of his sons as for anyone else.

If word of his trip to town got back to the Pitchfork, it was sure to sharpen the tension which seemed to hang forever between him and his father. The shirking of duties and the flouting of a gun would become minor points in an ear-shattering argument, however, when Nate Wylie learned the purpose of Smoke's ride to Jackpine.

After resting a few more minutes, Smoke pushed his doubts aside. Squaring his shoulders, he nudged the bay down the last slope toward the level plain which led into Jackpine. He continued to study the town, his eyes squinted against the glare of the chalky alkali of the streets. The sun was past its midday zenith, and Smoke felt uneasy because he had used up so much time.

Puffs of dust, wafting upward from striking hooves like tiny smoke signals, drew his attention to two horsemen moving along the street. He watched them tie their horses at the rail in front of the Great Western Saloon, and a wry smile tugged at his lips. They were dressed in range garb, similar to the faded Levi's and wide-brimmed Stetson worn by Smoke, and it gave him some comfort to know he was not the only working cowhand taking time off.

Even at this distance the clear Texas air allowed Smoke a good estimate of their size and appearance. One of the riders was an exceedingly tall man, so thin he looked almost frail. He strode across the boardwalk with a quick, fluid grace despite the awkward tilt of his stirrup-heeled boots. The other man, who kept a step behind like an attending servant, was a head shorter than his companion, his thick shoulders tapering to a narrow waist. Smoke dismissed them from his thoughts as soon as they disappeared through the batwing doors of the saloon, but he did not miss the glint of sunlight on the guns they carried.

As the horse picked its way down the slope, Smoke's gaze moved farther along the street and centered on the tall clapboard front of the Pioneer House Hotel a moment, then swung toward the jail, which was diagonally across the street from the Great Western Saloon. He spotted the familiar shape of Marshal Ben Toler. The marshal was only a shadow in the shade of the wooden awning which jutted out over the boardwalk, but Smoke knew enough of Ben's habits to visualize his position. Ben would be sitting with his chair tilted against the log wall of the jail, a keen-bladed knife skimming over a cedar stick, piling up shavings around his feet while he kept an eye on the street.

Smoke had viewed this scene from the ridge many times. It usually held little interest for him, but it seemed important to him on this day to know the lay of the land before he rode into town. He saw Ben Toler stir briefly, half-rising to peer at the horses in front of the Great Western. Apparently the lawman was studying the brands on the horses, and this was an indication the two riders were strangers in Jackpine. Otherwise, Smoke knew, Ben Toler would not have interrupted his whittling to stare at ordinary cowhands.

For the next twenty minutes, after reaching the level plain, Smoke lost his view of the town, except for the uneven silhouette of sun-bleached buildings outlined against the sky. The trail Smoke followed came into town from the east, turned into a meandering little residential road, and finally made a right-angle intersection with Main Street. He saw a few women sweeping dust from their porches or hanging out laundry. Most of them turned their heads away at sight of the stocky, dark-haired man on the bay gelding. Smoke smiled to himself. His reputation for associating with women of dubious morals was no secret in Jackpine, and he guessed that many of the town's housewives regarded his habits as less than respectable.

Their disapproval would be intensified in a few minutes if they watched him long enough to see him turn his horse toward the Great Western. Ned Arnold, the proprietor, was known to allow three or four professional girls to keep rooms on the saloon's second floor. Smoke meant to make only a brief stop there, just long enough to brace himself with one drink before he told the lawyer

John Bastrop he was thinking about breaking up his father's giant Pitchfork Ranch.

Smoke needed that drink even more before he reached the saloon. By the time he turned the corner beside Matt Stacy's blacksmith shop and came into Main Street, he was holding the bay to a slow walk. He had expected to finish his ride along a quiet, almost-deserted path that gave Jackpine the appearance of a ghost town on most weekdays, but such was not the case. A flurry of activity on the boardwalk about fifty yards away distracted him and Smoke was puzzled by what he saw.

He drew his horse to a halt and sat staring at the scene ahead, his hands folded on the pommel, his brow furrowed with curiosity. The three people gathered in front of Swain's Gun Shop, across the street from the Great Western, were moving about in jerky steps as though engaged in an unrehearsed dance. Then Smoke saw the reason for their strange behavior, and anger flickered in the lead-gray eyes beneath the shadow of his hat brim.

One of the trio was a young woman who was trying to get around two men who were blocking her path. The men had their backs to him, but their shape and size told Smoke they were the same two riders he had seen enter the Great Western Saloon while he was resting his horse on the ridge.

As Smoke watched, the tall, frail-looking man swept off his dusty black Stetson in an exaggerated bow and rasped out some sort of greeting which came to Smoke as a murmur. Apparently surprised, the woman backed away a step. She moved sideways, shuffled her feet in indecision, then her chin tilted upward and she made a determined effort to slip between the two grinning men. The shorter of the men, the big-shouldered cowboy with the waspish waist, grabbed her right hand and yanked her toward him. From the other side, the tall man slid a bony arm around her waist, holding her still.

A knot of muscle ridged along Smoke's jaw and he felt the pressure of his teeth clenching together. He straightened in the saddle and started to move the horse forward, then hesitated. He looked toward the jail. Marshal Ben Toler was still there. The lawman rose half out of his chair and remained in a crouch momentarily while he studied the activity in front of the gun shop, then sat down again and resumed his whittling.

Smoke relaxed, feeling a sense of relief when he saw that Ben Toler was watching. From the lawman's lack of interest, the scuffle must not have been as unusual as Smoke thought. Ben was often reluctant, however, to become involved in any situation that might resolve itself, and Smoke was not sure the lawman would regard a man's advances toward a pretty woman as worthy of his attention.

While he gazed at the lawman, Smoke could see from the edge of his vision that the struggle on the boardwalk was continuing. A small, flowered handbag dangled by its drawstrings from the woman's free hand, and she tried to swing it against the tall man's face. As she fought back, the man's arm tightened around her waist and she could not manage enough freedom to land the blow.

On that side of the street there were no buildings between Swain's Gun Shop and Ed Jarvis's General

Store, which was fifty yards closer to Smoke's position. The vacant lot was overgrown with weeds and waist-high sage, offering a few bare spots where children played Indian games and stray dogs bedded down. The tall man swiveled his head around, scanning the street, and made his decision. He stepped off the boardwalk, signaling his companion with a toss of his head, and they started toward the brushy area.

There was no outcry from the woman, but she fought them fiercely, trying to free herself from the man's grasp. She made no progress until she started hopping along on one foot, kicking with the other. The toe of her shoe finally struck the shorter man on the kneecap and he released her hand. Quickly, she whirled her body away from the tall cowboy, and his encircling arm was uncoiled. She tried to run, but the tall man was too fast for her. She had taken only a step when his hand clamped down on her shoulder. His fingers caught the inside of her dress collar. As he yanked her toward him, the blue-checked gingham dress tore away, baring one full, gleaming white breast to the mid-afternoon sun.

The ripping cloth freed her momentarily and again she attempted to run, but this time the stocky cowboy grabbed her. As he held her in a half-embrace the tall man laughed hoarsely and reached a cupped hand toward the naked breast.

A yowl of pain and a curse followed the move and the tall man straightened in surprise. The woman's teeth had snapped at the hand as it passed her face, and the tall man lost a sliver of skin as he pulled away.

Anger jerked at the rawboned shoulders and the tall

man laughed again, like a child enjoying a rough game. Ignoring her flailing fists, he pushed himself against her and wrapped both arms around her in a bear hug. He moved so suddenly that one elbow caught his friend in the mouth, staggering him and loosening the shorter man's hold on the woman.

She was beginning to tire, and the tall cowboy moved farther into the brush and weeds with her. His companion had dropped a half step behind, strolling almost nonchalantly as he watched the woman dig her heels into the ground, bracing and squirming and moaning softly.

It required all the self-control Smoke could muster to remain still while the men tugged and pawed at the slender, shapely woman. His eyes kept flicking from the trio on the boardwalk to Marshal Ben Toler, and back again. The lawman stayed where he was, and Smoke took that as a cue not to interfere.

For a while Smoke concluded that Ben knew the people involved and that the scuffle amounted to little more than a couple of cowboys teasing one of the girls from the saloon. They came closer to him as they moved into the vacant lot and Smoke knew the men were not joking. He had a clear view of the woman's face—a strikingly beautiful face with full red lips and creamy skin—framed by hair so black the sun struck blue lights from it. She was not one of the saloon girls. Smoke was acquainted with all of them.

Her identity did not matter. The two strangers meant to take their pleasure with her against her will, and even a saloon girl deserved better treatment. Smoke cast one final look toward Ben Toler, scowled, and kicked the bay into a gallop. While he was still some distance away, he yelled, "Hold up, strangers! That's a lopsided match you've got going there. Turn the woman loose."

By the time the words were out of his mouth he was drawing to a halt at the edge of the field. He swung out of the saddle, dropping the split reins to the ground so the horse would remain in place. Two long strides carried him across the boardwalk and into the tangled weeds, a mixture of anger and anxiety in his face.

The shorter man looked around first- -a youthful, even-featured man with deep dimples in his cheeks and a cleft chin. "Somebody's hollerin' at you, Jesse," he said.

"Dammit, I hear him, Chub!" Jesse shouted. "Get rid of him!"

Chub shifted his grip on the woman's arm. "You're the gunhand, Jesse," he said uneasily. "You get rid of him. He looks like he's ready to stomp on somebody."

Still clinging to the girl with one arm, Jesse turned to face Smoke Wylie. He was a tall, emaciated man in a hide vest, trail-worn Levi's, and run-over boots. His small black eyes were set close together alongside a sharp nose, and they were gleaming with desire. He wore an ivory-handled Colt holstered waist-high on his right side, and he looked like a man who knew how to use it.

Jesse slung the woman around, using her as a shield, and snapped, "Stay out of this, cowboy. It's personal."

Smoke kept moving toward them, the thumb of his right hand hooked in the waistband of his Levi's. The

13

tips of his fingers were only a few inches above the walnut-butted Colt tied low in an oiled holster. The two men in the field halted again. Both of them turned to look at Smoke, and Chub yelled, "This is none of your business, cowboy."

Less than thirty feet separated Smoke from the trio. He could see doubt and a trace of fear in Chub's handsome face, but the man called Jesse was not afraid. He mouthed a string of curses, angered by the interruption.

"What are you trying to do, mister—prove that two men can hold down one woman?" Smoke's gaze could not ignore the rounded breast exposed by the woman's torn dress, but his question was whipped out like a slap in the face.

A moist smile spread across Jesse's face, but there was no humor in it. He chewed absently on a wooden matchstick, bobbing it up and down between his lips. He splintered the stick between his teeth, bending it into a V with his tongue, then spat it angrily to the ground.

"Why are you hombres shoving a girl around who isn't even half your size?" Smoke growled.

"Well, now," Jesse drawled in mock humility, "the reason is this. We aim to take her back here in the bushes and have a tumble with her. We've got a real craving for a woman and she ain't going to mind once we get started. You can have your turn too, if you'll just shut up about it."

Smoke stopped walking, his muscles taut. His senses were keen and alert. His nerves hummed with tension and his smoky gray eyes pried at Jesse's face as though nothing else existed in the world, yet Smoke was conscious of all the sights and sounds around him. Insects buzzed in the weeds around his feet and the greasy odor of frying potatoes filtered in from the direction of the hotel kitchen. He could feel sweat trickling from beneath the band of his Stetson and danger radiating from the fury in Jesse's black eyes.

"Don't push me, cowboy," Jesse warned.

A yapping dog ran by a few feet behind Smoke, but it did not distract him. He continued to glare at the tall, lean Jesse, challenging him. Smoke was little more than half the man's age and five inches shorter, but he looked bigger. Corded muscles broadened his shoulders and rounded his neck, rippling beneath his shirt with every move of his body.

"Let her go!" said Smoke. For a moment the vacant field was frozen in stillness, then there was furious movement. Realizing Jesse's full attention was focused on Smoke, the woman made her break. She slumped to the ground, and the sudden surge of her weight pulled her free of Jesse's grasp. She rolled quickly away, making a thrashing sound in the weeds. Chub started toward her, and it was then that Jesse went for his gun.

A twitch of Jesse's elbow gave him away. Smoke saw gunsmoke, and heard the echo of an exploding shell. Smoke's bullet tore into Jesse's right thigh just below the scarred holster. The impact of the slug whirled Jesse around before the sight of his gun cleared leather. Such were his instincts that Smoke was hardly aware he had drawn and fired the Colt until he saw the wisp of blue smoke curling up from his hand.

Jesse lay writhing on the ground, his face twisted in

15

pain. Blood oozed between his fingers as he clutched at the torn leg, but he did not cry out.

The woman was already on her feet and running toward the street by the time Smoke swung his gun toward Chub. The stocky cowboy lifted his hands and shouted, "I'm out of it! Don't shoot me!"

Smoke motioned toward the street with the gun barrel. "Fetch his horse, then both of you ride out of here."

"Hold it," Jesse grunted. He ripped the red neckerchief from around his collar and tied it over the leg wound to slow the bleeding. He struggled to his feet, then scooped up his gun from the ground and shoved it into his holster.

"I can get my own horse," Jesse said. He hobbled closer to Chub, grimacing, and put his arm across the shorter man's shoulder for support.

As they shuffled away Smoke turned so they would not be at his back, still holding the gun in his hand. At the edge of the boardwalk Jesse slowed and looked over his shoulder. "You shouldn't have shot me in the leg, mister," he said grimly. "You should've shot me between the eyes, because I'll be back to see you and that's where I'm going to shoot you."

A hint of worry clouded Smoke's eyes. "No reason to come back," he said. "It's over as far as I'm concerned."

Hate overpowered the pain in Jesse's face. "I'll be back," he repeated.

Smoke did not reply. He dangled the Colt on his forefinger for a few seconds, then, with a sigh of resignation, dropped it back in its holster. The excitement of the gunfight died quickly within him, and he was already worried about his father's reaction when he heard about the shooting.

Chapter Two

Voices buzzed around him, disrupting his thoughts, and Smoke started toward the boardwalk with a sinking feeling in his stomach. The sound of gunfire had attracted a crowd from among the few people who were in town, and they were babbling among themselves as they gathered at the edge of the field.

Far back in the group a voice said, "That hombre is some kind of a horse with a six-gun. I saw the whole ruckus and I mean to tell you he's fast!"

There was movement in the crowd as Marshal Ben Toler pushed his way through to confront Smoke. Sweat ran in shiny rivulets along the deep creases beside the marshal's tight lips. There was a stony glint in his china-blue eyes, but the anger in his face did not show in the quiet nasal drawl when he spoke.

"There's goin' to be hell to pay for this, Smoke," Ben Toler said. "Comin' in packin' a gun and shootin' people up. That's twice in about a year you've shot a man. You ain't supposed to be packin' a gun in town and you know it. Your pa told you that and he told me to make it stick. Now Nate's spurs are going to be diggin' in your back and mine too. I ain't got the stomach for this no more."

Smoke took a deep breath and let it out slowly. He did not want the disgust he felt toward Marshal Ben Toler to become evident. Years ago, at a time Smoke could barely remember, Ben Toler had been the ramrod at Nate Wylie's Pitchfork Ranch, and there was a strong bond between Nate and the marshal that Smoke had never quite understood.

"If I had listened to you and Pa I might be lying over in that field dead," he said. "That Jesse hombre meant to fight anyone who tried to take the woman away from him and he meant to do it with a gun. Why in hell did you just sit there and let them have their way?"

Ben Toler's chin dropped almost to his chest and his gaze darted from side to side. The small knot of people was still at his back and he did not like the fact that others had heard Smoke's accusing question. He was a hard-muscled man with the sloping shoulders so typical of those who spend too many years clutching the reins of a horse while peering between its ears at whatever trail lay ahead. Slowly, Ben Toler turned his head and glared at the lingering spectators. He stayed that way until feet began to shift uncomfortably and the crowd scattered.

"Where the hell were you, Ben?" Smoke asked again.

"I was watchin'," Toler said. "It wasn't worth shootin' somebody. I've known women to spend a whole summer or a whole year in a cabin by themselves, miles from nowhere, when their men were on roundup or trailin' cattle to market. Except for Indians, I've never heard of a man in the West forcin' his way with a decent woman, but when they come sashayin' along like they're askin' for a man, they usually get one. A man can spot the kind to take his pleasure with."

Smoke took a step forward, his hat brim almost

touching the marshal's sweat-faded Stetson. "That's pure sheep-dip. I wouldn't call those two saddle bums men. They're more like animals—trail-starved animals. If you're so good at sizing up things you ought to know that. She looked like a decent enough woman to me, not more than nineteen or twenty. She didn't have the look of a woman who can be bought, and I figure I know something about women. You were going to sit on your bottom and let them take her like a couple of rutting elk on a mating spree."

"Nothin' would have happened," the marshal said. "I would have been over here before it got that far."

"Like hell," Smoke snorted, and started toward his horse. He studied the street thoughtfully. "I saw her go into the Pioneer House. I think I'll walk down there and see if she's all right."

He had taken only a couple of steps when Toler said quietly, "I want your gun."

A fiery light danced in Smoke's eyes and his face was a shade darker as he came back toward the marshal. He planted his hands on his hips and squared his shoulders.

"I'm not going to give up my gun," Smoke said, "and I don't believe you're going to try to take it."

"I promised Nate I'd take up your gun if you came in again with it. Are you goin' to shoot me too?"

"No, but you'll have to shoot me to get this gun," Smoke said evenly. "I'll bust you up with my fists if you reach for it."

Their eyes met and held and there was no fear in either of them. Ben Toler was pushing fifty, but he had been hardened by blistering summers and bone-chilling win-

19

ters, years of wrestling steers and taming wild broncs. There was many a barroom brawl and trail-town face-down in his past. He had lost none of his toughness, but he knew the Wylies, and there was no back-down in any of them—particularly Smoke. He had watched Smoke grow from a quiet, morose child into a rugged, hard-muscled man with a quick smile, a quick temper, and a strange sadness that seemed to lurk always behind those lead-gray eyes.

Finally the marshal shrugged, but his stern expression did not relax. He said, "I'll let it go. It's too late now, anyway. But stay away from the hotel. Don't get mixed up any deeper. The girl's got folks down there, her ma and pa, I think. They showed up in a wagon two days ago. She came in on the stage last night. She'll be all right. You've got enough to deal with when Nate hears about the shootin'."

A look of concern showed in Smoke's face. "Are you going to tell him?"

"I won't have to. I saw Preacher Pardee nosin' around among the folks who came to see what the shootin' was about. Him and Nate bein' thick like they are, the preacher is probably on his way to the Pitchfork by now. It might go better for you at home if you'd give me the gun."

Smoke shook his head. "We might as well get things straight. Nate may lord it over everybody else on this range, but it's come to an end with me. I don't aim to be treated like a loco kid anymore. Ever since I was ten years old I've been wearing a gun out on the range. Nate's the one who started me doing that so I wouldn't get bit by rattlers or mauled by cougars. I've found out there are rattlers and cougars everywhere. Don't worry about any more trouble from me today. We're in the middle of our roundup and I'm supposed to be gathering cattle, but I needed to check on something with our lawyer. After I talk with John Bastrop I'll be heading back to the roundup camp."

The sun had tracked midway toward the western horizon and its searing heat was bouncing back from the matted weeds in the field. A buckboard clattered by and turned toward Ed Jarvis's General Store, the horses throwing up dust as they braced their feet to slow the wagon. From the corner of his eye Smoke saw the Widow Lovelace, who kept a sewing shop in her big white house at the end of the street. She paused briefly on the boardwalk near them, then hurried on. She had been curious, Smoke could tell by the way she kept looking back at them, and he hoped she would not guess the nature of their conversation.

"You've got a notion that Nate's makin' rules to punish you, but that ain't it," Ben Toler said after a moment. "He knows not many people throw down on an unarmed man. A couple of gunfights might not get you a reputation, but it could. There's a lot of talk around here about the way you handle a gun. Nate's afraid too much talk will bring in gunslingers who want to prove they're better than you. He likes his ranch and his cattle, but you and Gil are what he lives for. He's had enough put on him at times to worry the horns off a bull without a trouble-makin' son to bring him more grief."

Smoke gave the marshal a hard stare. "This probably

won't surprise you much," he said, "but I don't care how much grief I cause Nate. He's sure handed me plenty of it. He could have more than sons. He could have a complete family—Gil and me, and our mother. I'm sure Nate ran my mother off by being too hard on her—just like he's going to run me off. You were there, Ben. You know about that."

The marshal sighed and looked down at his boots. He said, "I don't know much about it. I was Nate's ramrod and that's all. I didn't mind other people's business then and I don't now."

Smoke whirled angrily and walked toward his horse, feeling the need to defy the marshal. "What's the woman's name?"

"Stay away from the hotel. You're just goin' to cause more trouble. I don't know her name. I just saw her come in and the stage driver told me she was meetin' her folks here. I figured it had to be the couple with the wagon, them bein' the only strangers at the hotel."

"Don't you ever ask old Henry Bain about strangers who check in at the hotel? It seems to me you'd be wise to keep an eye on these outsiders who keep coming in."

Another sigh escaped Ben Toler's lips. "I try to keep the streets safe and people from killin' each other. Aside from that I listen to complaints from the townfolks, lock up rowdy drunks, and mind my own business."

Smoke gave the marshal a skeptical smile as he swung into the bay's saddle. "Yeah, I noticed, Ben. I noticed you're keeping the streets safe."

Turning the horse with a tug of the reins, he sat staring a moment toward the Pioneer House Hotel. Then he changed direction and sent the horse cantering up the street to the hitching rail at the Great Western Saloon.

Smoke walked slowly as he pushed through the batwing doors. He stopped briefly while his eyes adjusted to the dim light inside the saloon, then moved on to the far end of the bar. With the rooms above providing insulation, it was considerably cooler there than on the street. The sweet-sour odor of the sawdust floor, mingled with tobacco smoke, sweat, and spilled whiskey, was a pleasant change from the drifting dust outside.

He asked for whiskey and swung his glance around the room while Ned Arnold filled his glass. Matt Stacy, thick-shouldered and heavily muscled from his years at the anvil, was nursing a drink at the other end of the bar. Next to him stood Ed Jarvis, the slender, pale-faced owner of the General Store. They had been watching Smoke, but shifted their attention to their drinks when he looked toward them.

The only other customers in the bar were two cowboys seated at a table near the front window. Smoke did not know them, but remembered seeing them among the crowd which had been attracted by the shooting. From their gestures, and the speculative look one of them gave him, he surmised that they were still discussing it.

Ned Arnold, his round, flat-nosed face solemn and flushed from the heat, leaned forward and spoke quietly. "Are you all right?"

"I guess so." Smoke looked shaken. "I seem to get mixed up in every scrap of trouble that comes down the road. Where did those hombres come from, Ned? What kind of hardcases are you letting hang out in your bar these days?"

The saloon man rubbed his pudgy hands across the front of his stained white apron. "They say they're with a trail herd coming through on the cutoff. I don't know who's ramrodding the outfit, but he's bossing one wild bunch of drovers."

His high-pitched voice strained with exasperation, Ned Arnold told Smoke what he had heard from the cowboys who had drifted in and out of the Great Western during the last two days.

From passing the time with the drovers, Ned had learned they were moving a herd of cattle northward to the Colorado range. Their outfit was the Triangle T, out of south Texas, and thirty days on the trail had brought them only as far as the rolling hills country around Jackpine.

The Triangle T had swung westward off the Chisholm, taking the cutoff to pick up the Goodnight-Loving Trace which would lead them to Colorado. In earlier days, before the Comanches were pushed onto reservations farther north, they would have traveled southward first to avoid raiding parties, then northward through the deserts of New Mexico Territory. It was only after the danger of Indian attacks had been reduced that the herds had come this way. The shorter route had brought additional business to Jackpine, but with the new prosperity had come more strangers and more trouble.

The vastness of the land had begun to take its toll on men and animals, and the Triangle T trail boss had decided to rest the herd for a few days to allow the cattle to recoup some of their weight loss. Their camp was only a two-hour ride west of Jackpine, and the cowboys were permitted to come into town a few at a time to relieve their boredom.

"I ain't had nothing but aggravation from that bunch all week," Ned concluded.

"Then mine wasn't the first hassle?" Smoke asked.

"Not by a long shot. It's been right hairy around here. The first two to come in weren't half bad. They played a little poker, sat around and drank some, and then rode away. Later on, the hardcases started. Three of them came in together, loud, foul-mouthed, and in a helling mood. They started a brawl at the poker table. Hank DeKalb, my old swamper, ain't got half-sense and he tried to break it up. They almost stomped his guts out. Knocked him around pretty bad. He's still laid up in his cot in the back room. After they left, a big fat geezer with a mouth full of gold teeth beat hell out of one of my girls upstairs. Claimed she didn't show any spirit in bed. Said he didn't get his money's worth from her."

Smoke's eyes narrowed. He took a long sip from his drink. "I don't like people who beat up on women, Ned. I'm glad I wasn't around when it happened."

Ned Arnold poured himself a small drink and gulped it down. "I'm glad you were here today. Maybe that bunch will stay out of town for a while. The two you tangled with was the worst of the lot, especially that tall drink of water called Jesse. Chub just walks around in his partner's shadow, I think, but Jesse griped about his drinks and everything else that caught his eye. He said

25

he once shot off a barkeep's ear for selling him bad whiskey. He never took his eyes off me until that good-looking girl came along. He just stood there drinking and chewing on matches. He'd break them into little V shapes with his teeth and spit them across the bar at me. I was afraid of that man."

Smoke shook his head. "Why did he go after the girl the way he did? He could have got him a woman right here."

"Not today," Ned Arnold said. "After Lorene got beat up, the girls scattered to rooms all over town. They don't come around now until after dark, after they know there ain't no Triangle T riders in town. Jesse and Chub went sort of crazy when I told them there wasn't any women in the place. They were getting ready to bust up the place, then they saw that pretty woman coming down from the Pioneer House, and said she'd do fine. She is some kind of woman—just about the most beautiful human being I've ever seen!"

"Maybe the prettiest anybody's ever seen," Smoke agreed, recalling his few quick glimpses of the shapely figure, the full lips blazing against tawny skin. "She's one stranger who ought to be welcome here."

Washing out the glass he had been using, Ned set it aside and changed the subject. "Nate went on a tear about the last shooting you was mixed up in. What's he going to say about this ruckus?"

Smoke chuckled drily. "Things you wouldn't want to hear. Things I don't want to hear either."

The saloon man frowned. "Something tells me you ain't even supposed to be in town. You told me last week

26

the Pitchfork was starting roundup. What brought you to Jackpine?"

Smoke's chin lifted. "You've always had a habit of minding your own business, Ned. A man shouldn't break a good habit."

Ned Arnold's face colored and he opened his mouth to mumble an apology, but Smoke was already turning away. He picked up his glass and walked to the nearest table to finish his drink.

Smoke was stalling for time, postponing the completion of his business in town. He had been drawn into a fight he did not expect and did not want, and it had complicated his plans. It had taken him all night, tossing restlessly on his blankets at the roundup camp, to make up his mind to have a talk with Lawyer John Bastrop about his rights at the Pitchfork. Now he was not sure it was a good time to force a showdown with his father.

Ned Arnold's reminder that today was not the first time Smoke had been involved in gunplay had added to his indecision. A year ago Smoke had shot a drifting gambler through the shoulder during a poker game at the Great Western.

He had not been playing, but he had watched as the game progressed. In the game were Matt Stacy, Ed Jarvis, one of the riders from Jerry Mead's spread, and a drifter who had ridden into Jackpine looking for work. Smoke knew little of the others, but he knew Matt and Ed had lost more than they could afford—or should.

He had kept his eyes on the gambler, a soft-talking man in black broadcloth who called himself Mason Jordan. When the gambler started to rake in the biggest pot of the evening, Smoke said, "Don't let him have the money, boys. He's cheating you. Every time he fiddles with that fancy watch chain on his vest he palms a card he needs."

The gambler wasted no time with protests. "That'll get you killed, friend," he snapped, and his right hand was moving all the time, darting inside his frock coat for a hidden gun.

Smoke's move was so fast the other players did not see him draw his gun, but they heard the shot. The gambler flipped backwards to the floor, his hand still inside his coat. Ben Toler found an old Philadelphia derringer in the gambler's pocket when he came in to inquire about the gunfire. The marshal heard the details from the others at the table and found no fault with Smoke's action. It was the next day that Nate Wylie made one of his rare appearances in Jackpine and issued his ultimatum about Smoke carrying a gun.

Although the discussion was held in Ben Toler's office at the jail, Nate's booming bullhorn voice had carried out on the streets and half the town had heard him. Among those listeners was Ned Arnold, and it was not long before he told Smoke the details of the conversation. He had already warned Smoke, Nate declared that day, and now he was warning the marshal. If Ben Toler valued his job and his hide, he was never to let Smoke Wylie walk the streets of Jackpine with a gun on his thigh.

Smoke had obeyed his father's order until today, but he had never lived easily with the embarrassment of it. Each time he came to town he felt his blood warm and his face burn when he saw covert glances inspecting his waist, followed by sly grins when the onlookers noticed he was without a gun belt.

His resentment toward his father had festered like a sore inside Smoke. He was unhappy with his life, and had decided during the night he would try to change it.

Deep in thought, Smoke was not aware that Matt Stacy and Ed Jarvis had left their place at the bar until he saw them standing across the table in front of him. Matt was brushing a meaty palm through his tousled red hair and Ed Jarvis had his hands jammed into the pockets of his moleskin pants, his watery brown eyes blinking nervously. They both looked ill at ease.

"That was a good thing you did out there," Matt said. "I felt real sorry for that girl, but I didn't know what to do."

"I guess you think we're a couple of cowards, just standing in here and watching while she was about to be raped," Ed Jarvis murmured.

Smoke smiled reassuringly. "Don't let it bother you. I don't think you're cowards. A man ought to give some thought to how he wants to die and what he wants to die for. That Jesse hombre wouldn't mind killing you to get what he was after."

Matt Stacy's big blacksmith arms dropped limply to his sides. "I'd take pleasure in buying you a drink, Smoke."

"I'll pass on it, Matt." Smoke pushed his empty glass aside and stood up. "I'd better do what I came to do, then get back to the cow business."

Turning, he lifted an open hand toward Ned Arnold in

farewell, hoping the gesture would indicate he no longer felt offended by the saloon man's earlier questions, then he went outside, a step behind the two townsmen. He climbed aboard the bay and rode up the street toward Lawyer John Bastrop's office.

Chapter Three

As he walked away from the vacant lot after the gunfight, Marshal Ben Toler felt like his steps were slowed by unseen weights. There was also a heavy feeling in his chest as he reflected on his encounter with Smoke Wylie. Their words had revived old memories that were not things Ben liked to think about.

Following any difficulty in Jackpine, it was the marshal's custom to record the details in a journal kept in his office. He was a thorough, dedicated man in all that he did, and if questions should arise he wanted to have the answers at hand.

Ben's nerves were raw. He felt the need for a drink, but when he saw Smoke Wylie heading for the Great Western, he pushed aside the urge and went on to the jail. He was unusually cautious and tense around Smoke these days and his discomfort annoyed him.

Inside the stuffy office, Ben cleared a space on the rolltop desk, dipped a pen in the inkwell, and began writing. He wrote slowly, taking particular care in recording the details of the shooting incident involving Smoke Wylie.

After a while he pushed the journal aside. He stretched his legs beneath the desk and sat staring at the sunlit street outside, thinking about the shooting. Nate Wylie would, at some time or another, give Ben a tongue-lashing for not taking away Smoke's gun. He dreaded to face it, but he owed his job to Nate, so he would hold his temper and accept the rancher's criticism.

The outcome of the gunfight did not disturb him. The man who had been shot for mistreating the girl was the kind of hardcase Ben despised. Men such as Jesse knew the West well and they feasted off its weaknesses. When they saw something they wanted they took it by force—another man's beef, clothes off a line, or a woman's body. They ran roughshod over the weak with little fear of reprisal because much of the land was still sparsely settled and men who wore badges were often hundreds of miles apart. Only occasionally did the hardcases find someone strong enough to stand up against them. Jesse had met such a man today—Smoke Wylie. Ben was not sorry Smoke had put a bullet in the man's leg.

As a matter of fact, Ben thought, Smoke might have done him a favor. Ben had kept his eye on the trio in the vacant lot. He had every intention of putting a stop to the struggle before the men could drag the girl out of sight, but he kept hoping she could free herself so his intervention would not be necessary. He could not find her without fault in the incident. He had seen her walking along the street, her thrusting breasts straining against the buttons of her gingham dress, and he could not believe her swaying, rhythmic stride was completely natural. The way she moved her body seemed deliberately contrived to entice a man.

It was not the shooting which made him want to sit

alone and try to shake off a nagging sense of dread. It was Smoke's bitter reference to Ben's presence at the ranch when Nate Wylie's wife left that stuck in his mind.

The subject had come up in a casual way at other times, when there was no tension between them, and usually while they were sharing a drink at the Great Western. Ben had suspected for a long time that Smoke believed the marshal knew more about his mother than Ben was willing to tell. During the four years since he had returned to Jackpine after a ten-year absence, the marshal had tried to avoid the subject, but Smoke was always leading him to it—prying, pressing, and flying into a rage when Ben answered virtually every question with a simple, "I don't know."

Once, in an unguarded moment at the Great Western, Ben made the mistake of saying, "I can't tell you that."

Smoke's mind was too quick to miss the slip of the tongue. He had asked when Ben had last seen Cora Wylie, and the reply was a certain giveaway. Smoke expected the marshal to say he had last seen Cora at the ranch, but Ben's response was an indication that he had seen her somewhere else since she left the Pitchfork.

By the time the words were out of his mouth Smoke was flying across the table at him, his hands reaching for Ben Toler's throat. Angry accusations of lies and betrayal gushed from Smoke's mouth.

"You slippery, lying old lapdog!" Smoke shouted. "You had a hand in helping Nate run her away! I know damn well you've been hiding something from me."

As tables and chairs splintered beneath them, Ben felt Smoke's fingers clamping around his throat. He tried to squirm away, but he was no match for Smoke's size and strength. Ned Arnold and two other men grabbed Smoke and pulled him away. He let them get him to his feet, then flung them aside with a swing of his arms. Before they could recover their balance, Smoke's gun swung up and Ben thought he was going to die.

"For God's sake, Smoke!" Ned Arnold yelled, but Smoke did not look at him. He kept the gun pointed at the marshal's head for a full minute, his chest heaving and his arms shaking, then he lowered the gun slowly to his side. Suddenly he grinned, slammed the gun into its holster, and reached down to help Ben Toler to his feet.

"You ought to lock me up for being a damn fool," he said sheepishly. "Pa would want you to do that and I won't put up a fuss if you do."

Ben Toler dusted himself off and shook his head. "Not tonight. We'll let it pass. I know how you feel."

Smoke shrugged and held out his hand. "No hard feelings?"

Ben shook his hand. "No hard feelin's."

There was not much Ben Toler could tell that would give Smoke Wylie any comfort. At Nate's insistence he had sworn never to discuss Cora Wylie with anyone. It was generally believed around Jackpine that she'd simply tired of the West and gone home to live with her folks—a story that Ben suspected had been planted among friends by Nate Wylie. Ben did not want to break his word, but he knew Smoke would not rest until he knew all there was to know about his mother.

He pushed back his hat and rubbed the sweat from his face with his pocket bandanna. He wondered what had brought Smoke to town this time of day. Why would he leave the range in the middle of a roundup to talk to a lawyer? Ben shuddered and rose to pace around the office.

Smoke's remorse over losing his mother had gnawed at him so long he no longer made any secret of the bitterness he felt toward his father. When he mentioned Nate Wylie's name, a look akin to hate came into Smoke's eyes.

For the lack of any honest explanation from his father, Smoke blamed Nate's tough and arbitrary nature for Cora Wylie leaving the Pitchfork. He had lived with it himself and he was sure it was too much for any woman to endure. He resented Nate Wylie for that and he wanted him to know it. He could not fight his father as he might some other man, but Smoke found ways to get even. He patronized the saloon girls, often drank too much, fought at the drop of a hat, and spent money recklessly at the poker tables—all practices a prosperous and respected rancher like Nate Wylie found offensive to his dignity.

Although it was clearly self-defense, the marshal had sometimes wondered if the shooting of the gambler at the Great Western had come about by accident, or if Smoke had interfered in the game purposely to goad the man into trying to draw on him. Did Smoke know there was a gambler in his mother's life, or was it merely a coincidence?

Ben dismissed such farfetched thoughts from his mind. Smoke would not satisfy a desire for revenge against the wrong man.

There were times when Ben Toler felt he ought to defy

Nate Wylie and tell Smoke what he could about Cora Wylie, but it was really up to the rancher to be frank with his son about family matters. Nate had not done that. He considered the loss of his wife a sign of failure and he could not face the humiliation of it.

Rather than talk about Cora Wylie, Nate let Smoke think what he wanted to think. If Nate would tell Smoke the truth, Ben reflected, it might heal the breach between father and son, and everyone would be happier. Ben was worried. He could not shake a premonition that violence was about to explode around Smoke Wylie and the Pitchfork Ranch.

As he passed the window on one of his trips across the office, movement around the entrance to the Great Western caught his eye. He saw Matt Stacy and Ed Jarvis come out and amble down the street toward their shops. Smoke Wylie came out a step behind them. He swung aboard his horse, and Ben watched him until he passed beyond his line of sight.

For several minutes Ben Toler stood before the window, but his mind was no longer on the activities outside. He had carried the burden of Nate Wylie's trust alone too long, and he was trying to determine where his responsibilities were supposed to begin and end. He needed to share his thoughts with someone—someone both understanding and trustworthy. Tugging his hat close to his eyes, Ben locked the jail and walked along the boardwalk toward Abigail Lovelace's big clapboard house at the end of the street.

He found her sitting in a slatted settee on the front porch. Balls of yarn were laid out beside her and her fingers were working knitting needles in and out of a half-finished wool muffler. Ben smiled, knowing the muffler would be his when the blue northers started blowing along Jackpine's streets in the winter months ahead.

"I'm glad you came, Ben," Abigail Lovelace said as he sat down in a wicker chair in front of the settee. "I was worried about you."

"Oh? Why so?"

She frowned. "That gunfight scared me. When I saw it was that troublemaking Smoke Wylie, I was afraid you'd have to tangle with him. He's a dangerous man."

Abigail Lovelace was in her mid-forties, but her skin was still creamy and unlined. The few gray strands which laced her blond hair gave it a shimmering sheen. She looked cool and desirable in the soft shade spread by the tall post-oak which grew beside the porch. Ben had adequate living quarters in the rear section of the jail building, but he had taken all his meals at Abigail Lovelace's house since his return to Jackpine.

He looked at her affectionately and tried to wave her concerns aside. "Smoke's not a bad person, Abigail. He's just got some notion he has to look after everybody who's bein' mistreated. I think that's because he figures his pa has mistreated a lot of people, includin' him, and he's supposed to make up for it."

"Well, I'm glad you quit work early anyway," said Abigail. "It must have been a hard day for you."

Ben stretched his legs and sighed. "I'll be goin' back directly. Right now I need to talk to somebody."

"I'm glad you chose me," she said, smiling.

Ben studied the floor, searching for a place to start. He

said, "You never have asked me why I left the Pitchfork and stayed away from these parts so long."

The knitting needles slowed and she lifted her gentle brown eyes to meet his glance. "No. I knew you would tell me some day if you wanted me to know."

"I went on an errand for Nate Wylie. I went lookin' for his wife."

Abigail nodded knowingly. "That was my guess, but I didn't know whether you went with her, or left after she did, and I didn't want to know. That's why I never asked."

"Well, I didn't go with her," Ben said. "Nate came to me a few hours before dawn that day. He told me Cora had cut out on him. She'd been gone two-three hours by then, since sometime around midnight, Nate reckoned. He was really tore up, half out of his head. One minute he was sobbin', then cussin' at Cora, then cryin' like a whipped young'un again.

"Cora had asked him for some money to get away on, but Nate was too mad to give her the time of day. Later he cooled down some and that's when he woke me. Cora was the mother of his boys, Nate reasoned, and he owed her somethin' for that. I told him that maybe Cora would come back later—that family spats had a way of blowin' over. He didn't want to hear none of that. He said he never wanted to lay eyes on her again."

Abigail frowned. "But he sent you after her."

Nodding, Ben said, "Nate wanted to do what was right—hold up his end, as he put it. He handed me a roll of bills, two thousand dollars in all, and told me to hunt Cora down. I was to use what I needed for expenses and give her the rest. Nate wanted to know where she was. He said he couldn't stand the thought of her bein' a laundress for some soldier, or maybe takin' to some brothel just so she could get food and shelter. He wanted her to keep in touch so he could see that she didn't want for anything within reason. Nate thought I might catch up with her somewhere in Jackpine, but I wasn't to give up, whether it took a day, a week, or a year. He told me not to come back to the Pitchfork until I found her."

Ben paused and cleared his throat. Abigail put her knitting needles aside and leaned toward him. Her voice was a murmur of sympathy as she said, "But you failed and didn't want to face Nate Wylie. You didn't find her."

"Oh, I found her all right," Ben said.

His eyes narrowed and his nasal drawl was muted as he recalled the events that followed after he accepted Nate Wylie's assignment. In the gray light of dawn Ben packed his gear and rode away from the Pitchfork Ranch. He didn't find Nate Wylie's wife in a week, and he didn't find her in a year. But Ben stuck to the trail. A hundred times, around isolated campfires, at stage stations, brothels, noisy saloons, and cowtown cafes, Ben described the woman and listened for clues that might lead him to her.

Finally a drifting bronc-tamer told him of a beautiful auburn-haired woman who worked as a singer at the Elkhorn Saloon in San Antonio. By the time Ben arrived there the woman had gone. She had used the name Lucy Long, but after talking with the bartender at the Elkhorn, Ben knew the woman who called herself Lucy Long was really Cora Wylie.

Her constant companion during her stay there, the bartender told Ben, was a thin, smooth-talking man who rented a small shop near the old Alamo mission, and claimed he was an eye specialist from the East. The man and Lucy Long had made a hasty departure, catching an eastbound stage, when the good doctor's customers discovered the ten-dollar spectacles he sold them were nothing but plain glass.

Next Ben picked up her trail in a remote crossroads trading post near the Nueces. She had worked in a cafe there, and her companion had dropped all pretenses of being a doctor. He'd dealt poker at a saloon on the edge of town, but those who stopped there had never had enough money to make it worth his while. Both Cora and the gambler had moved on several weeks before Ben reached the Nueces.

Finally, just as Ben was ready to give up the search, one night he came face to face with Cora Wylie. It was in a boisterous saloon just south of Tule Canyon. Ben had stopped to rest his horse for a night and a day, and was strolling along the boardwalk to loosen his sore muscles when he heard a singer's voice coming from the saloon. He went inside and had to thread his way through a score of jostling cowboys before he could see her.

She was working from a makeshift platform of rough boards jammed into a corner to the left of the bar. Light from two lanterns above her head cast a coppery halo around her auburn hair and softened the contours of her full figure, which was outlined in provocative detail by the skin-tight green dress she wore.

There was no doubt about his luck this time. Ben's heart raced triumphantly. He was looking at Nate Wylie's wife, Cora.

She was twisting and bouncing around the stage, showing off her body, and singing at the top of her lungs. She was having a good time with the cowboys, blowing kisses at them as they laughed and whistled and clapped their hands. There was nothing romantic about the song, "Sweet Betsy from Pike," but it was a lilting trail song that touched a chord among those in the room. The song ended, and Cora paused to study the crowd before she turned half around, preparing to leave the stage. She turned quickly forward again and her eyes met those of Ben Toler. For a moment her mouth opened in a circle of surprise, then her full, sensuous lips broke into a friendly smile.

She rushed from the stage and came toward him. Behind her, beyond the circles of light created by the lanterns, Ben saw someone move. A man had been standing there in the shadows throughout the woman's performance, Ben realized. The man backed away and slipped through a doorway behind the bar. Ben saw only enough of him to know he was tall and thin and wore a high beaver hat.

"Ben Toler!" Cora's voice sounded happy as she came up beside him. "It's so good to see you again! What in the world could cause you to stray so far from the Pitchfork?"

"I've got something for you. It's from Nate."

"Oh?" Her face colored and a frown pinched her brow, but it was quickly gone. She smiled again and appeared to be embarrassed. "Then wait for me here," she said. "I've got to change my dress so I can move around better. I'll be right back."

She gave his arm a squeeze and hurried through the doorway where Ben had seen the man leave earlier. Without asking questions, Ben could guess the identity of the furtive figure behind the stage. It was the gambler he had been told about months ago on the Nueces.

Ben never saw Cora Wylie again. He waited at the bar for half an hour. Then he knew she was gone. The bartender checked her room, but there was no sign of her. She had slipped through a back door into an alley behind the saloon and disappeared.

For most of the night Ben scouted the town, but he learned nothing. Almost sixteen months had passed by this time, and ten was tired of the trail. He had spent eleven hundred dollars of Nate's money, just about what he would have been paid as ramrod of the Pitchfork. He found a bank which could mail a draft, and returned the remainder of the money to Nate Wylie. Later, he sent a letter telling the rancher the search was over.

Ben did not return to the Pitchfork. He had failed to establish a lasting contact with Cora, as Nate had ordered, and Ben was reluctant to face the rancher's disappointment and anger. He wanted even more to avoid the atmosphere which would prevail at the ranch. Nate had never been an easy man to work for, but now that the rancher's marriage had broken up, Ben feared conditions would be unbearable.

After he returned the money Ben took several different riding jobs, slowly working his way back toward

41

more familiar territory. In the spring he signed on as ramrod of the Bar C, just north of the Leon River, and he learned to like it there. The spread was not as large as the Pitchfork, but he had a good crew and the owner treated him like a member of the family.

Ben might have remained at the Bar C until he died if he had not received a letter from Abigail Lovelace. He did not know how it ever reached him, but he was glad it did. The letter had been forwarded from town to town and was more than three months old. Ben decided as soon as he read it that he would go back to Jackpine.

The letter was not very sentimental, but Ben read hints from it that he was sure Abigail Lovelace meant for him to find. Abigail began on an apologetic note, saying he probably would be surprised to hear from her, but that she thought he might like some news from around home. She mentioned a few trivial happenings, then added that she seldom wrote letters while her husband was living, but since his death four years ago she seemed to have more time on her hands.

The next day Ben Toler said his good-byes to the Bar C. He had been in love with Abigail for years, but there had been nothing more intimate between them than courteous smiles, an occasional chat on the street, and a few dances together at neighborhood gatherings. She was Dr. Adam Lovelace's wife and she appeared to love him dearly. Ben respected both of them too much to make any overtures to Abigail, but now she was a widow, obviously lonely, and he wanted to be near her.

His reaction to the letter was the only detail of his rambling years that Ben did not reveal to Abigail Lovelace.

When he had finished the story he stood up and hitched at his gun belt, feeling fatigued from the telling of it.

Shaking her head, Abigail Lovelace said, "That's an awful lot to give to a man like Nate Wylie just for wages."

Ben shrugged. "I was a drifter and a drunk when I heard about the Pitchfork losin' its foreman and I applied for the job. Nate took me on when nobody else would. He gave me so much responsibility I didn't have time to think about drinkin' and carousin'. When a man puts his whole spread in your hands it makes you feel like somebody, and I decided to *be* somebody. You might say Nate saved my life. I can't ever repay him for that."

"I see," Abigail said. "Why did you decide to tell me this after all these years?"

"I need a woman's instinct," Ben said. "I've been thinkin' I ought to tell Smoke what I know about his mother, but I'm not sure it would change anything. What do you think?"

Lifting her knitting materials back into her lap, Abigail shook her head firmly. "When you start trying to help with a family's problems, you're never sure which one in the family you should help. You can't win at it. Pick the wrong one and it sets them all against you. Your instincts are as good as mine in a thing like this. Something has kept you from speaking up all these years and I'm sure you know what it is."

Ben rose and stared off into the distance for a moment. "Yeah, I know what it is."

Abigail did not inquire further, but Ben continued,

43

"Yeah, I know what it is, all right. In all that time I was lookin' for Cora I was never sure in my own mind why Nate wanted to find her so bad. Maybe he wanted to look after her needs, like he said, and maybe he didn't. I kept thinkin' he might want to find her so he could do her some harm. Like you say, Nate's a hard-willed man. He's not a man to let somebody do him wrong and get by with it."

Abigail looked up at him, her eyes clouded with worry. "Stay out of it if you can, Ben."

The marshal spread his hands and stared at his finger-nails, his craggy face looking older than it had only an hour ago. Straightening, he touched Abigail's shoulder reassuringly and stepped off the porch. "I'd best keep an eye out for a while in case some of those Triangle T riders come back, but I'll be back in time for supper."

As Ben reached the boardwalk after leaving the dirt path which led to Abigail's house, two cowboys came out of the Great Western and strode across the street to intercept him. They touched their hat brims politely and the taller of the two said, "We don't make a habit of buttin' in on another man's game, Marshal, but seem as how a woman was mixed up in it . . . well, if you need any witnesses, we saw how that gunfight started a while ago. I know them two jaybirds who were pawin' at that girl too. I rode with them a spell down on the Rio Grande. Their names are Jesse Slater and Chub Morgan. They're mean cusses. Jesse grabbed for his gun first. We saw the whole thing."

"Appreciate you," Ben said. "I saw it too, and the victim didn't stick around to lodge any charges. I'll just put it down as a personal fight and forget about it."

He went on toward the jail, but he knew he would not forget anything about this day. His instincts told him Smoke Wylie was going to cause a lot more trouble for somebody.

Chapter Four

John Bastrop's law office was on the second floor of the Plainsman's Bank, which was the only brick building in town. A walled-in stairway led from a doorway at the corner of the building to the floor above, and Smoke Wylie went up the steps two at a time. He was eager to complete his business and get out of Jackpine. He might have been able to come and go without notice if the shooting had not occurred, but now there would be no way to keep his visit a secret.

Smoke had visited the lawyer's office many times on errands for his father. His clearest memory was of the unusual odors created by leather-bound books, parchment paper, ink pots, and pine panels. He was aware of the many smells the moment he opened the door and stepped inside the office. John Bastrop looked up from a cluttered desk, his quill pen poised over a stack of papers.

"I prefer that people knock on my door before they come bursting in here," he said brusquely. "There could have been a client here with confidential matters to discuss."

"I don't see anybody," Smoke said. "I've got confidential matters to discuss myself."

45

The lawyer mumbled under his breath and waited for Smoke to continue. John Bastrop had lived in the West half his sixty years, but he clung to many of the dress customs of his Eastern origin. His stiff white removable collar contrasted sharply with the wilted appearance of his pin-striped shirt. A set of green sleeve garters bloused the limp fabric above his elbows to hold the cuffs away from his wrists. He was a prim little man with a thin neck, sharp features, and gold-rimmed spectacles perched near the end of his pointed nose. Smoke did not like his pretentious manner, but the lawyer had a reputation for being both honest and shrewd.

"If it's business, let's get on with it," Bastrop said.

Smoke was nervous. He hesitated until he was sure his voice was strong before he spoke again. He ran his tongue across his lips, took a deep breath, and said, "When I was just a little shaver, Pa told me he left some deeds with you. One was for me. I want to pick it up."

A touch of color tinged John Bastrop's cheeks and he began to shuffle papers around on his desk. He said, "You can't get the deed on a minute's notice."

Smoke leaned forward. "No? That's not the way I understand it. I've been told it was all set up. Don't start a lot of lawyer talk with me and don't try to stall me."

John Bastrop pushed at his glasses. "I only stall in court. I do as my clients instruct me. The deeds are here and you can have yours at the proper time."

"When will that be?" Smoke asked impatiently. "I thought the time was already past due if I wanted it that way. I was twenty-one more than—"

As he spoke, Smoke was rising slowly from his chair in front of the lawyer's desk.

"Now, now," Bastrop cautioned. "Just sit down and I'll explain the details."

Smoke glanced through the single window beyond the lawyer's shoulder. The sun was moving toward the western horizon and he felt pressed for time. "Do that," he said sharply.

"Nathan Wylie doesn't set much store by the legal majority—twenty-one, that is," Bastrop began. "He feels most young men go a little wild the day they reach that milestone. They usually want to do something foolish to prove their manhood—get drunk, take a woman to bed, or hit the trail for faraway places. He wanted you and your brother to have a chance to grow out of those impulses. The deeds are here and they may be exercised when you are twenty-two—not at age twenty-one."

"Fine," Smoke said. "I was trying to tell you I was twenty-one last year. My next birthday is less than two weeks from now—nine days, as a matter of fact."

John Bastrop twisted his hands together. "There's more to it. The deeds are set up similar to a trust, but not exactly. If Nathan dies before you boys, everything is automatic. The deeds are yours and you and Gil would each own a portion of the Pitchfork. Nathan wanted to be sure of that. As long as he's alive he must be given notice of your intention before you can claim your share of the ranch. If he thinks you are not yet ready to accept such responsibility, he can revoke the entire arrangement. However, if he lodges no objection within two weeks, I'm instructed to record the deed in your name. Is that clear?"

Nodding, his teeth clenched, Smoke kicked back the chair and stood up. "Yeah, that's clear. I'll take care of the notice. I want the deed ten days from now, but I should have known Nate would throw in a ringer."

The lawyer's face did not change expression. "Nathan Wylie wouldn't make a promise and refuse to keep it if he's dealing with an honorable man. By the way, the name on your deed is Zack Wylie—not 'Smoke.' I don't know the origin of your nickname, but I don't care for it. Knowing something of your reputation, I assume it's a euphemism for 'Gunsmoke' Wylie, in honor of the way you handle a gun."

"You assume wrong," Smoke snapped. "Pa named me Zack because he fought in the Mexican War with General Zachary Taylor and took a liking to him. Years ago Gil told Pa my eyes looked like smoke, and they teased me about it until the name stuck. That's all there is to that, but I don't care what name's on the deed as long as I get my share of the Pitchfork."

Bastrop saw the quick anger in Smoke's eyes and tried to be reassuring. "My guess is you'll get your deed if that's what you want," he said. "You'd have to do something worse than usual to cause Nathan to change his mind."

Smoke tugged at his hat brim as he walked toward the door. "Maybe I've already done that."

"It's strange—the difference in brothers," the lawyer mused. "Gil could have exercised his rights a long time ago, but he's never mentioned the deeds."

48

"That's not strange," Smoke said over his shoulder. "Gil would be content to live the rest of his life under Nate's thumb. He's just like him."

"I imagine your father is quite proud of that," Bastrop said quietly. "A lot of people would like to be like Nathan Wylie."

"Everybody to their own taste," Smoke said.

He hurried from the office and down the steps to the street. As he stepped into the saddle of his waiting bay, he turned his eyes toward the Great Western. He had planned to go back there for a final drink after visiting the lawyer, but he decided against it. There would be more questions about the shooting, and it was a subject he did not want to discuss.

Smoke rode slowly toward the open range. Behind him the sun was already growing pale, rimmed with a yellow haze. The dying rays painted a golden fringe on the pines, cedars, and scattered post-oaks that studded the ridges which rolled away from the town like pulsing, purple waves. He was in no hurry. By the time he reached the roundup camp, there would be no daylight left for work.

He let the horse pick its own way, with only a nudge of his knee now and then to guide it in the right direction. His thoughts were jumbled, all of them worrisome and depressing.

The trip to Jackpine had been taken on impulse and it was a mistake. His business at John Bastrop's office could have waited, but Smoke was not sure how much longer he wanted to live under the same roof with Nate Wylie. The deed in Bastrop's office offered him a way out, and he had been thinking about such a move for months. During the night he'd been unable to put it out of his mind, so he'd decided to do something about it.

It was an unfortunate twist of fate, he reflected ruefully, that the very day he defied Nate's orders about wearing a gun he would find a reason to use it. In his own mind, he had no choice. Under similar circumstances Nate or Gil would have done the same thing, but they would never admit that to him, Smoke thought.

He knew he had a natural talent for lifting a gun from his holster with exceptional speed. He'd discovered that at the age of seventeen. Nate had taught him to shoot when he was ten, and there had been a time when Nate was proud of his skill—particularly the time his gun speed might have saved the rancher's life.

He and his father were working cattle at the toe of Buzzard Ridge one day when Nate stepped off his horse to help a newborn calf which was tangled in a brush thicket. Nate's boots had barely touched the ground when Smoke heard the unmistakable dry clicking sound of a rattlesnake. It was coiled five feet away from the calf, but Smoke knew it could throw its poisonous body that far when it struck. His grab for his holstered Colt was spurred by desperation, and he shot off the snake's head in midair. He was sure of his gun speed, but it did not occur to him that he would have an occasion to use it against another man.

Twice in a short time Smoke had used that lightning speed against other men, and he feared he might have to call on it again soon. He could not forget the fury in the eyes of the gangling, grim-faced man called Jesse when he said, "I'll be back. . . ."

The night was two hours old when Smoke spotted the campfire, a flickering red-orange glow against the dark prairie. He had left the crew on the banks of East Creek, but the roundup plan was to work from there back toward the ranch headquarters, picking up cattle as they went. He'd estimated they would have moved about three miles westward, and his guess was close.

Food smells, scented with wood smoke, filtered through the still air, and he knew the riders were keeping some supper warm for him. He rode toward the fire with a feeling of guilt. There had been no ramrod, as such, at the Pitchfork since Smoke and Gil had become grown men. Supervision was divided among the Wylie family—Smoke and Gil, and Nate when he felt up to it.

This was Smoke's crew at the campfire, four tough, experienced cowhands, and he had gotten off to a bad start with them. They had heard Nate Wylie's instructions before they left the ranch two days ago, and they'd been uneasy when they learned Smoke was going to ignore them. He'd heard them grumbling beneath their breaths before he left.

As he neared the fire Smoke called out, "I'm coming in, boys. It's me—Smoke."

It was a rangeland custom to make yourself known when riding up to another's camp in the dark. At the beginning of a roundup men became edgy and short-tempered, and Smoke could not be sure one of them would not have a nervous trigger finger.

"It's about time," a man said, and Smoke recognized

51

the voice of Joe Santine. He had spotted him moving around in his easy, catlike strides beyond the fire—a wiry, dark-faced man with thick black hair spilling from beneath his hat and down across his forehead.

Smoke came into the light and stepped down from his horse. He had been in the saddle almost five hours, and the events of the day had added to his fatigue. He was hungry, but he was not sure he could enjoy his meal. The sick and empty feeling which had tortured him since he left Jackpine had his stomach tied in knots.

He glanced around the camp, at the open bedrolls with saddles piled at the end of them for pillows. Three of the men—Paul Mabry, Ed Slade, and Ike Yarby—were lounging on the edges of their blankets, smoking cigarettes and talking among themselves. Joe Santine stood just beyond the firelight, a tin cup filled with coffee in his hand. Slade, tall, quiet-spoken, and always polite, pushed to his feet. "I'll take your horse, Smoke," he said, and led the bay off into the darkness where the other horses were picketed.

Smoke nodded and fastened his gaze on Joe Santine's face. Most of the time the wiry man with the square shoulders and lean waist was quick to laugh and joke, and often talked so much that those around him had to walk away for relief. But his mood could change swiftly, turning morose and surly. He claimed to be descended from an Irish mother and Spanish father, but the high cheekbones and arched nose hinted of Indian blood somewhere in his background.

"I don't like a smart mouth, Joe," Smoke said sharply.

Santine lifted the cup to his lips and sipped the coffee,

looking at Smoke across the rim of the cup. He swallowed deliberately and tossed the rest of the coffee on the ground. He turned and put the cup on a stack of firewood behind him, then looked again at Smoke, his shoulders tensed.

"I don't like a man who goes off and leaves his riders to get saddled with whatever goes wrong with the roundup," Santine said. "There could be rustlers scouting around here, or cougars knocking down young calves, and who knows what. If Nate rode in to check things, he'd take the hide off of us for anything he didn't like. Some of us would probably get fired. A good boss would be around to stand up for his crew. I know Nate would raise hell if he knew you left us on our own all day."

Smoke glared at him and said, "That's family business, Joe, and none of your worry."

"The way you and Nate keep yapping at each other's heels is everybody's worry," Santine said. "A man can't be at ease around you. I get the feeling the lid's going to blow off at any time and we're going to get caught in the cross fire."

Smoke had held his temper in check as long as he could. He felt his nails bite into his palms as his fists clenched at his sides. "Nobody fights my fights, Joe, or takes the blame for my mistakes. If you don't like the way I do things you can pack your gear and ride out."

Surprise showed briefly in Joe Santine's face, then a thin smile tugged at the corners of his mouth. "Maybe I'll do that after a spell. I don't leave no place with something stuck in my craw. I'll have to get that out before I go."

"Meaning what?" Smoke asked.

"Meaning," Joe Santine said, his eyes brightening, "that I'll take a piece of your hide with me when I go."

Smoke heaved a sigh of disgust. "Are you saying you're going to fight me over this?"

"That's right." Santine's voice was soft, threatening. "It'll make me feel better either way it goes."

"Are you going to draw against me?"

Santine shook his head. "No. I know about your gun hand. I'm not stupid enough to draw on you, but I aim to knock you around some with my fists."

Smoke felt relieved. He did not want any kind of fight, and he was sorry he had pushed Santine to this point. The man had been with the Pitchfork almost four years, and he was good with a horse and a rope. He was the kind of man Nate liked to have around—confident, a little cocky, afraid of nothing, and willing to work long hours without complaining. Smoke did not want to lose him, but he could not back away from the choice he had given him.

Smoke watched as Santine carefully unbuckled his cartridge belt and laid his holstered gun on the wood pile. He was relieved that there would be no shooting. He suspected the wiry cowboy was better with a gun than he wanted anyone to know.

Smoke's bedroll, which was still unfurled, lay on the ground a few feet away. Someone had placed it near the spot where Ike Yarby had spread his bed. Smoke walked over and dropped his own gun on the bedroll.

Ike Yarby was sprawled on his blankets, propped up on one elbow, and eyeing Smoke from beneath bushy brows. Ike was a monstrous man, towering over six-foot-six, with massive shoulders and arms like fence posts. His early years had been spent trapping furs in the Dakotas, and his right forearm still carried the puckered scar left by a Sioux arrow.

"Ye got yerself into somethin' ye ought not be in, lad," Ike said quietly. "It ain't becomin' to fight yer own crew."

Smoke turned toward the fire without responding. Joe Santine stood ten feet away from the blaze, his feet braced wide apart, his fists clenched and moving in small circles at his sides. Drawing a deep breath, Smoke stepped toward him, his own right fist cocked. Santine hit him on the cheek so swiftly Smoke halted in amazement. The blow jarred his head. His skin burned like it had been grazed by a hot iron and tears boiled out of his left eye. Santine, dancing aside with catlike grace and speed, was only a blurred outline.

Smoke's head cleared and he went after him, recognizing quickly that Joe Santine was no ordinary brawler. He was good at this, relying on his quick hands and swiftness afoot. It did not seem possible that so much power could come from that small, lithe body. Smoke would have to do more than just throw blows at him; he would have to out-think him.

Smoke stood a step forward, then stepped back. Santine was already darting toward him, but Smoke's retreat disrupted the man's timing. Smoke brought his fist up from the level of his belt. The punch caught Santine just below the chin, then slid off the edge of his Adam's apple. Santine flopped backward. He hit the ground hard, but he bounced quickly to his feet.

Smoke braced himself for another charge, but it never came. The hulking form of Ike Yarby came between them. One of Ike's meaty hands clutched Smoke's shirt collar and the other twisted at the red bandanna around Joe Santine's neck. He held them apart as easily as a man might part the curtains over a window.

"Hurrah there now, the both of ye," Ike roared. "Ye got a lick in apiece and that's all I aim to stand fer. This here scrap is over!"

He kept his grip on them, glaring from one grim face to the other, tiny beads of sweat glistening in the reddish beard which covered most of his leathery face. Joe Santine tried to twist away and Smoke shoved at Ike's brawny shoulder. Ike hardly noticed their efforts.

Slowly Ike dropped his hands away, but he continued to watch them closely. As unpredictable as ever, Joe Santine laughed aloud. He reached around Ike to tap Smoke's arm.

"Hell, Smoke," he said, "if Ike ain't going to let me fight you, I reckon I'll stay on. I think I'll hang around till I get a chance to whip this big bull of a mountain man."

Ike Yarby threw back his head and a laugh rumbled in his throat as he walked back toward his blankets.

The characteristic loose smile was back on Joe Santine's face, and his anger appeared forgotten. Yawning, he said, "I reckon I'll turn in now, so I can get my sore bones in shape for chasing cows tomorrow."

During the argument and brief fight Paul Mabry had not moved. Smoke caught a glimpse of him squatting on his heels far back in the shadows. There was a frightened look on the youngster's face. He jumped to his feet now and hurried toward Smoke as though he needed something to do.

"You want some supper, Smoke?" Mabry was the baby of the crew, barely nineteen, and had not yet seen the violent side of many men. "We saved some stew for you."

Mabry started toward the iron pot nestled in the outer coals of the fire, but Smoke waved him aside.

"You don't have to wait on me, Paul. I'll get it. I'm as hungry as a goat. Something about a good fight helps my appetite—especially if it doesn't last too long."

The cotton-haired youngster grinned and walked back to his bedroll. The camp was at peace again, without tension, and Smoke liked that. He could hear quiet voices around the bedrolls, and the smell of tobacco flavored the air as men rolled a final smoke before turning in.

Joe Santine's voice rose above the others. "That thing with Smoke reminds me of a happening when I was down in Nacogdoches a few years back—"

"You ain't ever been in Nacogdoches," Ed Slade cut in, chuckling.

"Sure I have," Santine said. "I've got people down there. Anyway, this gambler comes in from New Orleans and takes a fancy to a paint horse I had at the time. He was riding a big black stallion and he said he'd bet me that—"

"Tomorrow, Joe. Tell yer tall tales tomorrow," Ike

Yarby called out with a groan. "I'm trying to get me some shut-eye over here."

A chorus of complaints drowned out Santine's protests and it grew quieter in the shadows. Smoke finished eating his stew and laid out his own bed. He stretched out on the blankets, lifting his knees now and then to soothe the aching muscles in his legs. The sky above him was a deep violet dome with stars tracking across it like glittering beads, and the vastness of it made him feel strangely alone. Sleep would not come easily to him this night.

Chapter Five

An hour after the others were asleep, Smoke was still wide awake. The continuous tossing around on his tarp had made him nervous and even more exhausted. Slipping on his boots, he walked a short distance from the camp so he could pace and unwind without disturbing the sleeping men.

He smoked only occasionally, but he carried the makin's with him, and he reached into his shirt pocket for the tobacco sack. He took his time rolling a cigarette, and had just lighted it when he heard the grass rustle nearby. He whirled around, startled, then relaxed when he saw Ike Yarby, who had spent too many years in Indian country to miss the slightest sound. Smoke's movements had not escaped him.

Ike came up beside him, grinning through his beard. "Ye been thrashin' around like a bull in a buffler waller. Do ye need somebody to talk to?"

Smoke took a deep drag on the cigarette, the first he had tasted today. It made his head feel light and he rubbed his eyes, scowling. He threw the cigarette down and ground it under his heel.

"I remember this place, Ike," he said, gazing out over the land. "Nate made me ride out here with him and the rest of you the night he burned those settlers out. He said he wanted me to learn how to handle anybody who ever tried to squat on the Pitchfork graze. We rode half the night and came in on them at dawn. It was awful the way those folks were running around, screaming and begging while they watched everything they owned burned to ashes."

"That was twelve, maybe fifteen years ago," Ike Yarby grunted. "He was fair with 'em. Nate had me come over a week ahead of time and tell 'em to get out or be burned out, but they held tight. He left 'em horses and wagons to get out with. That's fair dealin'. Most Texans I know would have buried 'em here. They were on Nate's land."

Smoke's eyes narrowed as he looked at the big man beside him. "Nate doesn't know whose land it is. He's got a hundred thousand deeded acres, and uses twice that much government land like it's his own. Nate can't own everything. Other people have a right to something."

The bitter tone of Smoke's voice drew only a shrug from Yarby. He did not waste his time explaining the customs of the country, because Smoke had grown up with them. Surveys of the sprawling Western frontier were so sketchy and poorly drawn that even state land agents did not always know where the boundaries lay between deeded land and government graze. The land belonged to the first man to settle on it if he was strong enough to hold it against Indians and interlopers. They called it possession land, theirs by right of continued use, and men such as Nate Wylie would hold it until the government said otherwise. Most of the large ranches in the West had grown from possession land.

"That's not a sight a boy ought to see," Smoke murmured. "I'll never forget that night, and it's one of the things that makes it hard for me to feel the way a son ought to for his father."

Lowering himself, Ike squatted on his heels and spat into the grass. "They were fools, lad. Four families out of Miss'sippi, claimin' they could plow up the prairie and grow cotton here. I hold no shame fer my part in it. Fact is, Nate likely done them folks and their young'uns a favor by runnin' 'em out. They would have starved to death before cotton ever growed here."

"The West needs people and families if it's going to amount to anything," Smoke said stubbornly. "That can't happen if Nate has his way."

Ike plucked off a grass stem and began to chew on it. "That ain't the burr under yer saddle, Smoke. Yuh've got bigger troubles than what happened way back then. I could spot it in yer face when ye rode in tonight."

Smoke let his breath out slowly and nodded. "You're right. I've got big troubles."

He sat down beside the man, feeling the need for companionship. He told Ike about the shooting incident in Jackpine and about Jesse's threat to search him out for another showdown.

"Nate's going to raise hell about that," Smoke said.

"That he will," Ike agreed. " 'Less'n, of course, ye beat him to the punch."

Smoke shrugged listlessly and asked, "How can I do that?"

"Ye don't wait on him to jump ye first," Ike said. "Ye ride back to the ranch and tell him in his teeth. Ye ask him how he would have played out his string in yer spot, and see if he can give ye a good answer. Sometimes a man confessin' his mistakes takes all the thunder out of them that hold him responsible."

"I can't do that right away," Smoke said, turning the suggestion over in his mind. "You heard what Joe Santine said about me dodging my responsibility. I don't want the rest of you feeling the same way. Starting at sunup I aim to get this roundup moving the way it should. I've got to shape up and do my share, but you give good advice, Ike. Maybe in a day or two I'll go back to the Pitchfork and have it out with Nate. By that time he'll probably know why I went to Jackpine in the first place and we'll have a real showdown."

Ike Yarby rose from his heels and moved away without a sound. Over his shoulder, he said, "Don't wait too long. If Nate sends a rider to fetch ye, he's got the upper hand from then on."

Smoke waited a few minutes and then followed Ike back to the camp. He felt like he could sleep now.

For the next four days Smoke gave his full energy and attention to the roundup. It was hard, repetitious work, but it was a part of range life and a man could lose himself in it. They were in the saddle at dawn and did not quit until darkness was nearly upon them. Sometimes they worked in teams, sometimes alone, riding sweeps and circles, pushing the cattle together into a growing herd.

They had no permanent camp. They moved their sleeping places as the herd moved, always working their way toward the Pitchfork headquarters and the holding grounds. It was Nate's custom to work the range in sections, bringing in a few hundred head at a time, then cleaning up another area. Smoke's crew had started at the eastern boundary of the Pitchfork graze while Gil and another crew worked toward them from the west. Nate, with another four or five men, would gather those closer to the ranch and prepare the holding grounds. Later, Nate would hire extra riders to help castrate calves, brand yearlings, and make a preliminary count before the cattle broker arrived to take the herd to market.

Despite other faults they might find in him, no one on the Pitchfork had ever accused Smoke of lacking skill when it came to working cattle. As the roundup progressed he seemed to be everywhere at once, doing the work of two men, and there appeared to be a driving urgency in everything he did.

Around the cook fire at night there was little talk now. The men were bone-tired, grimy with sweat, and dried out by the scorching sun. All they wanted to do was wolf down their food, wash off some of the dust when they could find a stream nearby, and drop on their blankets. At mealtimes Smoke noticed that Joe Santine usually tried to sit near him, grinning often and making casual conversation about the day's chores. He made every effort to show Smoke he held no grudge because of their earlier disagreement.

Although he tried to be concerned only with the roundup, Smoke scanned the prairie often, expecting at any moment to see a rider loping toward them with a message from Nate Wylie. He awoke each day with a feeling of anxiety. On the fifth morning he decided he could not stand the waiting and watching any longer.

After breakfast Smoke called Ike Yarby aside and said, "I'm riding in to see Pa today. You keep things moving along. I don't know what's going to happen when I get home, and I may not be back by tomorrow—maybe not at all."

Ike Yarby ran his hand through his beard. "Good luck to ye, lad. I'll handle things here, and there won't be no more complaints. I jedge we've got better'n four hundred head, and we ought to pick up another hundred in a couple of days. They're on home range, standin' real good, so we've got no problems. We'll just keep walkin' 'em with the grass and addin' on a few as we go."

"We should be at Middle Creek in three days," Smoke said. "We'll leave this bunch there and move on to South Basin."

"The crew knows we're gettin' closer to South Basin, but they won't complain about ye leavin' this time," Ike said. "They learned somethin' by the way ye handled Joe Santine."

A scowl crossed Smoke's face. "Are you worried about waiting this long to get to South Basin?"

Ike nodded. "Some. One thing ye can say about yer

63

pa. He knows things about the seasons and about cows. He was on edge about South Basin and was dead-set on us goin' there first. This is the wettest spring we've had in nigh twenty years. It gets soft and messy down there where the coulees and little ravines open up on the flats. Cows are ornery. They always do what they ain't supposed to do."

"Are you hinting I'm as thick-headed as a cow?" Smoke chuckled, trying to shake off some of his apprehension by teasing the big cowhand.

Ike Yarby opened his mouth to explain his remark, but Smoke continued before he could speak. "Maybe Nate had some kind of hunch, but it doesn't make sense to start the roundup so close to home. We've always started at the farthest point and worked back. I figure I'm old enough to decide how to work my own crew."

"If ye say so," Ike said, and a small, uncomfortable smile parted his beard.

Smoke tightened his cinch and stepped into the bay's saddle. He swung the horse around to look down at the other men, who were busy cleaning up their plates or tying bedrolls behind their saddles.

"I'm going back to the ranch for a talk with Nate," he told them. He wanted no mystery about his leaving this time. "Ike will be my segundo until I get back."

Busy with their horses, Ed Slade and Paul Mabry merely looked around and nodded. Joe Santine moved up next to Smoke's horse, a frown on his dark face. He said, "Hang tough when you get there," and Smoke knew Ike Yarby had told the men about the trouble in town.

As he rode, Smoke spotted a few deer, a pair of foxes, and dozens of jackrabbits running through the brush patches along his path. He made good time, but he did not push the horse enough to tire it. It had taken the roundup crew a day and a half to reach the outer range at East Creek, but they had been leading extra horses and pack animals loaded with provisions, extra ropes, and spare harness. Smoke made the trip much faster, helped by the fact that the distance was shortened as the roundup worked its way back closer to the ranch.

He crossed Middle Creek about noon. Two hours later he topped out on a bare ridge and looked down at the Pitchfork headquarters spread across the valley. Sunlight glinted on the windows of the main house—a plain, unimposing structure of hewn logs. A short distance to the rear of the house was another small log building which served as the kitchen. A half-dozen corrals of varying size were scattered around the area, two of them adjoining large hay barns. At the south side of the house was the long, low-roofed bunkhouse, capable of accommodating twenty men. Beyond that were other outbuildings—a blacksmith shop, a tool shed, and the privies.

In the crystal-clear air the layout appeared to be only a few hundred yards away, but the ranch was still two miles away. From his elevated vantage point Smoke could see an unusual amount of activity at the ranch. Four horses stood with reins drooping at the corral nearest the house and men were moving around the yard. The men were too animated to be casual visitors. Their arms moved in emphatic gestures, and their booted feet were stamping the ground so hard that small dust clouds floated around them.

Smoke meant to pause on the crest of the ridge, rest his horse a few minutes, and smoke a cigarette before he approached the ranch, but he was too curious to wait. He nudged the horse with his heel and headed down the slope. Something had happened at the Pitchfork, and Smoke had a premonition it was something bad.

The men at the corral were so engrossed in conversation they did not see Smoke until he appeared at the far side of the enclosure and reined his horse toward them. He knew all of them—but what were they doing here?

In the center of the group was Nate Wylie, his wide-brimmed hat bobbing up and down as he turned from one man to another, speaking to them in a low, hard voice which came to Smoke only as an angry rumble. With him, listening intently, were Wade Stone of the Bar W, Jake Fentriss of the Turkey Track, and Jerry Mead of the Circle M. Even Jerry Mead's blond, green-eyed daughter Hetty was crowded into the ragged circle, her pretty face flushed with excitement. That was to be expected, Smoke told himself. Sometimes Hetty Mead behaved more like a man than half the cowhands on the range.

Surprisingly, Gil Wylie, who was supposed to be gathering cattle on the western boundary, was also there. Gil stood apart from the others, his back against the corral poles, the heel of one boot hooked over the bottom rail.

The brothers had been close companions most of their lives, but there had been little warmth between them in the past year. Since the shooting of the gambler in Jackpine, Gil had nagged Smoke about his behavior as much as Nate, and Smoke felt the two of them had united against him. At the moment, however, he preferred Gil's company to the others. He pulled the bay to a halt and stepped down beside his brother.

"What's going on here?" he asked. "Looks like a war party over there."

Gil's square-chinned, craggy face was almost drained of color. His sandy eyebrows, bleached almost white by the sun, were drawn close over his walnut-brown eyes which always shone with coppery flecks when he was angry or scared. Smoke saw the copper flecks in them now.

"That's what it is—a war party." Gil spat into the trampled dirt at his feet. "Pa wants to ride across Deadline Ridge and hit the sheep settlements. He wants to kill twenty or thirty sheep to even a score, he says. If he does that the sheepherders will hit us back sooner or later and we'll have to go after them again. You know what that means."

"Yeah," Smoke said, his face sober. "A range war that could last a long time."

Gil tugged nervously at his hat. "Something that will get a lot of people killed—maybe us among them— unless you can talk Pa out of it. I can't."

The voices ten yards away from them were growing louder. Smoke glanced uneasily toward the knot of men. Everyone seemed to be talking at the same time. Smoke could understand a word only now and then, but he heard enough to know they were in a dangerous mood.

Farther away, halfway between the corral and the

kitchen, he saw two men he had not noticed earlier. One was the ranch cook, Charlie Ray Jones, his hands twisting at the apron around his skinny waist. Smoke felt a surge of resentment as he recognized the other man. It was Elijah Pardee, his squat, pear-shaped form shrouded in the soiled white linen duster he wore winter and summer.

Smoke turned back to his brother. "You're getting ahead of me. What stirred them up? We've always got along with the sheepers. What's Nate trying to get even for?"

Gil leaned forward and rested his arms on top of the corral fence. He lowered his voice. "Yesterday afternoon I found one of our yearlings butchered over near the ridge. Somebody had hacked off the right hind quarter and carried it away. The rest of the carcass was still there, so I—"

"Wolves could have done that," Smoke said.

Gil shook his head. "Wolves had been after what was left, all right, but the yearling had been shot. I picked up the trail of a single rider. He must have been skinning out the quarter as he went. I found patches of hide along the way, and some blood drippings. The trail went across Deadline Ridge. I rode as far as the top, then turned back. I figured I'd better tell Nate."

"Why didn't you just forget it?" Smoke said irritably. "You should have known what would happen when you told Nate."

Gil whirled around, his blunt chin drawn in close to his chest. It was a pose Smoke had seen Nate Wylie strike often.

"Nobody slaughters the Pitchfork's beef and gets away with it," Gil said. "Especially somebody who's too damn lazy to take the whole calf. I figured we ought to hunt down the man and make him pay his due. I sure didn't think it would mean war. We don't need that. Maybe you can make Pa see he's wrong."

A wry grin touched Smoke's lips, but he felt the same uneasiness he heard in Gil's voice. "I'll try," he said, "but you know he never agrees with me on anything. Besides, he'll probably kick me off the whole spread. I came home to tell him about a shooting I got mixed up in."

"He already knows about it," said Gil. "Looks like you're doing your best to make the whole Wylie family look like a pack of outlaws. But that's between you and Nate. Preacher Pardee brought the news. He was here when I got in last night. He's been here for days. Pa sent him and Charlie Ray to bring in the other ranchers after I told him about the dead yearling."

Gil started to say more, but he clamped his mouth shut as Nate Wylie moved away from the group and strode toward his sons. He was Smoke's height, an inch over six feet, but his shoulders were broader and he was beginning to put on weight around his waist. He carried a polished hickory cane and favored his left leg with a slight limp, the result of a riding accident six years ago. As he walked, he jabbed the cane fiercely against the ground. His lips were pursed so tightly his mouth was almost hidden by the thick brush mustache. The fury in his walnut-colored eyes was unlike anything Smoke had seen in him before.

Chapter Six

A full thirty seconds after Nate Wylie stopped an arm's length in front of his sons he did not speak. He stared at the ground, his cane drawing meaningless circles in the dirt. Muscles worked along his jaw and swelled his neck as he swallowed hard, apparently trying to get a rein on his temper.

Finally he glared at Smoke and said in a low, choking voice, "You must think you're a real King Fisher or John Wesley Hardin or one of them other loco killers. I've got one son who looks after business and one who looks for nothin' but trouble. I've been prayin' for you, Smoke, and so has Preacher Pardee, but it's done no good. I ordered you to leave off your gun, but you don't do a damn thing I say. You've got no respect for your pa, like the Bible tells you to and—"

"In the Bible," Smoke cut in, "it's something like, 'Honor thy mother and thy father,' but I don't have a—"

"Shut your mouth and listen," Nate snapped. "First things first. I hear you've gone and tangled with a couple of hooligans named Jesse Slater and Chub Morgan and you shot one of 'em. By damn, Smoke, you're a born troublemaker and I aim to see—"

"Seems like you've got worse troubles here," Smoke interrupted again. "Gil was telling me—"

"Hear me out, dammit," Nate Wylie roared. "You ain't switchin' me off and gettin' out of nothin'. You're like the prodigal son in the Book of Luke. His old man set that boy up good, but he went off and wasted every-

70

thing. You're wastin' every chance you have to be somebody, but by damn, I won't have you draggin' my good name and Gil's down with you."

Nate Wylie paused for breath, clenching and unclenching his fists. He was fifty-seven years old, but except for the gray in his hair and mustache, his age did not show. His broad face was unlined, his jaw square and hard. The smooth skin, usually a deep brown, was beet-red now, an indication of the high blood pressure Nate's doctor kept warning him about.

He was silent only long enough to make sure the group nearby was still busy with their talk, but Smoke could see Hetty Mead stealing a glance at them.

"Brother Pardee tells me the shootin' had somethin' to do with a woman. You're forever messin' around with some woman."

"Jesse and Chub were doing the messing," Smoke said flatly. "They had her clothes half tore off and were trying to force her into the bushes next to Ed Jarvis' place."

Nate's head lifted. He drew his chin in close to his chest. "Is she a good woman—a decent woman?"

"I figured her to be," Smoke said. "I talked to Ben Toler about her. He said she was a stranger in town."

A snorting sound came from the rancher's throat. "I don't hold with abusin' a good woman, by damn. Women have a hard time in these parts. They spend most of their time alone, work like dogs, and hold their breath to see what kind of life the man they've got can give 'em. The least they deserve is to be treated like somebody."

71

Nate's eyes swept the faces of his sons. He wanted his words to register with both of them. "I don't like you foolin' with the girls that come and go at the Great Western," he said, "but I've got no sympathy for them. They're in business, sellin' merchandise like their body was a side of beef, but by damn, if either of you ever start sleepin' with a decent woman, you're goin' to take her on as your lifetime responsibility. You're not goin' to ruin her name and then walk off and leave her when nobody else will have her. I mean you'll marry her or I'll head the posse that runs you out of the county.

He paused, his body shaking with emotion. He continued staring at Smoke and said, "It's a sorry son who can't be depended on to do a day's work instead of goin' off for a lark in town. I aim to go into that later, but there would've been no shootin' in Jackpine if you'd kept that gun in your saddlebag like I told you."

"Maybe not from me," Smoke said, "but Jesse Slater meant to do some. The man was crazy for a woman and was ready to kill somebody to have one. I didn't fancy ending up dead, so I shot him."

"Do you aim to keep packin' a gun in town?" Nate Wylie asked angrily.

"I do." Smoke's gaze did not waver before his father's stare. He wanted to say that he was going to need a gun because Jesse Slater had promised to come back looking for him, but he knew it was better left unsaid.

Finally Nate Wylie's shoulders relaxed and he jerked his head toward the group waiting nearby. "Come on over with the others. This ain't over between us, but we've got some other business to take care of first."

They did not have to move. Impatient with waiting, the other ranchers were already walking toward the trio at the fence. Wade Stone, a rawboned, red-haired man, was in the lead. Close beside him was short, stocky Jake Fentriss. Lagging a few paces behind them was Jerry Mead, a careful, thoughtful man who seemed less pleased to be there than did the others. Hetty was holding to his left arm, her face turned upward as she talked to him.

"Just a bunch of no-good, thievin', foul-smellin' cutthroats," Nate Wylie said, waving a hand in the general direction of Deadline Ridge. "I prayed over them last night, seekin' the Lord's guidance. I didn't get a message, but the message had already been sent. Preacher Pardee pointed it out to me right there in Exodus where it talks about an eye for an eye and a tooth for a tooth."

"We want more than one eye, Nate," Wade Stone said solemnly. "If we let those sheepherders get by with this we'll all be losing cows."

Nate Wylie's head bobbed in agreement. "One good yearlin' calf ought to be worth twenty sheep and lambs. I want us to ride over there with clubs and guns and leave plenty of dead woolies behind. They need a lesson to remember."

"He's right!" Hetty Mead shouted, her voice rising above the din. "Let's stop talking and get on our way."

She had moved up beside Smoke, but he was so upset by Nate's words he had not noticed her nearness. He gave her an annoyed glance, said loudly, "He's wrong. If you'll stop and think a minute you'll see he's wrong."

Nate Wylie took a step toward Smoke, his eyes

73

flashing. "By damn, you're goin' with the rest of us and stand up for the Pitchfork. I'll give a hungry man a beef, but I won't have one taken from me by a thief."

Instinctively, Smoke reached out and grabbed his father's arm. He could not remember the last time he had touched him, and the same thought must have coursed through Nate's mind.

"It's some kind of setup, Pa," Smoke said, dropping his hand away. "Can't you see that? First somebody takes only part of a beef, leaving the rest of it to the wolves, then drips blood all along the trail and drops pieces of hide to mark the way. That's too easy. No real thief would ever be that stupid. Somebody wanted us to find the trail."

"They got scared," Hetty Mead chimed in. "They left in a hurry and didn't cover their tracks."

"Stay out of this, Hetty," Smoke snapped.

Anger fired the green in Hetty Mead's eyes. She swung her arm around and tried to slap Smoke's face. He knew Hetty's nature and anticipated her reaction. Before her open hand could reach its target, Smoke's fingers closed around her wrist and held her immobile.

Ignoring his daughter, Jerry Mead stepped close to Nate Wylie. "That's been bothering me ever since I heard Gil's story. I think Smoke's right. It looks like somebody wants us to get in a squabble with the sheepmen and I don't think it's them. We ought to think on this, Nate."

"Nothin' to think on," Nate snorted. "Somebody butchered my beef. I don't care who it was, or why it was, I aim to make 'em pay for it."

74

Smoke nodded at Jerry Mead, grateful for his support. "There's plenty to think on, Pa. You've got a right to get yourself killed, but you don't have the right to get everybody else killed. Let me and Gil run it down. We'll scout across the ridge and try to find the person who's to blame. When we do we'll see he pays a price."

"Makes sense to me," Wade Stone murmured.

"Beats a war," Jake Fentriss agreed. "If Smoke and Gil will hunt for the thief, the rest of us can get back to our work while we wait to see how the land lays. We don't have a big crew like you do, Nate."

The talk went on for a while with Nate Wylie going from man to man, still urging them to act against the sheepmen. "Once it starts it won't be just Pitchfork beef they'll want. They'll be after your cows too, Wade. And yours, Jake, and yours, Jerry."

Nate was dressed in what he called his good clothes— pin-striped trousers, brocaded vest, white shirt, and black string tie. His black hat resembled those worn by Cavalry officers, except that the brim was straight and crisp. His attire set him apart from the other men, who wore faded Levis and flannel shirts, and Nate wanted it that way. He was the self-appointed leader on this range, and on occasions such as this he dressed for the role.

Gil and Smoke kept their distance from the group, studying the expressions on the ranchers' faces. Smoke noticed that Nate's tones began to mellow as doubts killed the excitement and eagerness displayed earlier by his neighbors. After a few minutes, Nate moved away from the others and beckoned to Elijah Pardee, who was still standing out in the field with the Pitchfork cook.

As Pardee started forward, his white duster grabbing at his ankles, Nate went out to meet him. They stood together for several minutes, heads close, then Nate rejoined the group. It was the preacher's opinion, he told them, that it would not be right for all the sheepmen to suffer for the sin of one man—the lone rider whose tracks Gil had found. Nate said he would abide by that decision and would give Smoke and Gil a chance to hunt down the thief.

"But mind you this," Nate warned as the other ranchers drifted toward their horses. "They'd better find me a man. If they do I'll either hang him or horse-whip him within an inch of his life and send him back so them sheepherders can see him bleed. If they don't find the guilty man I'm going to make an example with dead sheep! I'll want all of you back here to help with that."

Saddle leather creaked and hooves scuffed the ground as the visiting ranchers mounted to leave. They held their horses in check for a few moments and exchanged final remarks with Nate, then Wade Stone and Jake Fentriss rode away. Jerry Mead lounged in the saddle, holding the reins of his daughter's pinto while he waited for her to join him.

Hetty lingered at Smoke's side, gently rubbing the wrist he had grasped when she tried to slap him. The anger was gone from her face and her green eyes were soft when she looked at him. "Be careful, Smoke," she said. "If what you believe is right you could ride into an ambush."

He started to reply, but she did not give him a chance.

Suddenly her lips were on his, moist, warm, and alive with feeling. She whirled away as quickly as she had moved against him, and walked to her horse. Smoke stared at her back, admiring the smooth curves of her body which were outlined by her snug-fitting Levi's and open-collar red shirt. Taking the reins from her father, she swung easily into the saddle, jabbed the pinto with her heel, and left the corral grounds at a gallop. A half smile on his face, Jerry Mead looked across at Smoke, shrugged, and followed his daughter.

Gil Wylie said, "Pa listened to you this time. I'm glad you showed up. You bought us some time."

"He didn't listen to me," Smoke said with a shrug. "He listened to Jerry Mead. None of them had a heart for a sheep-killing, but they do what Nate tells them."

As they talked, Nate Wylie came toward them. He had only a slight limp, but it caused him to move in a rocking, uneven gait and his face registered an occasional grimace of discomfort.

Speaking slowly, grimly, he went over his instructions one more time, repeating most of what he had said earlier. "You're not to handle it yourselves," he concluded, his eyes set on Smoke's face. "You'll bring the scalawag to me when you find him—if you find him."

The rancher switched his glance to Gil, and said, "I'm countin' on you to see that Smoke don't do nothin' foolish with that quick gun of his."

He turned abruptly and walked away from them, his big shoulders squared stubbornly, his cane barely tapping the ground as he moved. Charlie Ray Jones had gone back to his kitchen, but Preacher Pardee remained nearby, shifting his weight from foot to foot while he waited for Nate Wylie.

"Do you want to head out now?" Gil asked.

Smoke glanced at the cloudless sky, marking the position of the sun, and nodded. "Yeah, let's get on our way. We've still got four hours of daylight. I've got to get a fresh horse, and I'll saddle one for you if you'll ask Charlie Ray to pack us a sack of grub."

"Why do we need food?" Gil asked, frowning. "We ought to be back some time tonight."

"I wouldn't count on it," Smoke said. "There's no way of knowing where this trail's going to lead."

For a moment Gil studied his brother's face, spotting in Smoke's eyes a cloud of worry he had not noticed before. Without further comment he turned and walked toward the cook shack.

At the corral next to the nearest hay barn Smoke roped out a sleek black mustang which he sometimes used as a cutting horse and switched the bay's saddle to it. He put a rope halter on the bay so he could lead it, then saddled Gil's roan. When he led the horses outside he found Preacher Pardee standing fifteen feet beyond the corral gate. Smoke stopped, wondering why the man was there. The noise from the horses in the corral had drowned out the sound of the preacher's approach.

Eli Pardee was barely five feet tall and weighed almost two hundred pounds. He claimed to be in his mid-thirties, but his bearing and appearance were those of an old man. His shoulders were stooped and he moved in short, shuffling steps. His close-set blue eyes looked out through puffy slits in a flat-nosed face creased by folds of fat. His breath came out in wheezing, whistling bursts, and his voice was a nasal twang.

Sweat rolled off Smoke's face and dripped from the strands of hair which poked out from his hatband. He was tense, edgy, already tired, and in no mood for small talk. He nodded curtly to Pardee and walked on past him, but the preacher fell in step beside him, his breath noisy as he struggled to match strides with Smoke.

Smoke stopped after a few steps. "Do you want something from me, Preacher?"

"I'd like to talk a moment," Pardee said, breathing hard from the mild exertion of the short walk.

There was impatience in Smoke's eyes as he waited for the man to recover his wind. He wondered how the preacher managed to get around the country. Pardee was a circuit rider, serving congregations in a dozen towns and hamlets along a looping hundred-mile route that swung out from Jackpine and back again. He showed up at the Pitchfork about every three months, staying sometimes for as long as two weeks, going into town once or twice to deliver a sermon at Jackpine's only church.

"Have you been eating good, Preacher?" Smoke asked pointedly.

"Very well, praise the Lord," Pardee replied. "I'm always treated well at the Pitchfork. Your pa is a good and hospitable man. He shall reap his reward in heaven."

"Yeah," Smoke said indifferently. "Did you have something to say to me?"

"We need to talk about your soul," Pardee said, his voice rising fervently. "We must talk about the sins you commit when you fornicate with the girls at the Great Western Saloon, when you shoot your fellow man on the streets, when you defy your father's guidance. You're bringing Nate Wylie great pain, and the Bible says you are to honor thy father . . ."

Smoke spat into the dirt, turned toward his horse, and left Pardee's voice trailing off into the air. He stepped into the black's saddle, holding the bay's lead rope and the reins of Gil's roan. He said, "I'm in a big hurry, Preacher. You'll have to give me that sermon some other time."

"Wait!" Pardee pleaded. "I know there's still hope for your salvation. I don't wish to damn you without offering praise for the good things you do. There's a struggle between good and evil going on inside you, my son. I can sense the struggle you're having with the devil, but you can cleanse your soul by letting the good spirit shine through and repenting for your sins while I am your witness. Let the good spirit shine!"

"You must have me mixed up with somebody else, Preacher. Nobody around here has accused me of doing good deeds."

"Not true, praise the Lord," Pardee said. "There's a girl at the Great Western named Amy Sue Buckner, for instance, who knows a side of you few people have seen."

"What about her?" Smoke asked quickly.

"The story came to me from some of those other poor wretches at the Great Western," Pardee said. "They seek me out when the burden of their sins becomes too much to bear. They long for forgiveness and salvation and they also talk a lot about you. I've been enlightened. Some of the girls tell me it's not always lust that takes you to the Great Western. They say you're the kindest person they know—that you're more of a friend than a lover. One of them—I forget which—told me about Amy Sue. She said you'd taken her under your wing and that you've urged her to give up her sinful ways and get married. She said you've been giving Amy Sue money for food and rent, but that you never . . . uh, never have relations with her. I know you're a terrible sinner, but I also know there's a good heart under that tough hide of yours."

Smoke looked down from the saddle, a bemused grin on his face. "Did you ever see Amy Sue, Preacher?"

"No," Pardee replied. "No, she's never sought my counsel."

"If you ever saw Amy Sue you'd understand." Smoke shook his head. "The poor girl is as ugly as a wet sheepdog. There's no way she can earn a living doing what she's doing, so I give her money. There's no way you can earn a living doing what you're doing, so Nate gives you money. Think on that, Preacher, and see if there's much difference."

Lifting his gaze across the field, Smoke saw Gil walking away from the kitchen, a lumpy sack thrown across one shoulder. He kneed his horse around, tugged at the animals behind him, and rode to meet Gil, leaving Pardee standing with a flushed face.

Chapter Seven

It was six miles from the Pitchfork to the foot of Dead-line Ridge, and the brothers covered most of the distance in silence. There had been a few minutes of closeness between them in the ranch yard when they banded together to oppose Nate's plans, but now it was gone, and they could find little to talk about.

As they rode, Smoke stole an occasional glance at Gil's face. Worry was written in the hard line of his brother's jaw and in the knotted fist which gripped the reins. Gil's interest went beyond an effort to prevent some of the ranchers from being killed in a range war, Smoke knew. He did not want any of the sheepmen killed either.

Gil had friends on the other side of the ridge, and Smoke had guessed long ago that one of them was a girl. Nate Wylie was unaware of it, but Gil made frequent trips across the ridge, sometimes staying overnight—something few cattlemen would ever do. It irritated Smoke that his father hounded him about his fondness for women while Gil's nighttime forays went unnoticed.

They rode for more than an hour, moving up the grassy humpbacks which led to the ridge, before Gil asked about the extra horse. If they took a prisoner, Smoke explained, he planned to rejoin his roundup crew while Gil tied the cow thief on the mustang and took him back to face Nate Wylie.

Presently Gil asked, "How's it going in South Basin?"

Smoke had hoped to avoid any discussion about the roundup. Nate had been too enraged over Smoke neglecting his work to check on details, and even now Gil's question was posed merely to make conversation.

"We haven't been to South Basin yet," Smoke said reluctantly. "We started on East Creek like we always do."

Gil's bleached eyebrows pushed down close to his eyes and his lips tightened against his teeth. "That's not what you were told to do. When are you going to learn to follow orders? You must like to get Pa's dander up."

Smoke shook his head. "I didn't change the plan just to rile him, but if I'm responsible for it I ought to be able to decide how to handle my part of the roundup. There weren't any orders. Nate just said he'd start in South Basin if *he* was doing it."

A snort of disgust came from Gil. "When Nate says anything about range work it's an order. He expects you to do what he'd do because it's his ranch and he knows more about cows than either of us. If it floods down there and some of the steers get crippled while you're trying to pull them out of the bogs, Nate'll run you off the place."

Anger darkened Smoke's face. He said sharply, "He may not get a chance to run me off, but you can quit fretting about South Basin. By the time I get back, Ike Yarby and the others should be down there. Are you going to tell Nate I ignored his suggestion when you get back?"

"I tell him what he needs to know," Gil said, and spurred his horse ahead. He went about a hundred feet, then slowed again. He leaned sideways in the saddle, studying the ground.

As Smoke came alongside, Gil pointed to places where he'd spotted the blood drippings the day before. Most of them were gone now, faded by the sun, but they found a few rust-colored spots in the grass as they moved higher on the ridge.

Smoke felt his pulse quicken. He also felt his anger building. Only a man who had grown up on the range, taking his living from it, knew how much work and sweat it took to raise a single steer. It was not a possession to be given up easily to someone who had done nothing to earn it. In the last few hours Smoke had begun to realize that his hate for anyone who violated the Pitchfork property could be as intense as that of Nate and his brother.

The country grew rougher as they rode northward, broken by gulches and dry washes. They had to work their way around clusters of sandstone boulders which had broken off over the years and rolled down in the gullies. Part of the trail was hidden by mesquite and hackberry thickets, but Gil knew the way and the ride was not difficult.

There was still plenty of daylight left when they reached the series of switchback trails that led over the ridge. It was cool and peaceful under the pines and cedars as they rode in and out of timber. The only sounds were the occasional ring of a horseshoe striking stone and the chattering of a flock of magpies farther up the slope. Looking through the trees, Smoke saw three vultures soaring in a circle off to his left, their fingered wings fluttering as they descended somewhere out of sight.

After an hour of climbing they came to a small level park and stopped to rest their horses. Gil sat down on the ground a few feet ahead of Smoke. He leaned back on his hands and blew the sweat off his nose. Smoke stayed close to the horses and took out his tobacco to roll a cigarette. He held the tobacco sack out toward Gil, but his brother declined with a shake of his head. Smoke stood and smoked quietly for a while. From the clearing he saw the vultures again, but there were only two of them this time. One of them was apparently on the ground feeding on something.

The sheep settlement was not yet in sight. From the park a hard-packed trail, which apparently was used often by the sheepmen, ran up a second slope that crested about a mile farther north. This was as far as Gil had followed the thief's trail. He had been unable to find any signs of blood or pieces of hide after he reached the clearing.

A quiver of excitement ran through Smoke as he realized they were nearing their destination. The trail from the park was uncluttered by rocks of any size and the timber thinned to small bushes. Smoke had been there only once since the sheepmen had come into the country years ago, but he remembered the settlement. A dozen or so small huts, each with a few lambing pens, were scattered across the flats beyond the ridge, and could be seen from the crest of the second slope.

Before the sheepmen came, the craggy hills were called Buzzard's Ridge. Nate Wylie had renamed them

Deadline Ridge, and the name was not without significance. It was the line between sheep country and cattle country—a boundary beyond which no sheepman dared let his stock stray toward the Pitchfork range if he expected to live in peace.

After a few minutes Gil pushed to his feet and Smoke turned to mount his horse. He stopped, his hand poised above the saddle horn as Gil said, "I want you to give me your gun before we ride down there."

Smoke let his arm come down slowly to his side and took a deep breath. He stared at his brother, his eyes smoky and narrow. "You're not going to get it."

Gil studied Smoke's face. "That's what I figured, but Pa expects me to see that you don't start something too big for the two of us to handle. You ought to humor me just once."

"Get this big brother stuff out of your head," Smoke said. "I'm fed up with you trying to boss me around like Nate does. I'm not a fool and it's none of your business where I go or what I do."

Spreading his hands in a hopeless gesture, Gil said, "You're driving Pa out of his mind. He never knows what you'll do next. Don't you care about him at all?"

"I guess I do," Smoke said, and his voice was strangely soft, almost sad. "I guess I feel like he's my pa, but I'm not sure I'm happy that he is. He owns half the range, half the town, and he's got his spurs into somebody all the time. We've grown up without a mother and he acts like we never had one. He must feel ashamed of the way he treated her, but he'll never tell us that."

Gil gave him a long, disapproving glance, then walked to his own horse and stepped into the saddle. As he started the roan up the trail he said over his shoulder, "That's what it's all about. It's not Pa's power you hate. It's what happened to our mother that you hold against him."

Smoke felt the blood rush to his face, but he started his own horses moving without replying. They had gone only a hundred yards when he stopped again. Ahead of him Gil pulled in his reins and twisted around in the saddle. "What's wrong now?"

Above them, and off to the left, the two buzzards circled lower and finally disappeared behind the trees a quarter of a mile east of the clearing they had just left. Smoke was looking in that direction.

"I think we ought to go back," he said.

Gil appeared annoyed. "Do you want to give up the search?"

"No. I think we ought to see what those buzzards are after."

Gil argued against the delay, suggesting that the birds were probably scavenging over a dead rabbit or some other small animal, but he did not protest strongly. He knew they were following a dubious trail, not at all certain it would lead them to a satisfactory conclusion. Their only plan was to ride into the sheep settlement, talk to some of Gil's friends, and hope they could pick up a clue. Gil was convinced the sheepmen would not lie to protect a thief—especially a thief who had angered Nate Wylie enough to jeopardize their lives and their future.

"Do you think there could be a body over there?" Gil asked.

"We won't know until we look," Smoke said, and turned his horses back toward the clearing.

Smoke took the lead, moving out of the park toward the spot where he believed the gleaming black carrion birds had settled to the ground. They had to cross back over the brow of the ridge, and after they were beyond the clearing the going was extremely slow. There was no trail, and they had to work their way through pine saplings and thick underbrush. The sun was low in the west. Pink and purple streamers pinwheeled along the horizon and the sandstone outcroppings reflected the blue and crimson hues.

After they had ridden about a mile, Smoke paused to get his bearings. Far off, in the valley below, he could see the rectangular outline of a hay barn on Jerry Mead's Circle M. Beyond the barn, where the stream turned eastward and eventually emptied into a tributary of the Brazos, the waters of West Creek glistened like a twisted mirror in the sunlight. Fifteen miles farther on, hidden by the hills, lay the town of Jackpine.

Scanning the ground ahead of him, Smoke cocked his ear for any sound made by the buzzards. He lifted the Colt from the holster and fired it into the air. The mustang nickered in alarm, tried to dance backward, and Smoke heard Gil fighting his horse behind him. The bay merely shook its head and stood still. A thrashing, fluttering noise came out of the brush fifty yards in front of them and the buzzards rose into sight, flapping their wings clumsily as they fought to gain altitude.

Smoke urged his mount forward, keeping his eyes on a spot where he could see a loose feather still skipping around in the air. He pulled up at the edge of an arroyo which was almost screened from sight by brush and boulders. He slid to the ground as Gil came up beside him. Together they walked around the edge of the gully, searching for whatever had drawn the buzzards there. Weeds and briars clogged the floor of the arroyo, but one patch had been trampled and beaten down flat by the vultures.

Almost at the same instant both voiced a startled curse. Lying in the flattened grass was the shank bone of an animal. The buzzards had picked it clean, but the size of it, and the remaining hoof, told them it had come from the yearling Gil had found slaughtered on the prairie.

"Whoever it was didn't kill the beef to eat," Gil said grimly. "They just threw it away, but they didn't mean for anybody to find it before the wolves and vultures got rid of it. It doesn't make any sense."

Smoke felt relieved. He said, "Somebody meant for us to do exactly what Nate had in mind—ride over the ridge with guns ready and start a war with the sheepmen. I'm glad we put the brakes on that notion."

"What do you make of it?" Gil's face was pale and his eyes held a puzzled expression. "We've never had any trouble from these people. Nate has seen to it. Why would somebody waste a calf just so we'd go gunning for the sheepmen? Who'd want to start that kind of feud?"

"Beats me." Smoke turned and walked toward the

head of the arroyo. "Let's see if we can pick up some sign around here. That hind quarter didn't walk up here by itself."

As the wash narrowed, with steeper walls where it slashed into the hillside, they saw that access to the arroyo was much easier at that point than the way they had come. Before long they found evidence of the rider who had discarded the beef quarter—a scratch left by a horseshoe on a flat rock, and a broken pine bough which had not yet turned brown.

Gil, walking bent at the knees, his head close to the ground, stooped and picked up something from among the rocks. He turned and held out his hand for Smoke to see. It was a wooden matchstick which was broken halfway through in the center and bent to form a V.

"It doesn't tell us much," Gil said.

A muscle jumped along Smoke's jaw and his voice was angry as he said, "It tells us all we need to know. I know who killed our steer. It was Jesse Slater. He's the man I had a run-in with in Jackpine. He has a habit of chewing matches and bending them this way between his teeth. He spat one on the ground just before I shot him, and Ned Arnold said he was spitting them at him while he was at the Great Western. Jesse Slater's been here. That's his match stick."

"Jesse Slater?" Gil murmured incredulously. "Why would a stranger like Slater be up here killing the Pitchfork's cows?"

Smoke took the match from Gil's hand. He studied it briefly, then wrapped it in a half dozen layers of cigarette papers, careful to preserve its shape. Afterward, he placed it in the tobacco sack and buttoned the flap of his shirt pocket so it would not fall out.

"Slater must have figured it would bring me after him. Maybe he planned to bushwhack me," Smoke said. "Or maybe he was hoping to get me killed in a range war, or at least make life miserable for the whole Wylie family."

"That's a hard way to get even, a pretty uncertain way," Gil reasoned. "It was pure luck that I stumbled on the dead yearling."

Smoke shrugged. He was not sure his speculation offered a logical explanation of the man's motives, but he was sure Jesse Slater had killed the Pitchfork steer.

"You can't figure a man like Slater," Smoke said. "I think he's a little loco, but I'll get some answers when I find him. I'm going after him and bring him in to face Nate if I can."

"How do you know you can find him?"

"I'll find him," Smoke said, studying the ground. He retraced their steps, going back to the rock they had seen with a horseshoe mark on it. After criss-crossing the trail a few times, he found what he was looking for—another broken match stick shaped like a V. He showed it to Gil, then placed it in the tobacco sack with the other one.

Smoke went back to his horse and began loosening the mustang's cinch strap, preparing to switch the saddle to the bay he had been leading.

"Leave me the food and take the mustang back to the ranch," he said to Gil. "Tell Nate what we found. Tell him I'll try to bring him a cow thief."

Gil grasped one side of the saddle, sharing its weight as he helped place it on the bay's back. "We'll do this job together. I'm going with you."

Straightening, Smoke looked into his brother's face, noticing the coppery flecks in Gil's eyes. "No, you're not," he said emphatically. "This is my fight. Jesse Slater promised to come back and kill me some day and he won't give up. If I don't find him, he'll find me. I don't like to be looking over my shoulder."

Finally Smoke convinced Gil that he should return to the Pitchfork. If both of them remained away too long, Nate might assume something had gone wrong and decide to lead the ranchers on a raid against the sheepmen. It was a chance neither of them wanted to take and Gil agreed reluctantly to let Smoke go on alone.

While he was tying his bedroll and the food sack behind the saddle, Smoke looked across the bay's back with a teasing smile on his lips.

"Since we're so close maybe you ought to spend the night across the ridge," Smoke said. "Nate probably wouldn't worry about us anyway. I know you have a girl over there."

"I had one," Gil said quietly, his face coloring. "Her folks sent her to college back East. She's going to be a schoolmarm. Some of our friends would be surprised to see how well educated some of the sheepmen are."

"Are you serious about her, or just sleeping with her?"

Gil rolled his tongue around in his cheek and said, "Oh, we get along about the same as you and Hetty Mead, I guess. Hetty's been in love with you since you were in grade school, but I can't understand why."

Smoke shrugged. He had started teasing Gil to ease his own tension, but he did not want to talk about Hetty

Mead. He checked the stirrups and stepped into the bay's saddle. As he reined the horse around toward the easier trail at the head of the arroyo, Gil asked quietly, "Is Jesse Slater good with a gun?"

A sober expression settled across Smoke's face. "That's what I'll have to find out. Maybe I was just lucky the first time, but I'll know more about it when I get back."

"If you get back," Gil said softly, but Smoke was already too far down the trail to hear him.

Chapter Eight

Nate Wylie was sitting at his cluttered desk in the parlor when he heard Eli Pardee come in from the ranch yard. Nate had changed his clothes and was in more familiar garb now—blue flannel shirt, a yellow neckerchief, and work-worn Levi's.

A hallway separated the parlor from a dining room on the other side. The house was spacious, but plain and modestly furnished. From the entryway, the hall led to bedrooms down the longer leg of the T-shaped building. Pardee paused in the hallway to catch his breath, then came into the parlor.

Nate closed the ledger he had been studying and watched absently as the preacher struggled out of the linen duster and hung it on an elkhorn rack beside the door. Pardee fanned himself several times with his stained derby hat, then put it beside the coat. He shuffled across the planked floor and eased himself carefully into one of the leather chairs beyond the desk. Sweat sparkled in the creases of his face and plastered his yellow hair close to his head.

"Had you a talk with Smoke before he left, did you?" Nate asked casually.

Pardee nodded. He picked up a bible from the table beside the chair and caressed it with his hands.

"I told you it would be a waste of your time and breath," Nate grunted. "Smoke don't listen to nobody."

"I'm beginning to wonder if he's as bad as he wants people to think. I've heard some stories in town—"

A scowl crossed Nate's face and his deep voice cut the preacher short. "He's bad, all right. You just don't know the cussedness in that boy, Preacher. It's like he's out to prove how bad he can be—drinkin', chasin' after cheap women, and gettin' mixed up in barroom brawls. Worse than that, he's always runnin' me down behind my back, I hear—even to old friends like Ben Toler. He's full of trouble and you can't tell what fool thing he might do next."

The preacher thumbed through the pages of the bible. Without raising his eyes, he said, "I was thinking about Marshal Toler as I came in just now. Perhaps you should ask his advice about your trouble—what to do about the dead beef. If he could find the poacher and hold him in jail for the county sheriff it might prevent bloodshed. It would be the proper thing, Brother Wylie, to have this matter settled by the authorities."

"No," Nate said flatly. "Ben's a town marshal and his jurisdiction ends at the town limits. He'd be willin' to stretch that, but by damn, I'm not. The county sheriff is a hundred miles away and we don't see him around here except at election time. I'll find the guilty man and I'll handle it."

"Judge not, lest ye be—" the preacher began to quote, but Nate's glare stopped him again.

"I'll handle it," Nate repeated sharply, and the fire in his eyes told Pardee the subject was closed.

While Eli Pardee concentrated on the bible, Nate turned his attention again to his ledgers, but he could not keep his mind on the figures he had entered in the books—estimates of what his herd would bring this year, how much his expenses would be, and where he would stand at the end of the season. His eyes hooded by his shaggy brows, he occasionally studied the preacher's face, feeling somewhat guilty because of the harsh way he had spoken to him.

Nate felt no firm bond of friendship with the fat, unkempt man, but he liked to have him in the house. Before meeting Pardee five years ago, Nate Wylie had had little interest in religious matters and knew very little about the Bible. Since then, however, he had found a measure of comfort in Pardee's readings and the messages of the Scriptures.

Their first meeting came by chance in the dining room of the Pioneer House Hotel on one of Nate's rare visits to Jackpine. At the time, Pardee was moving from table to table, talking with people about salvation and imploring them to save their souls. Nate watched him with a jaundiced eye. Most of the people merely glared at him, then dismissed him impatiently.

The hangdog expression on Pardee's perspiring face had aroused the rancher's sympathy. Nate invited him to sit at his table and drink a cup of coffee. From that meeting, Nate learned that Pardee was a circuit rider, that he traveled over a broad expanse of Texas and stopped in several towns. He also discovered that Pardee was a wellspring of gossip. The preacher enjoyed talking about the places he had been, the people he knew, and the hypocrisy he uncovered.

When Nate left Jackpine that day he invited the preacher to spend a few days at the ranch, and Pardee accepted. Afterward, Pardee made the Pitchfork his home whenever he came to the Jackpine area.

Nate's invitation was not entirely unselfish. He wanted information, and a man who traveled as much as Eli Pardee might be able to provide it. They had barely settled themselves in the parlor that first day when Nate gave Pardee a description of Cora Wylie and asked if he had ever seen her. Unfortunately, the preacher could not recall anyone who resembled Nate Wylie's wife.

It annoyed Nate that Pardee never volunteered an answer to the question he always knew was sure to come, that he always forced the rancher to ask it himself. As they sat in the parlor this day, Nate busied himself with his books and tried to wait the man out, but Nate was not a man of great patience. After they had been silent for ten minutes, he shoved his business papers aside and said, "Heard any news, Preacher?"

"I can tell you some interesting stories," Pardee said, "but I haven't seen anyone who looks like Cora Wylie." He rested the open bible on his knees and drew in a wheezing breath. "You've got to remember, Brother Wylie, that you described to me a woman the way she looked long ago. People change. They grow old, gain weight, lose weight, turn gray—and they die. We might not recognize her if she was sitting in this room with us."

Nate thought he detected a note of irritation in Pardee's voice, but he ignored it. He said, "Cora's eyes, her lips, and her smile won't change. You'll know her if you see her, and I'd sleep better if I knew whether she's alive or dead, rich or poor—livin' a good life or bad."

He sighed and looked down at the floor, shaking his head. "Sometimes you act like you think I'm a damn fool for tryin' to run her down after all these years."

Eli Pardee's jowls flapped against his wilted shirt collar as he shook his head in quick denial. "Oh, no, not at all, praise the Lord. We can't reshape the past, you know. We can repent for it, but we can't call it back. My thoughts and my prayers are on the present. I pray for your sons, and I'd feel better if you had asked the marshal to go with them."

Dishes rattled in the dining room across the hallway, and there was a sound of booted feet crossing the floor. Pardee twisted in his chair, trying to tilt his head so he could see through the doorway.

"We'll eat directly," Nate said. "Charlie Ray will give us a call when the food's on the table."

Leaving the desk, Nate walked to the front window and stared out over the prairie. His thick mustache was drawn close to his lips. Pardee's hint that he had not shown enough concern for the safety of Gil and Smoke had angered him. Any other man would have been told to get out of the house, or to mind his own business, but

Nate forced himself to hold his temper out of respect for Pardee's ministry.

More than he had with anyone since his wife left, the rancher had confided his innermost thoughts to Eli Pardee. He had talked with the preacher about his loneliness, his sadness over the strained relationship between him and his youngest son, and the emptiness of his life—a void he hoped his new-found interest in the Bible might fill. There were some things he did not talk about.

He did not tell Eli Pardee why he preferred to avoid advising Marshal Ben Toler about the threat of trouble between the sheepmen and the ranchers. Pride and ethics were involved, and Nate suspected Ben Toler would not welcome a call for help from the owner of the Pitchfork.

When he finally returned to the Jackpine range, Ben Toler's first stop was at the Pitchfork Ranch. He wanted his old job back, but Nate declined to hire him. Nate wanted no reminders of the past, and he did not want anyone to know of the mission Ben Toler had undertaken for him. In a moment of anger or idle reminiscence Ben might let something slip about the night Cora Wylie left the ranch.

Nate Wylie was a man who paid his debts, however, and he owed something to Ben Toler. He convinced Ben there was a more important job which needed filling— marshal of Jackpine. The town was small and had no lawman of its own, but Nate saw a need for one.

As more and more Texas ranchers trailed herds north to Colorado and Wyoming, taking the cutoff which passed near the town, Jackpine was experiencing a surge of growth. With the growth came crooked gamblers, cattle thieves, outlaws on the dodge, and drunken cowboys letting off steam. Someone was needed to protect the welfare and property of Jackpine's permanent residents, and Nate insisted that Ben Toler was the right man for the job. Nate told Ben he would speak to the Town Commission about it.

The proposition made sense and Ben Toler was happy with the job. It was only after he learned how much control Nate Wylie exerted over the Town Commission that he felt he had been manipulated like a puppet. The three-man commission was comprised of Ed Jarvis, owner of the General Store, Henry Bain of the Pioneer House, and Bob Elmore, the banker. All three of them owed favors to Nate Wylie and they did what he asked.

In his early years at the Pitchfork, Ben learned Nate had been instrumental in organizing the bank and owned a major share of it, but it was not until several months after the Town Commission hired him as town marshal that Ben found out that the rancher was also a partner in the other businesses. Sometime in the past, Ed Jarvis and Henry Bain had experienced financial hardships and come close to going out of business. They'd sought Nate Wylie's help. As security for the money he loaned them, the rancher had accepted a mortgage on their property. When they'd been unable to repay him, Nate had settled the loans by becoming their partner.

Bain and Jarvis were grateful that the rancher had saved them from disaster, but Nate's tactics bothered a man with Ben's principles, and he blamed the rancher for not letting him stand on his own. They remained friends, but there was a coolness in the marshal which Nate did not like to face. He would not ask favors from Ben Toler.

"Grub's on!"

Charlie Ray Jones's yell from the dining room cut through Nate Wylie's thoughts and he turned away from the window. Preacher Pardee squirmed out of his chair and started toward the hallway.

"Hold on a minute," Nate said. He went to his desk and took a small metal box from the bottom drawer. He rummaged through it for a moment, then returned it to its place. As he walked by the coat rack on his way to the dining room he dropped a double eagle into the pocket of Eli Pardee's linen duster.

"I reckon you'll be ridin' on in the mornin', Preacher," Nate murmured. "That's a little somethin' to tide you over until you come back."

"Bless you," Pardee said, and waddled toward the dining room. "Praise the Lord."

When they were seated at the table, Pardee cleared his throat and said quietly, "I'll keep looking. The Lord works many miracles and He leads me along paths which will help others. You'll recall it was me that put the Widow Lovelace on the trail of Ben Toler's whereabouts. I won't forget your interest."

"I'll be obliged," Nate said.

After supper they whiled away the early evening hours in the parlor with Preacher Pardee reading aloud from the Scriptures. Nate sat behind the desk and listened, but he rose occasionally and paced in front of the window. His thoughts were on Gil and Smoke, wondering what progress they had made.

The time passed slowly. It seemed hours before dusk came and Nate lighted the parlor's oil lamps. A night bird cried out its loneliness in the post-oak tree which shaded the front porch of the house. Nate had to force himself to concentrate on Pardee's droning, singsong voice as the man continued to read aloud.

Suddenly Pardee grew silent, his head cocked to one side. "I hear a rider coming," he said.

Nate nodded, grabbing his cane. The hoofbeats were muffled by distance, but they could be heard through the stillness of the evening. Nate hurried into the yard and walked beyond the corner of the house so he could see the corrals. The wheezing breath of Eli Pardee was close beside him.

At a hundred yards the rider was clearly outlined against the purple sky. "That's Gil," Nate said.

"He's alone," Pardee said.

Nate slapped the ground nervously with his cane. "By damn, that means Smoke is either in trouble—or he's gone lookin' for it!"

Studying the horizon as he rode, Smoke Wylie came off the western slope of Deadline Ridge with anxiety pressing at him. It had taken him almost an hour to travel to the end of the ridge, then find a passable trail which led him back to the prairie. He let the horse pick its way through the timber and outcroppings while he thought about what lay ahead of him.

What would Jesse Slater's reaction be when Smoke

found him and accused him of being a thief? And how was Smoke going to force the man to return to Pitchfork and face the judgment of Nate Wylie?

Slater was not a man who cowed easily. Smoke had learned that when he challenged him in Jackpine. Although Smoke beat him to the draw, there was no fear or lack of confidence in the tall, black-eyed man when he promised to return for another showdown. Now Smoke was searching for him, but it amounted to the same thing.

Slater probably would welcome such a meeting. At the time Smoke shot him, Slater was preoccupied with the girl. There was no way of knowing how fast the man could draw when there was nothing else on his mind. Smoke was sure of one thing—there was bound to be gunplay when he found Slater.

As the hills fell away behind him, the land flattened into a level plain and Smoke put the bay into a brisk canter. He skirted the southern edge of the sheep lands, keeping his eyes on the dying sun. Caught in the colors of sunset, scattered patches of sage glowed crimson against the waving grass. A thin plume of smoke spiraled upward a few miles to his left, marking the spot where Gil's roundup crew was camping for the night.

Shortly after dusk he passed one of the Pitchfork line cabins—a square, log building with a lean-to at the rear which provided shelter for both men and horses when they were checking on cattle during the winter months. A little later he forded West Creek and rode across a corner of Jerry Mead's Circle M range.

The Mead house was not visible, but it was not far

away, and Smoke wondered what Hetty Mead would say if she knew of his mission. A moment later a mental picture of the girl he had rescued from Jesse Slater and Chub Morgan came into his mind. Her unusual beauty and sensual carriage were enough to stir any man's blood, and Smoke had been unable to stop thinking about her. Despite his feelings for Hetty, he wanted to see the dark-haired girl again and learn more about her.

He did not know what lay ahead of him, and he was keenly aware that he might never see Hetty or the dark-haired girl again. He was sure he would find Jesse Slater. After he and Gil found the broken match sticks on Deadline Ridge, he'd recalled fragments of his conversation with Ned Arnold. "Triangle T riders . . . moving a herd to Colorado . . . resting the cattle about a two-hour ride from town . . ."

Under ideal conditions a trail herd could move only eight or ten miles a day. The cutoff which would eventually lead the drovers to the Goodnight-Loving Trace would take them north and west. Smoke's calculations told him the herd should be almost in a direct line westward from Deadline Ridge by this time, and that was the route he took.

Two hours after dark he stopped beside a wet-weather spring and made his camp. He did not want to challenge a strange crew at night. After rigging a picket line for the bay, he ate beans and cold biscuits from Charlie Ray's grub sack. He smoked a cigarette, unrolled his blankets, and fell asleep quickly, too tired from long hours in the saddle to worry about what tomorrow would bring.

At noon the next day he spotted the dust cloud stirred

103

up by the plodding cattle. Half a mile ahead of the herd a single rider jogged slowly along, twisting in his saddle once in awhile to look back at the dust cloud. Smoke guessed that the rider was the trail boss, scouting ahead for the easiest trail and the best grass. He was the man Smoke needed to see first as a matter of courtesy, and he galloped the bay at an angle that would intercept him.

The trail boss saw Smoke coming and wheeled his horse to ride back and meet him. Smoke stopped ten feet in front of the man, nodded, and asked, "Are you the ramrod of this outfit?"

"I own it," the man said. "My name's Grant Tillman. Are you lookin' for work, or just ridin' through?"

"Neither," Smoke said. "I'm looking for one of your men."

Chapter Nine

Grant Tillman spread his hands on the pommel and grinned. He appeared to be in his middle forties, a man with a relaxed manner and an easy Texas drawl. As he studied Smoke's face, seeing the hardness of the pale eyes, the grin faded. He pushed back his curl-brimmed Stetson, rubbed the sweat from his straw-colored hair, and fixed his hazel eyes on Smoke's walnut-handled Colt.

"Well, now, friend," Grant Tillman said without animosity, "nobody talks to my men when I'm on a trail drive until they talk to me first. I don't make a habit of answerin' questions for every drifter who comes askin' them. Has this man got a name—have you got a name?

I don't mean any offense, but you look like a hardcase."

Smoke ran his hand across his chin, realizing he had not shaved in two days. His face was covered with a thick black stubble, and he guessed he must present a sorry picture. He introduced himself, apologized for his appearance, then said, "I'm told the man I'm looking for is called Jesse Slater. He's a tall hombre who's got a habit of chewing on matchsticks."

"That's Slater." Grant Tillman spat between his horse's ears and stared thoughtfully at the land ahead of him. "I don't like the man much, but I had to pick up a crew in a hurry. I want to get to Colorado before winter sets in. I sold my spread to an Eastern syndicate, but kept my cows. Texas is gettin' over-grazed fast. All the good grass that's left is in Colorado and Wyoming. That's where I aim to settle."

Tillman spat at the ground again and asked, "Are you the man who put a bullet in Slater's leg?"

Smoke nodded. "I am. I wasn't looking for a fight, but he was trying to force himself on a woman he dragged off the street. When I tried to help her he went for his gun. He wasn't quite fast enough."

"That ought to settle it," Tillman said, a wary look in his eyes.

"That's what I figured," Smoke said, "but it didn't. My pa owns the Pitchfork Ranch over east of here, and I think Slater found out about it. He's been prowling around on our range trying to get even. He shot a Pitchfork yearling, butchered it, and wasted it. He tried to make it look like the work of some sheepherders, but it wasn't the sheepmen. It was Slater. If he's not trying to get me killed in a range war, I don't know what he's up to, but he's got to answer for killing that steer."

Surprise flickered in Grant Tillman's eyes and his back stiffened. "Have you got proof that Jesse Slater was the steer-killer?"

"I have." Smoke unbuttoned his shirt pocket and withdrew the broken matchsticks, both still holding the shape of a V. He held his palm toward Tillman so the man could see them.

The rancher swore under his breath. "He's had time to do what you say. Four or five days ago when we were restin' the cattle back a ways, another stranger rode out to see Jesse. He stopped his horse fifty yards or so from the camp and started callin' Jesse out to meet him. It wasn't on my time, so I didn't interfere. Knowin' Jesse, I figured he owed a poker debt or somethin' like that. They talked for a few minutes and the stranger left. They were too far away for me to see what the man looked like, but I thought at the time—"

"Did anybody get the man's name?" Smoke asked.

"No," Tillman said. "Jesse didn't talk much to anybody except Chub Morgan, and he didn't tell him much. Chub told me later the visitor was a friend who came out to tell Jesse the name of the man who shot him in case Jesse wanted to come back some time. I couldn't figure how Jesse could've made any friends here unless the man was a doctor he'd been to see. Jesse started complainin' about the wound in his leg the next mornin' and asked to go into town to see a sawbones. I let him go and he stayed away two days. Bein' in no hurry except to beat the weather, I held up the herd until he got back."

Squinting his eyes as he searched his memory for details, Tillman paused and looked again in the direction of his herd. His voice sounded angry as he continued, "My cook is pretty good at range doctorin', and when Jesse started complainin' again I asked him to look at Jesse's leg. The cook said it wasn't nothin' more than a clean flesh wound. He said Jesse was as able to ride as any of us, so it set me to wonderin' why he stayed in town so long. Like I say, he had time to do what you said. He lied to me at the outset—said he got hit by a stray bullet durin' a saloon brawl. He didn't mention a woman and neither did Chub."

Smoke lifted the bay's reins. "I'd like to ride back and talk to him if you can tell me which end of your herd he's working today."

"Just hold on," Tillman said. "I don't want to upset my whole crew. I'll fetch him. You wait here."

As the man rode toward the herd, Smoke stepped down from the saddle, leaving the horse's reins trailing. He rolled his shoulders back and forth a few times and flexed his fingers to relax his nerves and stiff muscles. Sweat beaded his forehead and glistened in the stubble on his cheeks.

He kept his eyes on the slow-walking cattle until he saw Grant Tillman emerge from the dust cloud with another rider trailing close behind him.

They stopped their horses fifteen feet in front of Smoke and Grant Tillman dismounted immediately. Jesse Slater kept his seat in the saddle for a while. His thin, angular face was sullen, but his black eyes were bright and alive. He seemed to enjoy sitting where he could look down on Smoke.

Slowly, an arrogant swing to his shoulders, he stepped down and faced Smoke Wylie. If the leg wound still bothered him he showed no sign of it. "The boss says you want to jaw with me about something. I don't want nothing to do with you, cowboy. I aim to let bygones be bygones."

The man's pretense of forgiveness only sharpened Smoke's anger. Smoke braced his feet, his right hand dangling loosely near the butt of his gun as he said, "You killed a Pitchfork yearling, carried off one of the hind quarters, and left the rest to rot. That makes you a cow thief. You're coming back to the Pitchfork with me and explain it to my pa—tell him why you tried to mix the sheepmen up in it. By the time Nate Wylie gets through with you, that bullet wound will seem like a flea bite."

"I ain't going nowhere with you." Slater's lips thinned to a narrow line. "You're talking tommyrot, cowboy. You've got no proof that anybody would believe."

"I believe him, Slater," Grant Tillman snapped. "I've seen you chew on too many matches." He nodded at Smoke and said, "Show him what you've got."

An ironic smile twisted across Smoke's lips as he watched a wooden matchstick twitch between Jesse Slater's teeth, then he took those from his shirt pocket and tossed them at the man's feet. The V-shaped pieces of bleached wood glistened in the bright April sunlight.

The tall man's mouth opened soundlessly, and the match he was chewing fell to the ground near the others. He took a half step backward. His shoulders tensed and he dropped a hand close to his gun. He stood frozen for a few seconds, then cast a questioning glance toward Grant Tillman and waited to see what Smoke would do.

"There's good enough proof for me," Smoke said, pointing to the matchsticks. "Habits are hard to be cautious about. You got careless and spat out broken matchsticks where you threw away the steer's hind quarter on Deadline Ridge. You're coming with me, Slater."

"Nobody takes one of my men away without I say so," Grant Tillman drawled. "I don't know your old man and how he might handle this. I don't want a hangin' to worry about, but I purely do hate a thief. Since he wasn't rustlin' for a livin', I won't let you take him if he'll make good for the yearlin'. That would be twenty dollars at market."

A curse of defiance came from Jesse Slater. "I'm busted, Boss. You know that."

"Yeah, I know," Tillman said. "I heard you tell Chub Morgan you had only six bits when the two of you were headin' for town the other day, but I can fix that. I'll advance Wylie twenty dollars on your pay if you'll sign the time book showin' it was done. I don't want nobody claimin' they were cheated when this drive is over."

Jesse Slater glared at Smoke Wylie. "I ain't signing nothing. As far as I'm concerned this cowboy can go to hell."

His face drawn and ugly, Jesse Slater turned his back as if to walk away, but he did not go forward. His body kept swinging around, describing a complete circle.

In the split second his back was turned, Slater's right hand dipped to his holster and his gun was swinging upward when he came around to face forward again.

Smoke had no time to think about a way to beat the man, but his reflexes took over and his right hand was blurred by speed. His Colt came alive in his fist, spurting flame and smoke in a startling roar.

He heard the sound of Slater's shot and felt a breath of heat as the bullet whistled past his throat, then he saw a mushy red spot blossom magically between the tall man's eyes. Slater did not slump to the ground. The weight and velocity of the .45 slug sent his body flying backward, bent at the belt so that his head almost touched his knees. His dragging boot heels made faint tracks across the grass before Slater flopped to one side and lay motionless.

For a dozen heartbeats Smoke stood frozen in his tracks, his eyes locked on the dead man. His stomach swelled with nausea and his face was cold and clammy. He had not known it could be like this—that ending a man's life so violently could shock the whole nervous system. His stomach retched and he turned toward the skittering bay, wanting to hide behind the horse and throw up.

"Hey, look at this!" Grant Tillman's shout of surprise took Smoke's mind off his sick stomach.

Slowly Smoke turned back toward the body. Slater's hat had fallen off and his dark hair was flared out around his head. Tillman had rolled the body over on its back and was kneeling beside it. He pointed to the pocket on Slater's hide vest. Two shiny coins had worked halfway out of the pocket. Moving closer, Smoke saw that Tillman was pointing to two double eagles.

The rancher pulled the gold pieces from the vest and

rolled them in his hand, scowling. "Jesse lied to me again. He was carryin' forty dollars in gold—a month's wages and more. How in tarnation would Jesse come by that kind of money?"

Smoke turned the question over in his mind, but he was too shaken to concentrate on the possibilities. The sound of running horses caused both men to rise to their feet and look toward the herd. Three horsemen were almost upon them and Smoke could see the alarm in their faces. They had heard the gunshots and were hurrying to find out what they meant.

The riders dismounted and rushed toward Jesse Slater's body, all asking questions at the same time. Grant Tillman raised his hands to quiet them. In slow, unemotional tones he explained what had happened, telling them the reason for Smoke Wylie's presence and of the events which led to the shooting.

There was no surprise among them. Rustlers and thieves often met swift and violent death in this country, and the Triangle T riders accepted Grant Tillman's explanation with little comment.

One of the men was Chub Morgan, and Smoke kept his eyes on him. Chub's handsome, even-featured face seemed the only one to register any sign of sadness. Small tears welled up in his eyes, but he quickly brushed them away. The others merely stared curiously at the body while Grant Tillman talked. Afterward, two of the men mounted their horses and rode back toward the herd, but Chub Morgan lingered near the lifeless form on the ground.

Smoke moved over beside the man. "I hope you don't

plan to take up Jesse Slater's fight with me. If that's on your mind I want to settle it now."

Chub Morgan looked at Smoke and started backing away. "You won't get any trouble from me," he said nervously. "Jesse is dead and I'm sorry he is, but I don't have any reason to fight for him. He didn't have any folks, no friends, and I don't either. He needed somebody to look up to him, no matter how mean he was. I did that and I don't even know why."

Grant Tillman joined them, rattling the gold coins in his palm. He showed them to Chub Morgan. "Do you have any notion where Jesse might have got his hands on these?"

"Maybe," Chub murmured. "Jesse told me he had a chance to even the score with the man who shot him and make a little money at the same time. He told me about it right after some dude rode out from town and talked with him privatelike. Jesse claimed the man didn't give a name and I never did get a look at him, but I think that's who Jesse met when he pretended he needed to see a doctor."

Smoke and Grant Tillman exchanged glances, nodding their heads. They were both thinking the same thing—Jesse Slater had not acted alone in trying to start a war between the cattlemen and sheepmen. He had no way of knowing the location of the sheep settlement, but someone in Jackpine knew about it, and whoever it was also told Slater that the name of the man who shot him was Smoke Wylie. There was no doubt in Smoke's mind now that Jesse Slater had been paid to slaughter the Pitchfork yearling and leave a trail that would throw suspicion on the sheepmen.

"I guess you're entitled to one of these double eagles for the beef you lost," Grant Tillman said. "I'll try to send the other one to some of his kin. We'll bury him here."

Ignoring the coin in Tillman's hand, Smoke turned toward his horse. Over his shoulder, he said, "I don't think pa would want the money. I figure we've been paid in full. Give it to Chub. He's probably due something."

Grant Tillman took a step forward as Smoke reined the bay around to leave. The rancher touched his hat brim in a farewell salute. "Luck to you, Wylie."

Smoke nodded. He wheeled the bay and sent the horse loping across the prairie. He was eager to put the Triangle T herd and the sight of Jesse Slater's lifeless body behind him.

There was an unusual amount of activity in the ranch yard as Smoke came within sight of the Pitchfork the next morning. Half a dozen men were clustered in front of the bunkhouse, and among them Smoke saw Gil and his father. He was puzzled only briefly before realizing Nate had planned to hire extra riders for the last sweep of the roundup, even though they would not be needed for at least two more weeks.

As he approached the nearest corral he saw Gil and Nate waiting for him. They had left the other men loitering around the bunkhouse chatting among themselves. Smoke kept the bay at a walk as he covered the last fifty yards, delaying the meeting as long as he could.

His return trip, through more familiar country, had been faster and easier. Feeling drained by tension and the long ride, he pitched his night camp early enough to get plenty of sleep, and took time at dawn to shave and take a bath in a nearby creek. He did not feel refreshed, however, and he appeared to have aged beyond his years. Hard lines creased the corners of his mouth and his eyes looked tired.

He dreaded to face Nate Wylie. It was Smoke's fight with Jesse Slater in Jackpine that had brought the threat of a range war to the Pitchfork. Now he had left a dead man on the trail behind him. Smoke had been forced to kill Slater to save his own life, but he felt it had served no other purpose. There would be no war, because the sheepmen were innocent, but a strange conspiracy appeared to be building against the Pitchfork. Slater had been used only as a pawn to satisfy the aims of someone else, but who had hired Slater to make it appear the sheepmen were raiding the Pitchfork beef—and why?

Smoke did not have any answers, and he feared his father would blame him for the danger hanging over their heads.

Nate Wylie did not waste time with greetings when Smoke stopped the bay and slid to the ground a few feet in front of him. The rancher set the polished cane between his feet and braced both hands on the curved handle.

"You didn't bring anybody back with you," Nate growled.

Smoke drew a deep breath and said, "No, I didn't. I killed him."

Spots of color appeared on Nate Wylie's smooth cheeks and his thick mustache bristled. "Was he the man who took my yearling?"

Smoke nodded. "He was the man."

Speaking rapidly, eager to unburden his mind, Smoke recounted the events of the day before. He told of his meeting with Grant Tillman and of Slater's reaction when Tillman tried to force the man to pay for the slaughtered beef. His voice grew louder and was filled with anger when he mentioned the two gold pieces which had fallen from Slater's vest.

"Slater wanted to get at me, all right," Smoke said, "but there's somebody in Jackpine who wants to get at all of us."

"That's your fault," Gil Wylie said angrily. He had remained near the corral fence, listening without comment until Smoke indicated that the Pitchfork appeared to be the target of an unknown enemy. "It's that damn gun of yours that's causing trouble. If you had listened to Pa none of this would have happened."

Smoke whirled to face his brother. "You mind your mouth!" he said grimly. "The next time you stick your nose in my business I'm going to knock it off. You and Pa carry a gun. What's so different about mine?"

"The difference is that you shoot people and we shoot coyotes and rattlesnakes. You're dragging us all into—"

"By damn, shut up, the two of you!" Nate Wylie's voice thundered across the yard, and Smoke saw the loungers around the bunkhouse stop talking and look toward them.

"Now," Nate continued, his voice a rasping whisper,

"I'll handle things from here on out. As soon as the roundup is runnin' good I'll go in and have a talk with Ben Toler. I'll ask him to nose around and see what he can find out."

Swallowing hard, his knuckles white as he grasped the cane, he swung a glance toward the men at the bunkhouse, then back to his sons. "I kept Gil here in case we had to come find you, Smoke, and I want him to stay around to help me pick a crew from them drifters over there. Then we all need to get back to pushin' cattle onto the holdin' grounds. You gettin' along all right in South Basin?"

Smoke cast a covert glance at Gil and said, "Ike Yarby and the rest of my crew ought to be moving in there— from East Creek today. That's where we started—East Creek, not South Basin."

"That's not what I meant for you to do," Nate said.

"Well, that's what I did," Smoke countered. "I know how to do my work and I want to be left alone while I do it. If we'd started in South Basin I'd have to deal with a tired and quarrelsome crew by the time we got to East Creek, so I worked the farthest boundary while the men were fresh. I've always done it that way."

A tremor shook Nate Wylie's frame. His neck swelled, and he chewed at the shreds of mustache which touched his lips. He raised a shaking hand and pointed a forefinger at Smoke.

"You don't pay me any more mind than if I was a fly on a horse's rump," Nate roared, "but you'd better learn somethin' and learn it good. The next time you go against me you won't have any more say about anything at the Pitchfork. You'll work here like any other hired hand or you can ride out on your own. I'll cut off your credit in town and you'll have to make do on drover's wages. That's my final word, by damn! Now get back to your roundup crew where you belong."

Nate Wylie walked toward the bunkhouse, leaving Smoke staring at his back. He tapped the cane against the ground as he went, but anger strengthened his steps and the limp was scarcely noticeable.

As he turned to follow Nate, Gil said urgently, "For God's sake, Smoke, do what he says. He's going to kick you off the ranch if you don't."

Smoke clenched his teeth and hitched at his gun belt. "We'll see about that, but I'm not going to argue with him today. I've got other things to do."

After Gil left to join Nate at the bunkhouse, Smoke turned the tired bay loose in the corral and put his gear on the black mustang again. He leaned against the corral poles for a few minutes and smoked a cigarette, trying to shake off his anger. He resented Nate's scathing threats and Gil's blunt accusations, but he admitted to himself they had good reasons to feel as they did.

Without further farewells, he rode away from the ranch yard, his head bowed in thought. Frustration and impatience put him in a surly mood. He wanted to take his share of the Pitchfork and get away from Nate Wylie, but he could not pull out and leave Nate and Gil to fight a battle he had begun.

Nate had taken the story about the gold coins in Jesse Slater's pocket too calmly, and Smoke was disappointed by his father's decision to delay any effort to find out where they came from. After thinking about it, he decided Nate's attitude could mean only one thing: Nate believed Jesse Slater had been working alone and that his only motive was revenge. In Nate's mind, the man's death had ended the fight and Smoke's quick gun was enough to discourage anyone else from challenging the Pitchfork.

Smoke did not think so. The plan to trick the Pitchfork into a war with the sheepmen was hatched in Jackpine by someone who either hated the Wylies or had something to gain from harassing them. Jesse Slater, craving revenge and money, had struck the first blow, but the man who'd hired him was still free and unknown. Smoke had an unsettling premonition that there would be no peace for him or the Pitchfork until he found Slater's accomplice.

A mile from the ranch yard he slowed his horse and looked back, remembering the anger in Nate's voice. His nerves quivered as he nudged the horse into a faster pace and turned it in a different direction. He could not wait indefinitely to find out who hired Jesse Slater—and why. It was possible that Ned Arnold or someone else had seen Slater when he returned to town and might know who met him there.

He might not learn anything that would help, but Smoke decided it was worth the trip. He turned his horse away from the trail to South Basin and headed for Jackpine instead.

Chapter Ten

The troubles which had hounded Smoke for the past week had started over a woman—a strange and beautiful woman he'd never expected to see again. Suddenly he met her for a second time about an hour after he left the ranch.

He had decided to take a shortcut across Lost Horse Hollow, choosing a cross-country trail that would take him into town in less time than the wagon road which ran most of the way between the Pitchfork and Jackpine. Lost in thought and worrying about the consequences of ignoring Nate's orders, he almost rode by without noticing her.

Relying on the mustang's instincts, Smoke was letting the horse choose its own path through the tangle of brush and cottonwoods which bordered the lower reaches of West Creek when he saw the animal's head lift warily. He became alert at once, feeling these days that he was always in danger.

For a moment he sat frozen in the saddle, but he heard nothing except the whisper of the stream as it washed against its banks. He rubbed a hand along the seam of his Levi's, touching the holstered Colt for reassurance. A few minutes later his nerves relaxed when he saw what had alerted the mustang.

A splashing noise in the creek guided his glance. He swung around at the sound, and through a ragged gap in the brush he saw the girl. It was only a brief glimpse, but it was a sight Smoke would not easily forget—a flashing picture of bare white shoulders and lithe brown arms which were quickly crossed to conceal her glistening wet breasts.

She discovered his presence at about the same time Smoke saw her. She was kneeling in the creek where it ebbed into a quiet pool at the head of a sharp bend, and the enjoyment of her bath was reflected in her enthusiasm as she threw the cold water over her naked body.

When she saw Smoke she ducked deeper into the water to conceal her body. Only her tanned, full-lipped face and shimmering black hair remained visible. Her mouth opened in surprise when she spotted the rider only twenty feet away. Smoke expected her to scream, but she made no sound. She clamped her lips tightly together, appearing more annoyed than frightened, and sat staring at him.

Smoke recovered from his surprise and managed a small grin. He said, "I'm sorry, ma'am."

It was only then that he recognized her as the young woman he had rescued from the two men in Jackpine. He did not know how to remind her of that brief encounter, so he said casually, "Well, what do I do now?"

Her lips puckered thoughtfully and her voice was throaty and calm as she said, "I hope you like what you saw, but it's the only look you're going to get. If you'll ride back behind the trees for a few minutes I'll get dressed and you can come back this way. I didn't know I was bathing in the middle of a busy trail—or do you make a practice of riding the creeks just in case you might spot a naked woman?"

The veiled accusation that he might have purposely spied on her sent blood rushing to Smoke's cheeks, but he did not reply. He rode back into the brush beyond the stream and stopped his horse. While he waited he scanned the horizon, picking out familiar landmarks. He could change his route there and pick up the wagon road to Jackpine, but it would take more time. Aside from the inconvenience, he did not want to miss an opportunity to become acquainted with the beautiful girl in the creek.

When he returned, she was sitting on a sandstone boulder at the edge of the stream. The expectant gleam in her eyes told him she knew he would come back. She was dressed in a buckskin riding skirt and a sky-blue blouse that clung tantalizingly to her full bosom as she worked a comb through the thick folds of her hair.

"I'm Ada Keller," she said as Smoke stopped his horse a few feet from the boulder. "If we're going to keep meeting this way I think we should introduce ourselves."

She laughed and kept the comb busy, but her eyes were taking stock of Smoke Wylie. Her glance passed approvingly over his muscular frame, then she looked directly into his eyes. She tilted her head slightly while she studied his face. Her expression brightened and she uttered a gasp of surprise.

"I know you!" she said, jumping to her feet. "I— I mean I remember you. You're the man who saved me from those two cutthroats who were going to—to rape me."

"I'm glad I showed up in time," he said, smiling. "My

name's Wylie." Smoke dismounted and stood beside her. He did not tell her that Jesse Slater was dead. He did not want her to think of him as a gunman.

The mention of his name brought a change to the girl's eyes, a look which could have been an expression of triumph or disappointment.

"I've heard a lot of talk around the hotel about the Wylie family and the Pitchfork Ranch," she said. "Could your name be Gil?"

Smoke shook his head. Something in the tone of her voice told him she expected a denial, and he wondered why she was pretending she had not learned his name after the gunfight. She was playing a game with him. He knew it, but he did not care if it allowed him to spend more time with her.

"No," he said. "Gil's the good boy in the family and I'm the other one. I'm Gil's brother, Smoke."

"Well, I'd bet you don't apologize much for being bad." She laughed and looked into his eyes again. "The manager of the hotel told me the man who rescued me was named Wylie, but I was too excited to remember which one. I'm sorry I guessed wrong. I was so scared that day I didn't take time to thank you. When the shooting started I just wanted to run away as fast as I could."

Her friendly manner put Smoke at ease. She seemed pleased by his company and wanted him to know it. There was a strange teasing, inviting look in Ada Keller's eyes which sent Smoke's pulse pounding while he stood close to her.

"Some might say I've got plenty to apologize for,"

Smoke said, "but I'm not good at that sort of thing." He frowned. "You should've learned something from what happened in town. It's pretty risky to ride out here in the brush by yourself just to take a swim."

She chuckled softly. "After you came up on me the way you did I'd say it could be dangerous, but I'm not here alone. My father's down the creek somewhere. I asked him to give me a little time to enjoy the water. He should be coming back any minute."

"I take it you folks are newcomers to these parts," Smoke said to make conversation.

She arched one eyebrow and smiled at him. "Wouldn't a red-blooded Texas man like you know if I'd been around here very long?"

Her expression grew serious and a yearning look clouded her eyes as she returned to her seat on the rock. "I hope we'll stay here for a long time. I hate the way we keep moving from place to place. I've never lived anywhere long enough to make any real friends. Every time we try to settle somewhere, folks act like we've got the plague and they run us off. It seems that if you don't own cattle in this country you're not entitled to anything at all."

She paused, appearing to be near tears, and Smoke felt an urge to put his arms around her, but she continued before he could move toward her.

"We came to Jackpine about a week ago," Ada Keller said sadly, "and since then my father's been looking around for some idle land. We found this stream today, and it doesn't look like anyone is using this place, so we've decided we'll settle here."

The tone of her voice aroused Smoke's sympathy, and he rose slowly to his feet, his fingers twisting unconsciously at the brim of the Stetson in his hand until he felt the crown crinkling in his fist.

Lost Horse Hollow was a broad patch of flatland, rimmed on three sides by low, moundlike hills. It had not been stocked with any regularity and was still open range, but Smoke knew it was looked upon by at least two men as future graze for cattle.

Bordering it on the north and east was Nate Wylie's Pitchfork Ranch, which already owned more grazing land than any other spread within a hundred miles. Westward was Jerry Mead's Circle M, but Mead had allowed the tiny valley to go unused because of the extensive clearing work necessary before cattle could be controlled there. Smoke knew both Nate and Jerry Mead would resist the efforts of any outsider who tried to claim Lost Horse Hollow.

"Good Lord!" Smoke exclaimed, relaxing his grip on his hat. "Are you folks squatters? Do you want to build a cabin and plow up the grass to raise crops here?"

Ada Keller sprang to her feet. Smoke tried not to notice that the sudden color in her face made her more appealing, or that her hair so close to his face gave off an intoxicating scent that reminded him of cactus blossoms.

"Why shouldn't we? Tell me that, Smoke Wylie!" Her voice quavered with emotion. "Texas wasn't created for cattlemen alone. I'd think you're smart enough to believe everyone has a right to choose his own way of making a living. Does anyone ever ride up to your door and tell you they don't like cattle and that you can't raise them anymore?"

Smoke stared at the ground a moment, and he could hear the echoes of Nate Wylie's voice booming in his mind. He raised his glance to Ada's face and said thoughtfully, "No, they don't."

Their glances met and locked for a few seconds. Then Smoke reached out for Ada Keller, pulling her into his arms as though it were the most natural thing to do. He meant to shock her, thinking of his impulsive move as a distraction for her bitterness. He braced himself for a struggle, expecting shocked resistance from the girl, but Ada Keller was also full of surprises. She rose on her tiptoes at the suggestion of his touch, pressing warmly and eagerly against him as his lips found hers.

"I owe you that for what you did for me," she whispered. "When I know you better I might not stop with just a kiss."

The rustling of brush behind them broke through the passionate roar of his pulse and Smoke released the girl abruptly. He turned nervously, expecting to see Ada's father.

"I've been looking for you, Smoke," Gil Wylie said. Smoke's brother had reined to a temporary stop on a cut-bank a short distance above them. As soon as he spoke he turned his roan and came splashing down the creek.

Smoke jammed his hat on his head and glared at Gil. He said, "I didn't expect you, but I should have. Nate must have figured I'd head for Jackpine to try and find out who was in cahoots with Jesse Slater, so he sent you looking for me. You're a regular trained dog. Just back off. I've already warned you about trying to boss me around."

Gil ignored Smoke's angry words. He halted his horse beside Smoke's ground-tied mustang, folded his hands on the horn, and stared stonily at his brother. He looked remarkably like his father—the same square jaw, blunt chin, and unyielding eyes.

Dismounting, Gil strode purposefully toward Smoke. He stopped with his hands on his hips, his gaze swinging from the girl's face back to Smoke. "You'll have to come with me, but your pretty little friend will have to go back where she came from. How you cheat on Hetty Mead in town is your business, but you can't mix it with work. Pa's going to raise hell when he finds out you're meeting these strumpets out here in the—"

Gil's words were cut short and his right hand flicked up to guard his face. Smoke sensed movement beside him, but he was unaware of what was happening until he saw Gil clutching Ada Keller's wrist and heard the girl cry out in pain. She had tried to slap him, but she was no match for Gil's quick reflexes.

"You son-of-a-you insulting low-life cowboy!" Ada shouted. "You're pulling my arm off."

Smoke's body shook with fury as Gil dropped Ada's arm and continued to stare scornfully at her. Suddenly Smoke felt the same revulsion toward Gil that he had felt toward Jess Slater that day in Jackpine, and he rushed forward to defend Ada Keller again.

"Stop hounding me, Gil," Smoke said. "You've got some apologizing to do. This is Ada Keller—the young woman who was being manhandled by Jesse Slater in town the other day. I just happened to see her as I rode by. You ought to know what you're talking about before you start calling people names."

Barcly glancing at the girl, Gil said, "Sorry if I offended you, ma'am." He kept his eyes on Smoke and said, "Get on your horse. We're leaving."

Smoke's fists knotted at his sides. "You can leave right now, but I'll come home when I'm ready. That'll be after I've settled my business in town and after I've checked with my crew in South Basin."

"Nate sent me for you," Gil said firmly, "and I aim to take you with me one way or another."

Gil took a threatening step toward his brother and walked straight into Smoke's fist, which came flying up from his side and smashed into Gil's mouth. The blow split Gil's lower lip and blood ran down his chin. His head rocked from the punch and he stumbled backwards, his arms windmilling while he tried to catch his balance. He fell at the edge of the creek and Smoke went after him, hoping to get him into the water where Gil's quickness would be hampered.

Gil's quiet manner was deceiving to those who did not know him. He was hard-muscled, tough, and afraid of nothing. A shocked expression furrowed his brow as he lay on the ground, but it was quickly gone, replaced by fierce determination. He jammed his hat back on his head and bounced to his feet, setting himself in a low crouch. Smoke tried to pile on top of him so he could shove him into the creek. It was too late to stop his charge when he saw Gil was no longer on the ground, and he ran almost head-on into him. Gil's head butted Smoke in the belly, stopping him in his tracks.

Pain shot through Smoke's spine. His ribs seemed to cave in around his lungs, and the wind went out of him with a gushing sound. He felt sick and dizzy. Before he could recover Gil jerked erect, his shoulders hunched forward. A fist slammed into Smoke's chin, jolting him so hard his vision blurred.

Smoke stepped aside, trying to guard against the other blow he saw coming, but Gil feinted with his left and hit him again with his right. The fist landed on Smoke's nose and he tasted blood in his mouth. Despite the pain, the blow seemed to shake the cobwebs from his mind. His vision partially cleared and he was able to catch his breath.

Dodging and weaving, he looked for an opening between Gil's poised arms. Even as he moved, he was rocked by a solid punch to the side of his head. He kept his feet under him, no longer concerned with trying to outmaneuver Gil. His only hope was to outlast him—to hand out more punishment than he took.

Gil's face was still a hazy vision, but Smoke struck out at it. He threw a fist into Gil's stomach and heard him grunt, then swung a backhand against his brother's neck. He kept striking and moving, but Gil's fists were all over him, stinging his eyes, hurting his ribs, and jarring his teeth.

Gil moved with the speed and grace of a matador, darting in and out, always punching, and shaking off Smoke's blows. Smoke stayed on his feet, eyeing his brother's face and jabbing at it every time he could get an opening. Both of Gil's eyes were bruised and his mouth was bleeding, but he kept coming, seemingly oblivious to the punishment he was taking. Smoke's breath burned his throat. He gritted his teeth against the ache in his ribs and wondered how long the fight could go on.

Gradually the battle slowed in tempo, but not in fury. They stood face to face, swinging and staggering. With another foe either of them would have given up long ago, but there was more than a disagreement in this. It involved family standing, whether one would enjoy an advantage over the other, and it had to be resolved.

The fight became a stalemate and the pain was more than either wanted to endure. They were punishing each other, but neither was winning, and that was why it was so easy for someone else to stop the fight.

Through the rasp of his own breathing, Smoke was vaguely aware of Ada Keller's plaintive cry before he felt hands pushing and shoving him away. He held back a feeble punch, realizing that the man in front of him was not Gil. Beyond the man's shoulder he saw Gil backing away, his head drooping while he gasped for breath.

"I've seen enough of this, gentlemen!" the man shouted. "Nobody's winning, but you're both going to end up as cripples if it goes on much longer. This kind of bloody brawl is the ugly side of life out here that I don't want my daughter to see."

Several seconds passed before Smoke could gather enough breath to talk. He rested his hands on his knees, drawing in deep gusts of air, and tried to shake the blood and sweat off his face. He had not won the fight, but he had made a point with Gil, just as he meant to do with his father. His life was his own and he meant to live it his own way.

Forcing himself erect, he looked around for his brother. Gil stood ten feet away, his arms folded across his heaving chest while he regarded Smoke with a disappointed look in his eyes.

"I don't want to go through this again," Smoke said between breaths, "but I'm not taking any more orders from you, and you can go home and tell Pa that. I'll tell him myself when I see him."

Gil frowned, his eyes narrowed. He shifted his glance briefly toward the man who had stopped the fight, then back to Smoke. "I didn't want to air our troubles in front of strangers, and you're too bull-headed when you're around a woman to listen anyway. I'm here because we need you at the Pitchfork and Nate wants to tell you why."

Smoke's bruised mouth twisted bitterly. "Nobody's ever needed me at the Pitchfork. You and Pa run everything and you know it."

Gil shuffled his feet impatiently. "You're going to get your chance. Those cows Pa told you to move out of South Basin at the start of the roundup may be dead before you can finish the job. He figures that's your fault and he wants to see what you can do about it."

130

Chapter Eleven

Gil's explanation was meant to stop Smoke's protests, and it had the desired effect. A feeling of panic turned Smoke's face pale and sober. "Has somebody shot more steers? Is that what you mean by dead cattle?"

"No," Gil said. "Nobody shot them and they're not dead yet, but it looks like they might die from blackleg. If that's what they've got it won't be just one dead steer. It could be a hundred, a thousand—or the whole Pitchfork herd."

Smoke eyed his brother skeptically. "Are you trying to pull something over on me? How do you know what's going on in South Basin?"

"I wouldn't ride this far to trick you," Gil snapped, his eyes fiery. "A few minutes after you left the ranch Paul Mabry showed up and brought the news. Ike Yarby sent him for some coal oil, turpentine, lard, and that sack of Indian herbs he keeps under his bunk. Ike's going to try to do something with one of his remedies, but he figured you'd want to be there. We got the stuff for Paul, then Pa sent me to find you. Since Paul didn't cross your trail I knew you'd headed for town, but I didn't figure on this."

Gil waved a hand toward Ada Keller and the gray-haired, overalled man who had interrupted the fight. "If your new friends have any notions about settling on this land you'd better tell them how dangerous that would be."

Gil turned and walked to his horse. He swung into the saddle, then looked down at Smoke, his bruised face set in hard lines. "I've told you what Pa wants and you can come home or keep making trouble for yourself. It's up to you."

"I'll be along right away," Smoke said quickly, and Gil put his roan into a gallop, rushing back the way he had come.

A strained silence fell over the creek bank as Smoke continued to stare at his brother's back, a worried look in his eyes. He shook himself out of his thoughts and turned his attention to Ada Keller and her father. "I'm sorry Gil said those things, but I think that was because he's mad at me."

"We all have our troubles, friend," the man said, his voice sympathetic. "I hope you won't take offense because I stepped between you and your brother. I'm Dewey Keller."

Smoke accepted the man's outstretched hand, but he felt uncomfortable. Keller was dressed in a style usually identified with dirt farmers—bibbed overalls, blue cotton shirt, and thick-soled shoes. His clothes appeared new, but they were ill-fitting. He was a slender man with gaunt shoulders, long legs, and a rich, sonorous voice.

Keller's palm was soft, like a woman's hand, and Smoke made the handshake a brief gesture. It was obvious that Keller had never known hard work, and Smoke felt a sudden resentment toward the man. His impulse was to tell Keller to move on—that he was not equipped to succeed as a farmer. That was what Nate Wylie would do, except that it would be an order rather than a suggestion. Smoke decided he would not interfere, determined not to imitate his father.

He forced a chuckle and said, "You sure didn't hurt my feelings any when you stopped the fight. I'd had about all that pleasure I could stand."

Dewey Keller nodded and smiled broadly. At one time his finely chiseled face might have been quite handsome, but now there were small pouches beneath his dark eyes and the skin sagged along his jawline. He patted the bib of his overalls as though unfamiliar with the arrangement of the pockets, finally withdrawing a slender cigar. It was an unusual luxury for a squatter, but Smoke had already gained the impression that Keller had enjoyed a finer style of living some time in the past and was trying to cling to it. His oratorical speech and stately bearing reminded Smoke of an actor or a lawyer, and he wondered why a man who appeared so confident of himself had been such a failure.

When Keller fumbled through his pockets for a match, Smoke stepped forward to hand him one of his own. There was an unpleasant odor about the man, unlike the smell of sweat left from hard work, and Smoke backed away to escape it.

Keller blew a ring of smoke and spoke around the cigar. "It's obvious that your brother doesn't approve of us, but I hope we can count on you as a friend. From what I heard at the Pioneer House, I believe you're the gallant young man who came to my daughter's rescue a few days ago. Some day we'll try to reward you. We're here to start a farming project, but we certainly want to avoid trouble."

While they talked Ada moved farther away, and Smoke feared she was still angry because of Gil's remarks. When he glanced toward her, however, she came back and stood beside her father. She put her hand lightly on Smoke's arm and said, "I think Smoke and I will get along together just fine."

The promise he saw in her heavy-lidded eyes was enough to dispel any misgivings Smoke might have had. He smiled, pleased by her show of friendship. Remembering her sadness when she told of the way they had been pushed from place to place, he felt drawn to her and wanted to help her. He did not care if Nate Wylie was offended by his actions, but he was uneasy about their presence in Lost Horse Hollow and confused about his own feelings toward the land.

He turned toward Dewey Keller and said, "You're never going to find a cattleman who feels good about a squatter living next to him. It'll be the same way at the Pitchfork. My pa can't get his fill of owning land, and I'm sure he's got plans for this place some day. If he had his way he'd own Texas, but I figure we need new people, new families and folks with new ideas, if Texas is ever going to be as civilized as it ought to be. I don't like the notion of everything being owned by just a few people. Nate's going to hate you, but I'll help you get a start here if I can."

"Splendid!" Dewey Keller beamed. He patted Smoke's shoulder, his dark eyes glowing. "You have the true spirit of a patriot, the dreams of a nation crying out for expansion. Yes, and a heart filled with charity. You're a good man and I'm pleased to know you."

Smoke shrugged aside the man's praise, admitting to himself that he had offered his help because of his sympathy for Ada and not to cultivate Dewey Keller's friendship.

As soon as he had made his commitment, Smoke wanted to get away from Lost Horse Valley. Nate Wylie was waiting for him at the ranch, and an unknown threat hung over the cattle in South Basin. He felt pressed for time, and frustrated because he would not be able to pursue any leads in town.

He was turning to leave when it occurred to him that Dewey Keller might provide as much information as he could have obtained in Jackpine. Moving back to face the overalled man, he said, "You've been around town for a while, so maybe you can give me a line on somebody I need to know about."

Dewey Keller rolled the cigar between his fingers. "It appears that I'm going to be in your debt, my friend. If I can do anything for you it'll be my pleasure."

To explain his questions, Smoke had to tell Keller about the events which had transpired at the Pitchfork, about the dead yearling and how he had tracked down Jesse Slater and killed him. Keller listened intently, exchanging glances with Ada occasionally, but he did not interrupt.

"Slater was working with somebody," Smoke concluded. "He came into some sudden money, and we figure somebody paid him to kill the yearling and make it look like the sheepmen did it. Ada must have told you what Slater looks like. I was wondering if you'd seen him around—maybe talking with somebody in Jackpine. He pretended to see a doctor, and I'm sure that's when somebody hired him to cause trouble."

"Hmm," Keller murmured. "What you say sounds possible, but you may be jumping to conclusions. I understand those drovers were a rough sort, capable of anything. Perhaps it was just Slater's way of settling things with you."

"It's not likely," Smoke said curtly. "He'd try that with a gun. He thought he could beat me. He might've gloated some over killing a Pitchfork steer, but he wouldn't settle for that unless somebody paid him to do it. I need to know who it was and why they're bent on causing trouble for the Pitchfork. When I know that I'll do some settling up myself."

Keller rubbed his hand across his chin and said, "I'm sorry I can't help you. We've spent most of our time at the hotel and haven't seen much of the town. My wife has been under the weather since we arrived—fatigue, I think—and she hasn't felt like getting out much. Ada and I have stayed close to keep her company, except for the last couple of days when we've been scouting around for a place to settle."

Smoke nodded, disappointed. "If you hear of anybody who talked with Slater I'd appreciate it if you'd let me know."

Keller rubbed the cigar against a stone, extinguishing the fire, and put the stub in the bib pocket of his overalls. "I owe you a lot for helping my daughter and I want you for a friend." He smiled and added, "You'd probably rather have Ada deliver the message if I learn anything."

Somewhere in the distance a horse whinnied, and Smoke let the man's remark pass without replying. He swung his gaze over the cottonwoods and brush which grew close to the creek. The sound came again, breaking off abruptly as though a hand had been placed over the horse's muzzle. The faintness of the horse's call told Smoke it was not very near the stream, but his eyes continued to search the horizon along the knolls which marked the beginning of Jerry Mead's Circle M range.

"What is it?" Dewey Keller had noticed the alarm in Smoke's face and his voice sounded frightened.

Keller's question was followed by a gunshot. A bullet whined over their heads and the crack of a rifle echoed behind it. Smoke grabbed Ada Keller around the waist and dragged her down with him as he hit the ground. Dewey Keller dropped beside them and they lay silently for a while, their heavy breathing blending in a nervous chorus.

"He's leaving," Dewey Keller said presently, getting to his feet. "Don't you think we should go after that rider and find out why we were attacked? It must be a mistake."

Smoke waited until the muffled hoofbeats of a running horse died away. He rose slowly, helping Ada to her feet. A knot of muscle jumped along the edge of his jaw.

"That was no mistake," he said grimly, "but I'm sure the shot was meant for me. The bushwhacker was far enough away to get a head start on us. We'd never catch up now."

He hurried to his horse, mounted, and nodded a cursory farewell to Dewey and Ada Keller. "Maybe I'll learn more about the bushwhacker when I get to the

Pitchfork," he said quietly. "That's where this has to be settled."

Smoke rode steadily toward the Pitchfork, disliking every mile of the way. He was tired, worried, and somewhat scared. He had ridden this range since childhood without any thought of danger, but now he felt the hairs on the back of his neck crinkle and he cast frequent looks along his back trail. He had a disturbing suspicion about the rifle shot, but he was not sure some unknown enemy was not stalking him.

Gil's report about the cattle in South Basin had shaken him and filled him with a sense of guilt. He wanted to ride there and see for himself what was happening, but it would be the wrong thing to do. Nate wanted to see him first, and it would be a mistake to ignore him any further.

Giving the horse its head after they cleared the knolls, he rolled a cigarette and smoked slowly, trying to settle his nerves. His mind was in turmoil, muddled by the puzzling circumstances which had placed his life in jeopardy. For the first time in years he was not sure about his feelings toward his father, and the resentment he had carried in his mind so long seemed less intense. Despite his belief that the Kellers had a right to a home of their own, their presence in Lost Horse Hollow aroused a grudging admiration within him for Nate's ability to acquire his land and hold on to it.

When they were younger, Smoke and Gil had listened with fascination while Nate told stories about his life. He came out of the Kentucky hills when he was sixteen, a homeless orphan who'd lost both of his parents to pneumonia during one hard winter. He was taken in by one family and another as he worked his way west, and at twenty-one he joined Zachary Taylor along the border. When the war with Mexico was over he remained in Texas. As the result of an unexpected bequest Nate became the owner of an old Spanish land grant—a tract of more than four thousand acres along Middle Creek.

With that as a base, Nate tracked down the owners of other land grants, most of which had been traded several times by disillusioned owners. The early settlers had been lured west by free land when *empresarios* were employed to encourage the colonization of Texas while it was still a Mexican state. For many of them it was not the dream they had envisioned. Scores of them gave up and moved away, unable to endure the grueling work, scorching summers, frigid winters, and loneliness of the untamed wilderness.

Even though the land was bought cheaply, Nate had to work three years before he could accumulate enough money for the down payments—two hundred dollars to each owner. He hired on as a drover on cattle drives to Abilene and Dodge City, rode shotgun for Wells-Fargo, and served for a year as a deputy sheriff in Caldwell. He held on to every dollar, finally settling on his land, which surrounded the three most dependable creeks of the hill country. For the next ten years every cent he earned from raising cattle was used to buy more land and pay off his debts.

Smoke never doubted that his father earned everything he owned by dogged determination and an unbending will, but Nate had no right to keep other people from trying to have as much—people such as the Kellers.

It was early afternoon when Smoke reached the ranch. He put his horse in a corral, then headed for the kitchen to see if Charlie Ray Jones had any food left from the noon meal. He could not face Nate Wylie on an empty stomach.

The bald, stiff-legged cook was full of talk and dire predictions. "All of them cows are going to die," Charlie Ray said in his cracked and gloomy tones. "All going to die. I know, because I've seen blackleg in my day. It was powerful wet in South Basin, so I hear, and them cows was grazing out into the bogs. That's how they get the blackleg—some kind of bug in the soil. When cows are standing in mud the bug has a chance to latch on and work into any sores or cuts, then a disease sets in that kills cows in a hurry. Old Nate's on a tear, Smoke. He's on a tear."

Charlie Ray rambled on while Smoke ate, saying little Smoke had not heard before, but he listened respectfully. Before age and rheumatism had relegated him to the cooking chores, Charlie Ray had been one of the Pitchfork's top hands, and there was not much he did not know about cattle.

When he finished eating, Smoke rose and slapped Charlie Ray playfully on the shoulder. He chuckled, making an effort not to appear unduly concerned. "Take a good look at me, Charlie Ray. It may be the last time you see me wearing my whole hide. Nate is waiting to take it off of me."

"He's got his dander up," Charlie Ray said. "Got his dander up good."

"That's not a real big piece of news around here," Smoke replied as he left the kitchen and walked toward the back door of the house, which was about twenty paces away.

Above the stone fireplace in the log-beamed parlor of the ranch house a foot-long model of a three-tined pitchfork was mounted on pegs driven into the mortar. It was made of pure silver, and Nate had paid well to have it molded in Matt Stacy's blacksmith shop. He considered it one of his most valued possessions. Whenever his mind was troubled, he toyed with the tines of the silver pitchfork, as though trying to draw on the source of power they represented. His power was water and cattle, and the silver tines symbolized the three creeks which fed his range. A tiny replica of the pitchfork was carried on the flanks of six thousand steers. The only reason there were not more was because Nate was content with that number at the present time.

Nate was fiddling with the pitchfork when Smoke entered the room. In one of the leather chairs to the rancher's left sat Gil, staring idly at the opposite wall. Smoke spoke to them, then stood with his back against the frame of the doorway which led to the entrance hall.

For a few seconds Nate Wylie remained in front of the fireplace, trying to get a leash on his temper. During the more than thirty years since the Mexican War, he had fought harsh weather, Comanches, and the invasion of squatters. He had survived the danger and violence of

141

the frontier, and it was maddening to find he could not control his own family.

He gave the silver pitchfork a tap with the tip of his cane and wheeled with surprising swiftness to stare at Smoke's battered face. His eyes burned with fury, contrasting sharply with his fine skin and short gray hair. When he spoke his voice was a rumble in his chest, and the softness of it was more fearful than his usual bellowing tones.

"I've gritted my teeth and put up with your wild ways, Smoke—the women, the poker playin', the hard drinkin', even the gunfights you were mixed up in. By damn, I won't stand for you ruinin' my herd, though. We could lose every cow on the Pitchfork because of you. We might save most of 'em if we get the sick cows away from the others before the blackleg spreads, but we don't have much time to get it done."

A film of moisture gathered on Nate's lips and he paused to wipe his mouth with the back of his hand. "I told you what to do," he continued, his voice rising, "and you didn't do it. Now it ain't up to you no more. I've put Ike Yarby in charge of your end of the roundup and I told Paul Mabry to tell him that. I can't count on you for nothin'."

Nate's hard brown eyes bored at his face, and Smoke knew there was more to come. The sickness in the cattle was a development Smoke could not have foreseen, but Nate's knowledge of weather and cow-country diseases had taught him to take precautions against the whims of nature.

Smoke swallowed hard, thinking of the embarrassment of meeting his crew again, and said, "I'll ride on down there and give Ike all the help I can."

Nate Wylie stalked across the room and dropped into the chair behind his desk. "You'll sit tight until I've finished with you. There's still the matter of a brawl with Gil here."

Smoke gave his brother a long look, the anger inside him visible in the sheen of his pale eyes. He crossed the room, put his hands flat on the desk, and met Nate's stony stare.

"I lit into Gil because he was getting ready to take a swing at me, but I didn't try to kill him. Gil takes your orders seriously. He hid in the brush up in the hills and fired a rifle at me because he couldn't whip me with his fists. Did you tell him to bring me home dead or alive?"

"That's a lie!" Gil came across the room in his swift, gliding stride. His fists were bunched and he moved around to stand in front of Smoke. "You act like a pig-headed fool most of the time, but you're not fool enough to think I'm a coward. I wouldn't shoot at you in the first place, but if I did you'd be dead. I couldn't miss a head as big as yours."

Nate Wylie's cane cut the air between them, causing them to draw apart. "Sit down, the two of you! We'll take first things first. Gil tells me he ran across a buckboard and some work stock down the creek a piece before he circled around and found you. Who are them pilgrims you were with, and what's their business?"

Taking a deep breath, Smoke hunched forward in the chair across from Nate's desk. He avoided his father's

143

demanding eyes and said, "I want to make a deal with you, Pa."

The rancher could read the mood of his sons by the way they addressed him—as "Nate" when they felt they were his equal, as "Pa" when they felt dependent on him. He lowered his glance, staring absently at the papers on his desk. He wiped a hand across his mustache in the manner of a man suddenly ashamed, but if he felt any shame it was for Smoke—not for himself.

When he looked up again his eyes had lost much of their ferocity. "It's not right for a man and his son to make deals in order to get along. By damn, a Wylie don't need to make deals with nobody. There are folks around who'd like to see us cut down to size so they could start pickin' at us with the hope of featherin' their own nest. I've learned the best way to keep peace is to be too big to fight and too strong to lose if you do. You'll learn that some day and you'll be glad you're among the strong."

Nate paused, moving his head from side to side in exasperation, then added, "Looks like somebody's studied up on you. They've found out you like to get under my hide—do things to hurt me or shame me. One sure way to split a team is to have one mule in the traces who's always kickin' them over. That's why you're to stay out of town and let me handle things. If you'll stick with me like Gil does, we won't have any trouble with outsiders—be they sheepmen, hired guns, or whatever. The time may come when we'll all have to stick together to hold the Pitchfork. If that time comes, you'll either be worth bein' called my son or you won't."

Chapter Twelve

Nate Wylie talked on about the Pitchfork, reviewing the hard times he'd endured at the beginning and how he wanted to build it as a heritage for his children and their descendants for generations to come. Reminiscing was Nate's way of calming his anger and easing tensions after the family had been at odds, so Smoke only half listened.

His thoughts drifted back to Lost Horse Hollow. He wondered if there was anything he could do to persuade his father to allow Ada Keller's family to settle there, but he knew it would not be easy to get Nate to turn his back on one square foot of land. Smoke remembered others who had sought concessions from Nate Wylie without success.

There were half a dozen other ranches around the Pitchfork, small spreads which had grown to their limit because Nate laid claim to all the open range for as far as any cow could walk from his boundaries to water in a day's time. This was the traditional rule for possession land, applied by the ranchers who reached it first, but Smoke felt it was unfair to new immigrants when one man controlled all the water sources.

Their nearest neighbors, Jerry Mead and Wade Stone, had made several visits to the Pitchfork in an attempt to get the rights to more land along the creeks, but Nate Wylie would not give up even a single blade of grass.

Smoke heard his name mentioned and his attention was drawn back to his father. Nate Wylie was saying,

"You don't have a feelin' for the land like me and your brother do, Smoke. You don't have any feelin' for anything except raisin' hell and causin' me trouble. I wish I could change that."

A pained expression wrinkled Smoke's brow and he looked away before his father noticed it. He said, "I've got feelings—feelings you don't know about. One thing you've told me is that marrying a good woman would settle me down. I've been thinking about that and maybe I've found somebody."

"Good!" Nate Wylie said. "Hetty Mead is a good woman—a pretty woman with a good head on her shoulders and a tough core inside that will bring out the best in a man. She'd be good for you."

Smoke shook his head. "I wasn't thinking of Hetty. I was thinking of the girl I met in town—Ada Keller."

Nate Wylie swore under his breath. "Ada Keller, huh? I reckon that's the woman Gil saw you with in Lost Horse Hollow. I don't know how to figure you. Sometimes I think you're just a born troublemaker, and other times I think you're addled in the head."

Nate's face darkened. His temper was boiling again, and his voice rose to a booming bellow. "You know nothin' about that woman. She might be a connivin' strumpet who thinks she can gain a foothold here through you. All Gil and me can figure is that she and her pa want to crowd in on our land because it's handy. You think I'm a hard-nosed old range hog, but I don't aim to be picked apart by folks who want to ride on my back like lice."

"It might do you good to practice some of that charity

you and Preacher Pardee read about in the Bible," Smoke said. "It won't hurt to make a friend by giving up something you don't need."

Nate became strangely calm. "There's a difference in people with backbone and people without any. I fought Indians, blizzards, wolves, and drought to hold this land. After I've sweated for it there's some who would like to move in and have it the easy way. There's land to be homesteaded in Arizona Territory and New Mexico, but that means a hard life at the start. Some don't want to work to get ahead. They want to profit from what I've done before they showed up."

Nate ran his hand across his brow, sounding tired. "We need all we've got and this country needs us. Maybe it ain't your fault, but you took too much after your ma. You let people turn you their way just because they shine up to you, and you can't understand that you don't need to apologize for bein' better off than somebody else if you earned what you've got. One night you'll get too much liquor in you and you'll end up married to some worthless woman just because she said somethin' nice to you. If that ever happens, I'll sure regret I was so proud of my sons when they was born that I split my creeks with them."

Smoke stared at his father in surprise. It was the first time in years Nate had mentioned his wife. Smoke's memories of her were dim, and no one had told him anything about her. Nate refused to speak of her, but Smoke realized she had left his father with a lasting sadness and an odd protective attitude toward all women. When Smoke was a child, Nate had shrugged his questions aside by saying, "She's gone away for a while."

Once, however, when Smoke was twelve, his father put an end to Smoke's questions, declaring angrily, "You've got no ma. You ought to know that by now, so don't ever ask me about her again!"

Nate Wylie dismissed the mystery of his wife's absence with curt words and a stubborn silence, but it was not that simple for Smoke. The cruelty of taunting children made him dread every day of school. Some said his pa was too mean to have a woman in the house, and that Smoke was a bastard child. Others whispered he was a half-breed Comanche who had been thrown on the Pitchfork doorstep by an angry squaw, but no matter how ridiculous the stories were, his schoolmates would not let him escape the feeling that he had been cheated out of an important part of his life.

Smoke suffered through the teasing in embarrassment and confusion, but Gil would not be badgered. When anyone mentioned his mother unfavorably, Gil lashed out with his fists and left his tormentors cowed and bloody. Word of Gil's schoolyard battles reached Nate, and he praised Gil for taking a stand against those who offended him without asking the reason for the fights. Even then Smoke lived with the same fury that fired Gil's fists, but he did not want to fight his schoolmates. He wanted to fight the man who was to blame for inflicting such torture upon him—Nate Wylie.

It was the years of frustration from being unable to forge a close bond with his father that had caused Smoke to ride to Jackpine the day he first met Ada Keller. His thoughts returned again to the deed in John

Bastrop's law office when he responded to his father's critical remarks, saying, "Maybe I care more for the land than you know, Nate—when it's my land. You might learn that if I ever take over West Creek and run my own spread."

Nate Wylie heard the quiet anger in Smoke's voice and a nervous look danced in his eyes. His instincts told him Smoke was scheming against him again. He had already voiced his misgivings about the generous arrangements he had made for his sons. He wanted them to share his pride in the Pitchfork, and when they were old enough to understand, he had told them of his plans for their future. Gil and Smoke grew up knowing that some day they would share in the ownership of the ranch.

A week after Smoke was born, Nate drew up his will, bequeathing West Creek to Smoke and East Creek to Gil. Nate wanted to be sure there would be no arguments in case he died before his sons reached manhood, so he left the proper deeds with John Bastrop, making a trust of the land bordering two of his water sources.

The deeds were prepared at a time of exuberance, and Nate did not expect them to be exercised during his lifetime. Gil understood his father's intentions, respected them, and never mentioned the possibility of splitting up the ranch. Smoke thought of it often, however, and he also wondered how Nate planned to dispose of Middle Creek.

Silence hung over the parlor for several seconds, then Nate glared at Smoke and said, "You'd best forget any notions about runnin' your own spread until you've learned to respect the land that feeds you. If you was to ride across Deadline Ridge and marry a sheeper girl, I'd just tell folks you were the foolish one of my sons, but if you ever come home with one of them—them professional girls—I'll swear Gil's the only son I've got and I'll treat him that way." He shuddered, as if the thought sickened him. "If makin' a deal is the only way to get along with you, I'll talk about it."

Smoke drew a deep breath and stared at the floor. His insides shook with apprehension. Nate's voice had changed, growing cold and impersonal.

"It's about Ada's family—the Kellers," Smoke said hesitantly. "You leave them alone and I'll do anything you say. I'll give you my gun and you can hold it until you feel like giving it back to me. I'll stay out of town and you can ask Ben Toler to check on Jesse Slater when you get to it. I'll work any way you want me to—take orders from Ike Yarby, or Gil, or whoever you say. You'll see me change and we'll get along all right."

He studied Nate's face, but he could read no reaction in it. In a firmer voice, Smoke said, "My brain's not as petrified as you think. I've thought a lot about what kind of Texas I want for my wife and kids. I don't want it to be the kind where two or three people own a whole county and nobody can move in without fighting for their lives."

Pushing to his feet, Nate Wylie limped across the parlor, letting the cane support more of his weight than usual. He stared at the silver pitchfork above the mantle for a while, and Smoke saw the back of his neck turn crimson. He turned and asked, "What do you think of them apples, Gil?"

Gil avoided Smoke's eyes, but he answered immediately. "Lost Horse Hollow is a pretty small patch of land. It's hemmed in by us and Jerry Mead's Circle M. There's nothing you can add to it until you go south and hit Wade Stone's Bar W range, and I don't see Wade ever selling out. That doesn't leave enough land for an honest man to make a living. Nothing rings true about those folks being there, and the best time to put out a fire is when it starts."

"You've whipsawed me again, Nate!" Smoke shouted across the room. "You got the answer you were looking for. Gil's never had a thought in his head that you didn't put there. But I do. I've been thinking since I was knee high that we know a lot of people and a lot of people know us, but we don't have a single real friend. One day we might be sorry about that and I—"

"And that's why you want the Kellers in Lost Horse?" Gil cut in. "Come off it, Smoke. You want the woman."

The discussion had lasted longer than Smoke expected and he was exhausted by it. He was emotionally drained and he had no anger left for Gil. All he could do was shake his head in denial. "You're wrong if you think that's all there is to it. I like Ada Keller, but I'm sick of being a part of a family who won't give anybody else a chance to do what we've done. Sooner or later everybody on this range will hate our guts."

Nate Wylie swore softly. "You can't make me believe that until I hear it from somebody besides you. There are folks around who will take from you as long as you'll give, but that don't make them your friend."

Nate's shaggy eyebrows pinched together and his voice rose in volume. "I've let you waste a lot of time here, but by damn we're not wastin' any more. It's time you got your carcass down to South Basin and see if you can save my cows. Gil sent two extra hands from his crew over to help out—Sam Dunn and Brad Lipps, I think it was. Now, get goin'!"

It ended that way. Another family quarrel was over and Smoke shoved to his feet with his hat in his hand. He strode toward the door, feeling the dejection of a man who had fought and lost.

He made a final effort. At the doorway he stopped and looked back. "What about the Kellers?"

"By damn, you tagged me as the worst kind of range hog before I could give you an answer," Nate growled. "I didn't say I was jumpin' at Gil's hunch. All I'm sayin' right now is that I'll think on your proposition."

Nodding, Smoke clamped his hat on his head and stepped out into the hallway which led to the front porch. Spurs jingled behind him, and he turned to find Gil following him. Everything had not been settled to Gil's satisfaction inside, and Smoke was not surprised that his brother fell silently in step, walking with him to the corrals a hundred yards away.

They covered most of the distance in silence, each busy with his own thoughts. There were many things about his brother Smoke did not understand, but he knew Gil had a soft heart and could not carry a grudge longer than an hour. There were times, however, when Smoke disliked him intensely.

He never received support from Gil when Nate was berating him for his misdeeds, and even worse, Gil often called Smoke's hand on matters his father might overlook. Gil's own behavior was not without fault. He harped about Smoke's attentions to the girls at the Great Western Saloon, but Smoke knew about Gil's many trips across Deadline Ridge. Gil had admitted he was in love with a sheepherder's daughter—a fact many cattlemen would consider shameful.

"About that fight we had in Lost Horse Hollow . . ." Gil began tentatively as they reached the corral. "I guess I pushed you into that. I'm sorry I overstepped my bounds. If I'd found you along the trail instead of hanging around kissing that girl, it would have been different. I'd have told you about the blackleg and gone on."

Smoke picked up his saddle and moved into the corral. The horses started milling, looking big-eyed and wild while they circled inside the fence. Smoke watched the horses, waiting for the bay to come around. He squinted against the fog of dust stirred up by the hooves and debated whether to answer Gil or leave him in silence.

The discussion at the house had made him feel like an outsider. The anger he had kept under control was in his voice now as he said, "Who are you trying to fool, Gil? Nate's plumb strange about women and he can pull it off, but you can't. We both know you don't worry about somebody taking advantage of a woman the way Nate does, so quit horning in on me. You brought up Hetty's name in front of the Kellers. I don't like that. Anything between me and Hetty is private."

"I didn't come out here to discuss your love life," Gil growled. "I don't want any hard feelings between us."

Smoke's eyes narrowed. "Why did you shoot at me then?"

A look of irritation showed in Gil's eyes, then faded. He stepped forward and put his hand on Smoke's shoulder. "If I was that much of a skunk, I couldn't look you in the face. When you told Nate somebody took a shot at you I thought you were making up a tale to throw him off the track, but if it really happened there's no telling what we're in for. Maybe something's going on with the sheepmen after all."

Shrugging Gil's arm away, Smoke grabbed the bay's mane as it came close to him. He busied himself with the saddle, hiding his nervousness. Gil's reaction convinced Smoke he was not lying about the gunshot, but it added to his worry. If Gil had not fired at him, he asked himself, who was it?

Blackleg!
It was a word which carried across the prairies with the same echoes of horror as a shout of wildfire on a dry range. Knowledge of its cause was vague and the treatment for it was purely guesswork. When it struck, the legs of cattle began to swell, then blood vessels burst beneath the skin and turned the legs black and ugly. Afterward there was the stupor of high fever, then death.

Nate Wylie was a wealthy man, but the loss of the Pitchfork herd would be a devastating blow. His business interests would provide him with some income, but he might never again know the power and prestige he had commanded for so long. Smoke had done many foolish things to punish his father, but the worst of them had come from unintentional negligence. Telling himself he did not possess the powers of a prophet gave him no solace. His deliberate disregard for Nate's authority was to blame for the disaster which threatened the Pitchfork, and he was tortured by a feeling of guilt when he rode into the South Basin roundup camp at dusk.

"Grab a bucket and a swab, lad," Ike Yarby said as Smoke dismounted beside him. Ike was sloshing a tin pail around in a wooden tub which Paul Mabry had brought from the ranch. "I've mixed me a potion I learned about on the Platte and we've been tryin' to wet down the sickest cows with it."

Smoke looked around the area. Ike had set up his mixing barrel on high ground, but less than a hundred feet away shallow water covered acres of land. Sprigs of grass poked through the water here and there. Soft mud, gashed by scores of hoofs, rimmed the pools, but the cattle had been driven away to dry ground farther on.

"We've cut some poles and tied rags to them for swabs," Ike continued as he stirred the liquid in the barrel. "We can brush it on the yearlin's and calves pretty good, but them longhorn steers is somethin' else. It's a wonder we ain't got somebody killed or got their guts ripped out. We've doctored a lot of cows already, though."

Smoke left his horse's reins trailing and reached for one of the pails piled near the barrel. "Do you think we have a chance of saving them, Ike?"

"Not if it's blackleg." The answer came from Sam Dunn, one of the men from Gil's crew. He rode up just in time to hear Smoke's question. "Did you ever see blackleg work its way through a herd?"

Dunn was a lanky, buck-toothed man who spoke in a nasal drawl. He smelled of raw turpentine and sweat and his face was gaunt with worry and fatigue. He stepped down, carrying a bucket in his hand, and walked toward the mixing barrel. "I heard about a spread in New Mexico Territory that lost five hundred head in three days. It's an awful thing to—"

"I know, Sam," Smoke said wearily. "I've heard tales about it all my life."

"If this thing gets off to a good start, your old man could wake up one day next week as broke as a one-eyed gambler," Sam Dunn mumbled. He filled his pail, balancing it carefully as he mounted his horse and rode away.

For the next few hours Smoke did not have time to think about the mysterious rifleman, the argument with his father, or Ada Keller. He rode away from the mixing barrel with Ike Yarby at his side, both carrying buckets of Ike's Indian-style medicine. He was eager to join the other riders and do what he could to help the stricken cattle.

Ike's crew had separated the cattle into two bunches. A hundred head had been moved far up the basin, and Smoke could see them grazing near the rocky benches and coulees which had channeled the spring runoff from the mountain snows into the lowlands. These were the healthy cows, those which showed no signs of infection. Closer by was a scene of activity so chaotic it made Smoke fear he had joined a hopeless fight.

Chapter Thirteen

Riders were circling a cluster of about twenty steers and calves, trying to cut out one at a time for treatment. Wasting no time, Smoke uncoiled the rope from his saddle horn and joined them. He did not have time to single out faces or talk to anyone. It took him a few minutes to learn the procedure, then he was a part of it.

It was dangerous, muscle-tearing work done with both haste and caution. Cattle milled in all directions, not quite ready to stampede, but nervous and skittish. Sweeping, needle-sharp horns slashed perilously close to horses and riders. Men pushed their horses in and out of the maelstrom, swinging ropes and splashing liquid at moving hoofs. Their tired and desperate curses mingled with the din of frightened animals bawling and banging against each other.

Smoke made a dozen trips to the mixing barrel, passing other riders as they went back and forth. Ike Yarby spent most of his time blending the ingredients. On his fifth or sixth trip, Ike delayed Smoke long enough to say, "Don't let Nate lay all the blame on ye for this mess. These cows have got old sores on them. Some of them have been that way for weeks. Startin' the roundup here might have made some difference, but nobody could swear to it."

By now Smoke was too tired to find any comfort in

Ike Yarby's words. He hurried away, leaving his bucket on the ground while he helped another rider push a few of the treated cows up the basin toward the healthy herd, then came back to the turmoil which surrounded the sick cattle. Joe Santine dashed up beside him, pointed at a mud-caked steer, and rode on with his rope swinging in a wide loop. Smoke understood what he wanted and spurred his bay to the other side of the steer.

One man could treat a calf by bulldogging it to the ground and tying it with pigging strings while he swabbed it with medicine. It took three people to do the same with one of the big longhorns. That was what Joe Santine had indicated to Smoke. Santine's loop settled over the steer's horns from one side and Smoke roped it from the other. With perfect timing, their horses braced their legs against the tug of the ropes and the steer was anchored between them.

"One on the rope!" Santine yelled above the clamor.

A slender, agile figure jumped down from a cutting horse near the struggling steer, sloshing liquid at the thrashing hoofs. As he kept his eye on the taut rope, nudging the bay around with his knees, Smoke found himself admiring the nerve and skill of their helper. A moment later he got a clear look at the rider's face, and almost tumbled from the saddle as surprise caused him to relax his grip on the saddle horn. The lithe, quick-moving rider was Hetty Mead!

Hetty swung back on her horse and was gone before Smoke could say anything. Afterward, he was too busy to keep her in sight. Santine was shaking his rope, loosening the noose around the steer, and Smoke had to do the same. Finally the ropes fell free, and Smoke's horse leaped sideways as the steer broke into a blind charge toward him.

Darkness came quickly to the basin. The work slowed, but it did not stop. They kept at it, and Smoke was pleased to see more and more cattle pushed away from the treatment area. They might have worked on into the night, but they stopped suddenly as a cry of pain rang out above the other sounds. Through the dust and gloom Smoke saw a flurry of activity ahead of him and sent his horse toward it.

A longhorn had gored Ed Slade in the left leg. Slade sat flat on the ground, his teeth clenched while he tore away tattered shreds of his Levi's to look at the wound.

Smoke pushed his way between two other men and squatted beside Slade. The horn had torn a ragged gash across the cowboy's thigh, and bright red blood glistened against his stark white skin. After staring at his leg for a moment, Ed Slade calmly reached toward the tin pail he had dropped when the steer came at him in the darkness. He found his swabbing cloth and rubbed it across the wound.

His face turned white and he whistled between his teeth as the liquid touched raw flesh. "Damn!" Slade murmured. "No wonder them cattle cut a sandy when this stuff hits them."

Slade got slowly to his feet and searched his pockets for another scrap of cloth. "It went pretty deep, but I'll tie something around it and it'll be all right."

He was already looking for his horse when Smoke said, "No more tonight, Ed. We're through for today.

We're worn out and it's better to have some dead cows than dead men."

Sam Dunn said, "I don't know about quitting until Ike Yarby says so. We was told to take orders from him."

"That's right." Smoke spoke slowly to keep his voice soft. He was annoyed that Sam Dunn called his hand, even though he had not argued about Nate's decision to remove his authority. "I think Ike will go along with me on this."

"I do," a deep voice said at their back. They had not noticed Ike Yarby's arrival until he spoke.

Ike flexed his massive shoulders and pointed his thick forefinger at Sam Dunn. "Yer takin' orders just like everybody else as long as yer a part of my crew no matter if Gil did send ye. My order to ye right now is to mind yer mouth. I'll work things out with Smoke."

His eyes on Sam Dunn's face, Ike said, "Nate sent word for me to handle things to suit myself, and right now it suits me to put Smoke back in charge. It's his job anyway."

Grinning sheepishly, Sam Dunn walked toward his horse. Ed Slade, grimacing from the pain in his leg, gathered up his hat and empty pail, and the others drifted away with him.

Smoke watched their shadowy figures as the men rode back to the mixing barrel where Ike had kept a fire going. Joe Santine came by to inquire about Ed Slade's injury, which he had heard about from the other riders. After assuring him that Slade's wound was not serious, Smoke assigned Santine the first night watch. Working in shifts, the riders would circle the sick cattle throughout the night to see that they did not join the healthy group farther up the basin until they had been treated.

Afterward, Ike and Smoke joined the crew at the campfire. Most of the men had already spread their blankets, lying quietly on their backs to let the weariness seep out of them. Paul Mabry, his youthful face haggard and sweaty, had started preparing food for the evening meal. Someone met Smoke and Ike at the edge of the firelight to take their horses to the picket line, but Smoke was too tired to notice who it was.

Only now did he become aware of his own exhaustion. He had been in the saddle since sunup, and he felt like he had covered half the Pitchfork range. Besides the physical energy he had spent, the mental agitation from his argument with Nate, his strained relationship with Gil, and his concern over the Kellers added to his fatigue. He was not in the mood for idle talk, so he eased himself to the ground in the darkness beyond the circle of light cast by the fire.

Ike Yarby came over and sat down beside him, gave him an oblique glance, and said, "Paul Mabry brought back all the news from the Pitchfork. I hear ye killed a man. Did he butcher up yer face that way too?"

Smoke sighed disgustedly. He should have guessed that Charlie Ray Jones would pass on all the news while Mabry was at the ranch, telling him about the dead yearling and the incidents which followed its discovery. Everyone for miles around would soon know Smoke had killed Jesse Slater.

"You might as well hear about it from me," Smoke

said, rubbing a finger gingerly over the lump beneath his left eye. "Charlie Ray will find out, and he enjoys showing off how much he knows about the family. I had a fight with Gil, but it's not worth talking about."

Ike politely changed the subject. "We've still got a lot of sick cows, but we've done good this day. I don't allow yer pa is goin' to end up broke. Matter of fact, I don't think——"

"Maybe it'd be a good thing for everybody if he got taken down a peg or two," Smoke murmured.

A clucking sound came from Ike's throat. "Them's mighty harsh words, lad. Why do ye keep runnin' down yer pa?"

It was a question Smoke should have ignored, but the bitterness he had forgotten for the past few hours was beginning to burn inside him again. "Nate doesn't give anybody room to breathe. He'd like to keep Texas like it is forever—wild and backward. Nate's got enough power to keep people out and he uses it. Sometimes I think Nate's heart is made out of a branding iron."

"Yer forgettin' one thing, lad," Ike said firmly. "It was yer pa's own decent nature that got him his start. If ye want to hold onto anything in this country ye've got to be hard as rock. Nate's all that, but he'll stick by ye in hard times if yer worth it. Ye know the story on that."

Smoke took out tobacco and papers and rolled a cigarette, growing silent for a while. He lay back on his side, propping on one elbow, and smoked thoughtfully. Nate Wylie had gained lasting respect in this part of the West from a single act of mercy, but that was a long time ago. It had happened during the war, when Nate was fighting with General Taylor to ensure the independence of Texas. After one of the final battles he had been scouting alone, looking for stragglers, when he came across a gutshot soldier. The man had been deserted by his comrades when they fled in defeat, but Nate stayed with him. Although he was an American, the soldier had fought with the enemy, as had many others who had sworn their allegiance to Mexico while Texas was a part of it.

The soldier's insides were spilling out and there was no way he could survive, but Nate would not let him die on the lonely desert without the company of another of his kind. He stayed with him through the night, and when the man knew the end was near, he asked Nate to bring him the personal papers from the saddlebags on his dead horse. In them was a Spanish land grant, issued by one of the early *empresarios* who had tried to colonize Texas through the lure of free land. The soldier had long since lost touch with his family, and he signed over the grant to Nate in gratitude. It was from that acreage on Middle Creek that Nate built the Pitchfork.

Presently, Smoke crushed the fire from his cigarette and stood up. The aroma of frying bacon and boiling coffee captured his attention and he started toward the campfire. Ike Yarby remained on the ground a little longer, stroking his beard and looking up at Smoke with calculating eyes. "For the time bein' let's just keep our minds on them cattle. Yer pa has give ye a mighty good life and ye owe him somethin'."

"He's ruined my life," Smoke said bluntly. "Every man here knows he's got a few good friends, but I'm not sure I've got even one. Most men keep their distance with me because they're afraid of Nate's money, or his power, or they've got some kind of grudge against him. Women hang onto me because they figure I've got some of Nate's money to spend. I try to fool myself about it, but that's the only reason—"

"That's a lie, Smoke Wylie!"

The interruption came from the darkness at his back, but Smoke recognized the voice immediately. He wheeled, feeling embarrassed because he had forgotten that Hetty Mead was among the roundup crew. He did not turn fast enough, however, to dodge the tin pail Hetty threw at him. The pail hit him above the knee, stinging his thigh before it caromed off toward a buckboard parked nearby.

"Damn wildcat," Smoke growled, rubbing his knee. "I wasn't talking about you, Hetty. What're you doing here?"

Hetty Mead stepped closer, pushing her short blond curls away from her damp forehead. Smoke was reminded of soft mountain moss when he looked into her green eyes, a startling contrast against the deep tan of her flawless skin. Since childhood, she had lived with the conviction that she was a disappointment to her father because she had not been born a boy. She had spent her life trying to prove she was the equal of any man when it came to riding, roping, or doing a hard day's work. At the moment she was as grimy and tired as the other riders, and there was a smudge of dirt across the bridge of her tilted nose.

She pushed at the hem of her flannel shirt, trying to

164

keep it in the waistband of her Levi's. "I hang onto you when I can and it's got nothing to do with your pa's money. I heard what you said. You ought to be ashamed for insulting me and for—for talking about Nate the way you do. I didn't come here to win any favors. I'm just trying to be neighborly and help out, but if you can't be decent to your own pa, I can't expect you to appreciate anyone else."

Her voice was sharp with anger, but Smoke was in no mood to defend himself. He found himself comparing Hetty with the exciting, dark-haired woman he had met in Lost Horse Hollow. He had known Hetty since their days together in grade school, but only in the past two years had he stopped thinking of her only as a neighbor. Hetty made no secret of her affection for him, and it took little encouragement for her to slip into his arms and kiss him passionately, filling him with desire.

Even in Hetty's presence he could not push the image of Ada Keller from his mind. He could not picture Ada with sweat dripping from the tip of her nose and tufts of cow hair stuck to the seams of her clothes. Ada was different, not truly a range-bred woman, but one whose touch went through a man like a jolt of hard liquor, lifting his spirits and setting his mind afire with daring dreams.

"You ought to be the last person to be taking Nate's side," Smoke said. "If he wasn't so selfish he'd have sold Jerry Mead more graze along West Creek years ago so the Circle M could feed a bigger herd. You'd be a lot better off, have the kind of nice things you deserve."

Again he ran his eyes over her rumpled range clothes,

looking away as color flooded Hetty's cheeks. She took a deep breath, and Smoke was about to explain that he wanted the best for her when she leaped at him.

Had he been less distracted by other problems, he would not have been surprised by the attack. He knew Hetty was not inclined to suffer through anger in silence. Once, when he had promised to take her to a dance, then changed his mind and sat in on a poker game at the Great Western instead, she'd almost scratched his eyes out the next time he saw her. That appeared to be her aim now.

There was little a man could do when an infuriated woman was kicking at his shins, slapping at his face, and tearing at his hair all at the same time. Smoke finally managed to grab Hetty's arms and pull her so close to him she could not fight.

She pounded feebly at his chest, uttering little screeching sounds through her clenched teeth. "Turn me loose, Smoke! Turn me loose, or I swear I'll lower my sights the next time. I hate to be in the same county with you, much less in your arms. Let me go!"

Hetty jabbed him with an elbow, wrenched fiercely at his arms, and Smoke released his grip, fearful of hurting her.

She stepped away from him, twisting at the buttons which had become unfastened down the front of her shirt to bare the high swell of her breasts. She stared at him, the corners of her moist lips trembling. "I'm sorry I don't dress to your standards. There's one thing I'm sure of—Nate Wylie wouldn't look down on anybody who has to work cattle instead of primping in front of a mirror. You keep trying to live down the Wylie name, but you'd do better if you tried living up to it. You've turned into a sorehead and it's making you and everyone around you miserable."

"I know what I want," Smoke said. "It's just not the same thing Nate wants."

Hetty's face sobered, and her eyes softened as though she had read his thoughts. Smoke started to smile, expecting her to put her anger aside and laugh at him as she had done many times before after a quarrel. Hetty's expression did not change. She turned and walked away. Over her shoulder she said, "I know what I want, too. It used to be you, but I don't think it is anymore. I'm going home."

Smoke started to follow her, but Ike Yarby blocked his path. The big mountain man had walked a few paces away, pretending no interest while Hetty and Smoke argued, but now he clapped a restraining hand on Smoke's shoulder. The force of the thick fingers was like a vise.

"Ye've just run off a mighty good hand, so don't make things worse," Ike said firmly. "It was Hetty who brought the extra rags we needed, along with a mighty helpful notion."

"What kind of notion?" Smoke asked.

"A notion that maybe our cows don't have blackleg," Ike replied. "She told us they had some Circle M cattle one time which had an ailment that looked like blackleg but turned out to be something else. It was hoof rot. We just took it in our heads that these cows have blackleg and got too scared to think about anything else. A good

167

germkiller can knock out hoof rot, and I've made me up the strongest there is. We still have a lot of sick cows to doctor and some waitin' and watchin' to do. Let's get some grub in our bellies and rest up for another day."

Smoke held back a little longer, and Ike waited quietly beside him. His gaze still on Hetty's back, Smoke watched her slender figure move through the murky light toward the picketed horses. Far off in the darkness he could hear the lowing of restless cattle, and he wondered if Joe Santine was having trouble keeping them bunched. He lost sight of Hetty, but before long the hoofbeats of a galloping horse told him she was riding away from the camp. He was sorry he had offended her, but Hetty's own behavior was beginning to puzzle him.

Reflecting on the way she had tossed the pail at his head, he suspected something more than his words had angered her. She was much too observant to miss the cuts and bruises on his face, but she had not inquired about them. Did she know about his fight with Gil?

Their stormy argument had lasted only about two minutes, but Smoke found himself trying to recall every word that was exchanged. He was sure he had allowed something important to escape his notice—something that Hetty had said that did not fit with the rest of her remarks. Whatever it was had struck him as odd at the moment, but now the words were buried somewhere in his memory and he was too tired to force his mind to recall them.

Smoke rubbed his hand across his forehead in frustration and started walking toward the campfire.

"I think I must have died some time around noon and

nobody bothered to bury me." Ike chuckled dryly as he fell in step beside Smoke. "I hate to think about sunup, but I might get lucky and die in my sleep."

Smoke smiled and slapped him on the back. "You might not be missed if you do. Knowing Pa and Gil, I figure we'll have help by tomorrow. Gil will probably bring some of his roundup crew to make sure we're separating the cows like Nate said—and to bury the dead. Nate wouldn't want dead cows lying out in the open where the disease might get spread by vermin. Maybe we can fool them. If Hetty's right about this being hoof rot we might keep them all alive."

Ike brushed at his beard. "Maybe, but it's still touch and go. We might bust our backs and still find out we've got blackleg on our hands. If it is we'll need all the gravediggers we can get."

Chapter Fourteen

Ten bearded, hard-muscled men sat around the campfire, sucking at the dregs in tin coffee cups and puffing at the stubs of their after-breakfast cigarettes. They had finally gotten a full night's sleep, and the tired lines had faded from their faces. The irritation which had edged their voices for the past three days was replaced by good-natured joshing.

Eastward, the heavens were being prodded awake by pink fingers of light, and the rising sun transformed the sage and naked rock of the western hills into a rainbow of colors. The early morning dew lifted the odor of damp soil and fragrant weeds into the heavy air. Above the hubbub of the camp came the sounds of cattle munching grass. The men cocked their heads to listen and exchanged relieved smiles.

Joe Santine rose, stretched, and flipped his cigarette into the fire. He hitched at his belt and said, "That's what I call a right pretty sight—a big Texas sun shining on cows that don't need me to wash their dirty feet any more."

Some of the men chuckled, enjoying Santine's good spirits. They laughed easily now and Smoke laughed with them, sharing the relief from worry and uncertainty. He had sweated through fourteen-hour days— bulldogging calves, swabbing roped steers, and dousing Ike's homemade remedy on every cow with a discolored hoof. The fear of failure had numbed his mind until he could think of nothing else, but now the nightmare was over.

Gil Wylie arrived as Smoke had predicted, bringing three men with him. Smoke's crew had gambled on a girl's hunch and won. The cattle's ailment turned out to be hoof rot instead of blackleg and the infection was under control.

Smoke did not savor the victory alone. He usually sat apart from the others in idle moments, assuming they were more at ease in their own company. In the past, the Pitchfork riders had made no secret of their preference to work under Gil's supervision. Any newcomer to the Pitchfork soon learned that Gil was Nate's right-hand man. When there was a tough job to do, Nate assigned it to Gil, and when he wanted companionship on an evening ride, it was Gil who rode with him. The cowboys were more comfortable with Gil because they felt that an order from him was the same as an order from Nate. They had heard talk of Smoke's quick temper, his ready fists, and quick gun. They were wise enough to sense the tension in the air when Smoke was around his father, and it aroused a fear of the unknown in them.

The attitude in South Basin was different. Smoke had worked himself to the point of exhaustion every day, driven by guilt over not having moved the South Basin cattle from the swampy land at the start of the roundup. The others had read the fear and desperation in his face and it was contagious. They tried to match his grueling pace—wanting to help, wanting to claim victory over the enemy which manifested itself as a swollen hoof.

When it was over they accepted Smoke as one of them—a man whose skill and stamina they had been unable to surpass. They had faced the threat of disaster together and it drew them together as a unit—as friends. Smoke had won their respect and they wanted him to know it. Both Brad Lipps and Sam Dunn—riders from Gil's crew—kept offering him tobacco for a cigarette, and every time his coffee cup got empty someone walked by with a heated pot to fill it.

For the first time in years Smoke found pleasure in the companionship of the Pitchfork crew. He let his gaze sweep over the basin, settling on the gleaming coats of the Pitchfork longhorns. The cattle showed no signs of illness. The sense of triumph he felt was new to him, but he was sure Nate Wylie had experienced it each time he paid off a debt or beat back a Comanche raid in the early years.

A rider crossed his vision and Smoke's thoughts returned to the present. Gil had ridden away soon after breakfast for a final inspection of the herd before he left with his crew. He rode high in the saddle, his head turning frequently so he could see every steer as he cantered toward the camp.

Gil swung down a few feet from Smoke with a smile on his face. "Everything looks great this morning. Nate's as bad as I am for raising hell before he knows what's going on. He'll have to eat crow when I tell him all the cows are alive."

Smoke rose, meeting his brother's smile with a frown. "Since it was my back he was jumping on, don't you think I deserve the satisfaction of telling him the score?"

"You sure do," Gil said. "I didn't mean to take credit, but I thought I'd ease his mind. It's your place to tell him, so I'll just head for my camp and let you talk to Pa."

Gil turned toward his horse and swung into the saddle. He turned to wave good-bye and saw Smoke staring at the rifle which rested in the boot beside his saddle. He slapped at the rifle butt and said, "I hope you're not thinking what I think you are. I thought we'd settled that business about the bushwhacker. You know I'd never use this rifle against you."

"I don't know what you'd do to stay on good terms with Nate," Smoke said flatly.

A surge of anger turned Gil's forehead red. His back stiffened and he loosened one foot in the stirrup as if he might step to the ground, then yanked at the reins, slow-walking his horse to the campfire. It was a signal for the men from his crew to head for their horses, and in a few minutes all of them were gone.

Afterward, Smoke continued to gaze across the land, deep in thought. The experience of the past days was a reminder that only hard and dauntless men could survive these times in the West. Besides the strength demanded by the work, a man had to wage an ongoing battle with Nature. He had to be able to smell a winter storm coming, sense a drought in the offing, and guard against minute pests which could lay eggs in a scratched hoof and destroy a herd. He felt a grudging admiration for Nate Wylie, who had learned to read the sky, the winds, and the sounds of the earth so well.

Nate had enjoyed many successes, but he also had known disappointment. Long ago, while prowling with boyish curiosity through his father's desk, Smoke had found plans for an elaborate manor house. It resembled the drawings of the elegant Southern plantations Smoke had seen pictured in books. The house was never built, and he wondered why a man of his father's means continued to live in the plain log house which he'd built when he first settled on the Pitchfork.

When he was older Smoke understood why the stately house had never become a reality. It had been planned for his mother, and after she left Nate felt no need for it. Smoke felt that Nate had deprived her of something she would have enjoyed, and his feeling of loss grew more intense.

He stirred to his feet and shook off the depressing memories, determined to let nothing detract from this day of triumph. The men were not pressed by anxiety anymore, but there was work to be done. The roundup in South Basin was not finished and Ike Yarby, Ed Slade, Joe Santine, and Paul Mabry were beginning to grow restless near the dead campfire.

He walked over to join them. "Another day ought to clean up the strays, Ike," he said. "I'll leave that up to you and the boys while I go home and talk to Nate."

Joe Santine brushed at his hat brim, his glance sliding toward Paul Mabry. Santine spat between his teeth and looked away. "Are you sure you'll be back, Smoke? We're getting sort of used to you."

Smoke grinned, pleased that his run-in with Santine was forgotten. "Who knows about me, Joe?" His face grew serious and he added, "Maybe I won't be back. If things don't go well at home I might not be living at the Pitchfork anymore."

Santine dismissed Smoke's pessimism with a wave of his hand. He picked up his saddle, ready to ride out to the herd, and Paul Mabry followed. Ike Yarby waited until the two men had walked beyond earshot before he said, "There's somethin' on yer mind besides watchin' Nate eat crow, lad. I can tell by yer eyes. Can an old mountain man be of help?"

Smoke shook his head. "Just wind things up here. Nate's put on extra hands to help with the branding and tallying when you get to the holding grounds. Thanks, but nobody but me can settle what has to be settled between me and Pa."

"I hope you ain't goin' to be ornery with him," Ike said, frowning. "I thought ye might have changed yer way of lookin' at things after what we've been through here."

Smoke managed a wry grin. He started toward the picket line and Ike walked with him. "How things go will depend on how ornery Pa is," Smoke said. "I met some folks who want to settle in Lost Horse Hollow and I want to help them. They need it. I tried to make a deal with Nate so he'd leave them alone. If he takes me up on it I'll be back. If he turns me down I might leave the Pitchfork for good."

Ike grunted in surprise. "That would be a damn' fool thing to do, lad, bow up yer back to help some pilgrims get a toehold here. Ye shouldn't go against yer pa over somethin' like that."

"It's more than just the settlers," Smoke said. "It's a whole lifetime of things, but maybe I'm just looking on the dark side. Pa might see things my way for a change."

His parting remark was not spoken with conviction. Smoke was thinking aloud, trying to dispel his own doubts, but his faint hopes died the minute he arrived at the Pitchfork.

As he rode toward the post-oak which shaded the front porch of the T-shaped house, he saw two ground-tied horses standing in the yard, their heads drooping against the glare of the midday sun. Their presence filled him with an uneasy curiosity. He recognized the horses. The long-legged sorrel belonged to Jerry Mead and the pinto was the horse Hetty usually rode.

Leaving his bay tied in the shade of the tree, Smoke moved quietly to the porch and sat down on a wooden bench. He did not want others to witness his conversation with Nate, and the presence of the Meads made him fear there was more trouble afoot. They were not frequent visitors, although Nate occasionally invited them to Sunday dinner.

After his wife left, Nate avoided the company of women when he could, but he was fond of Hetty Mead. He found it as easy to discuss cattle, horses, range conditions, and market prices with Hetty as with her father, and he welcomed her as a family friend. Jerry Mead ran a small spread, hired only a skeleton crew, and his visit to the Pitchfork on a working day would have to be for a special reason.

The reason soon became clear. Voices drifted through the half-open window at Smoke's back, and he listened to the discussion inside with growing anger.

"I hate to be pushed into trouble over a handful of land that's been ignored for years," Smoke heard Jerry Mead say. "This man Keller rode over to my place and cussed me out for building a dam that'll cut off his water in Lost Horse. He was talking about knowing people in Austin who would give him some kind of license or rights to open range, and how he would have the sheriff on my back. First it was the sheepmen, Nate, and now it's these squatters. It looks like we're just itching to get ourselves into a war with somebody. I'm falling behind in my work. I don't know which way to jump anymore and I can't sleep for worrying over this mess."

Smoke went into the house in swift strides, no longer concerned that the Meads might witness a family quarrel. Those inside heard the thump of his boot heels, and were staring at the doorway when he entered the parlor.

Nate Wylie stood with his back to the fireplace, the silver pitchfork framed above his head like a crown. His stubborn nature would not permit him to pamper his high blood pressure or the bad leg, and it was apparent he had already been riding today, probably to check the holding grounds.

Smoke's lead-gray eyes were like winter storm clouds against the deep brown of his face as he stopped in the middle of the room. Jerry Mead rose from the horsehide sofa along the back wall with the spring-like motions of a man expecting bad news. Hetty remained seated. Her glance met Smoke's briefly, then wavered and dropped to her hands, which were clasped tightly in her lap.

Nate was the first to speak. He leaned heavily on his cane, his weight causing the shaft to bend like a bow. "How many dead cows do we have?" he growled, his eyes hooded by his bushy gray brows.

"None!" Smoke spat out the answer, but he did not feel the satisfaction he had anticipated a few hours ago. "It wasn't blackleg, but I can see that's not important to you right now. Getting rid of the Kellers means more to you than half the Pitchfork herd. I heard Jerry talking when I was on the porch. While I was doctoring the cattle I kept hoping you'd do something I wanted for a change, but you're not going to take my deal, are you?"

"The price is too high," Nate said. "Squatters are like locusts. You let one move in and they'll swarm all over you. If we let them people set up in Lost Horse there'll be squatters on every corner of the Pitchfork before the year's out. I won't stand for that. I aim to nip it in the bud."

Smoke shuffled his feet and fiddled with his gun belt while he fought to control his anger. "Those people have had it hard and they want to get a start somewhere. I told them I'd try to help them. I figured there'd be some peace between you and me if you'd back me up, but I was a fool to think you'd ever do anything my way."

Avoiding his son's eyes, Nate limped to his desk and dropped heavily into his chair. "It's that gal you're tryin' to shine up to. Women are always on your mind. One day you'll learn it's not smart to give up too much just to please them. They'll take all you've got, and if that ain't enough they'll go lookin' for more somewhere else."

He paused and turned apologetically toward Hetty. "I'm not talkin' about people like you, child."

She smiled, glancing at Smoke with a fiery look in her eyes. "I know the kind you're talking about," she said.

Smoke did not look at Hetty, but he was aware of the harshness in her voice. He stared at his father and said, "You like this kind of thing. You want everybody to know you're the kingpin around here and that it's dangerous to cross you. You'll hound the Kellers just to prove it."

"He's making a heap of trouble for me too," Jerry Mead said quietly. The rawboned rancher shifted his hat from one hand to the other and sleeved the sweat from his face. "I agree we can't let a whole bunch of strangers move in on our graze, but we ought to wait and see where this is going to lead us. One family can't hurt us much."

Smoke felt helpless. There would be no compromise from Nate Wylie. Smoke could see that in the stubborn set of his jaw and the unblinking brown eyes. He had burned his brand on this land long ago, and he would let no one deface it. Swallowing against a dry throat, Smoke turned to Jerry Mead and asked, "Where'd he ask you to build a dam?"

Mead looked uncomfortably at Nate Wylie, obviously uneasy because he had spoken out against him. Nate saw his reluctance and supplied an answer of his own.

"It's not much of a dam—not much of a job either," he said gruffly. "I asked Jerry to throw some rocks and dirt across West Creek where it crosses his land above Lost Horse Hollow. There's a cut through a line of hummocks there and it can't be more than thirty-forty feet across. Once the water backs up a couple hundred feet, the creek will spill over into a little arroyo and cut a new channel, then flow east across the Circle M. It'll be better for Jerry—give him water where he didn't have any before."

He shifted his eyes to Mead, letting the Circle M owner feel the full weight of the disapproval in them. "I sent him word two days ago, sent two men to help, and the dam's half built. Now Jerry's gettin' cold feet and wants to give up because Keller rode over and raised hell when he saw the water dwindlin' away."

Jerry Mead kicked at an imaginary object on the planked floor and said, "Dad-blame it, Nate, I don't like the smell of it. I'm trying to work a roundup and I can't find time to brand my cows. Every time I've tangled with a stranger who knows how to talk fancy, I've found somebody sharp enough to raise a big stink. I'm going to give up that dam and do my own work."

Stepping closer to Mead, tapping his cane for emphasis, Nate said, "By damn, you'll finish that dam or live to regret it. West Creek supplies all the water you've got and it rises on the Pitchfork. You'll either cut off the water to Lost Horse Hollow or I'll build a dam above your spread."

The look on Jerry Mead's face was a mixture of pain and dismay. "I can't believe you'd do that to a friend."

"He'd do it," Smoke said.

"Don't ever force my hand, Jerry." Nate's voice was threatening. "My men are still over there workin', and I want you to go on back and see that your crew does its part."

The dispute was settled. Nate Wylie was going to have his way and Jerry Mead knew it. He stared hard at the Pitchfork owner for several seconds, then turned and headed for the door. He looked back, signaling Hetty to follow him.

Hetty had remained quiet during the discussion, looking alternately at her hands and the floor, refusing to face Smoke. She rose, but did not follow her father immediately. She crossed the room and laid her hand on Nate's arm.

"I'm still your friend," she said softly. "I know you wouldn't push my father unless you thought it was the best thing for us. He'll understand after he thinks it over."

Nate patted her hand, but the hard lines around his

mouth did not relax. He was watching Jerry Mead's back, his body hunched forward like he might go after the Circle M man and offer a farewell handshake.

Smoke was watching Mead too. He asked bluntly, "Why do you let him order you around?"

Mead laughed dryly. He gestured over his shoulder with his right thumb. "See that Pitchfork up there? Nate used to say the three prongs stood for the lucky three— West Creek, Middle Creek, and East Creek. That's all the year-round water there is north of Jackpine and Nate owns it all. He could starve me out if he was a mind to. That's why I do things that go against my grain."

He continued toward the door, saying, "Come on, Hetty. We'd better finish that dam if we expect to go on running a ranch in these parts."

He went outside, and Smoke heard Hetty take a deep, shaky breath as she started to follow. She had to pass within three feet of him to reach the doorway, but he could tell by the tilt of her chin that she meant to walk by without acknowledging his presence.

His pulse quickened as she neared him. For this visit Hetty had swapped her range clothes for more feminine attire, and Smoke was struck by her fresh, girlish beauty. Her brown cotton riding skirt was fitted to show the full curve of her hips, and her green-striped blouse reflected the emerald hue of her eyes. Smoke had not forgotten about the argument at South Basin, but still her coolness puzzled him. It was unlike Hetty to make so much of a brief quarrel or to side with anyone against her father. He was sure something else had ruffled her feelings.

She was directly beside him, her eyes fixed straight

ahead, when Smoke reached out to grasp her arm. He expected her to shake loose, but she stopped, her lips pressed tightly together as she looked at him.

"I need to talk with you," Smoke said. "Wait for me outside."

Hetty did not reply. She lifted his hand away with exaggerated tenderness and walked on through the doorway, leaving the room in oppressive silence.

Chapter Fifteen

After the door had closed behind the Meads, Smoke moved over to the front window so he could see what Hetty was going to do. Her father was already in the sorrel's saddle, looking down at his daughter as she picked up her horse's reins. Mead said something to her, nodding in the direction of the house, and Smoke surmised he was complaining about the task Nate Wylie was forcing him to perform.

Smoke could not hear their voices, but he saw Hetty shrug impatiently and step into the pinto's saddle. She was not going to wait for him. As they sent their horses galloping away from the house, Smoke crossed the room to stand in front of his father's desk. He said with a quiet viciousness: "If you weren't my pa I'd beat hell out of you for making me look like a fool with the Kellers."

Nate Wylie looked up, his eyes squinted. "By damn, I am your pa and I call the shots where the Pitchfork is concerned, so you can drop the tough talk."

Smoke whirled and started toward the door, then

turned and came back. His voice thick with anger, he said, "You deceived me. You let me believe you'd think about giving the Kellers a chance when I offered you a deal. That was just to get rid of me so I'd go to South Basin and work my butt off for the Pitchfork. As soon as I was out of sight you got together with Jerry Mead and started that dam. You and Gil are always cutting me out of decisions around here and doing things to suit yourselves. How long do you think I'm going to stay around and put up with it?"

Nate's patience had been exhausted in his discussion with Jerry Mead. He shoved to his feet, folded his arms across his chest, and glared at Smoke. "Put up with me—put up with the way I run this ranch?" he demanded, his voice rumbling in his chest. "You'll put up with it until you get to be a better man than I am. I decide what's good for the Pitchfork and what's not, and you'll take orders from me as long as you stay here. You've got no choice!"

Smoke started to reply, but changed his mind. He became strangely calm. He had a choice his father had overlooked—his claim on West Creek. Nate still held the power to cancel the deed, however, and Smoke would not risk challenging him in his present mood.

Smoke's birthday had passed without notice while he was busy with the stricken cattle in South Basin. He had met the age requirement specified by Nate and was eligible to receive the land which had been set aside for him, but he would have to choose the right time to exercise his rights. Cutting his ties to the Pitchfork immediately would not benefit the Kellers. He needed to be where he could watch Nate's moves.

After waiting a few seconds to see if Smoke was going to continue the argument, Nate sat down and began thumbing through a month-old copy of *The Galveston News* which lay on his desk. His temper cooled, but he still had other things on his mind. Finally he pushed the newspaper aside and asked again about the condition of the cattle in South Basin. They talked stiffly for about five minutes about the work, and the success of Ike Yarby's Platte River medicine.

Nate's mood slowly changed. He inquired about Smoke's estimate of the number of cattle stricken, how they were treated, and how the men had performed. He prolonged the conversation, trying to ease the hard feelings which had grown between them. Smoke's answers were curt, almost indifferent, and he found it hard to continue the conversation. His thoughts were on the dam Jerry Mead was building above Lost Horse Hollow. Even as his father talked, Smoke mapped a plan to thwart Nate's efforts to squeeze out the Kellers, and he was eager to get away from the house and put it into effect.

Finally they gave up their efforts at conversation. Smoke tugged at his hat and walked toward the door. He said, "I need some rest and time to think. If you don't trust Ike Yarby to finish up in South Basin, you can send Gil down there. I'm going to do my thinking in town today."

Surprisingly, Nate Wylie offered no objection. "Gil's busy with his own crew, but I trust Ike enough to leave him alone. You've earned a day off, and I don't mind you goin' to Jackpine if you won't push on your notion of somebody payin' Jesse Slater to start trouble. I'll handle that with Ben Toler. I don't want you shootin' up anybody else."

"That's not what I had in mind," Smoke said, and went on through the doorway.

He reached Jackpine in mid-afternoon. Halfway down Main Street he reined around a plodding freight outfit and passed before the Great Western's hitching rack. A gaunt, bearded old man who had been lounging in the shade of the saloon awning spotted him and perked up with a toothless grin. He called Smoke's name, hoping to be treated to a free drink, but Smoke waved him away and rode on.

He stopped at Dulaney's Ranch Outfitters Store and dismounted without bothering to fasten the bay's reins to the tie-bar. Next door, at Olson's Boarding House, a red-haired woman in a low-cut dress came out and started along the boardwalk. She hesitated, looking him over and smiling. From her appearance and the direction she took, he presumed she was a new girl at the Great Western, which probably meant one of the others had moved on. He hoped she was replacing Amy Sue Buckner, who desperately needed a husband to care for her.

Seeing the invitation in the girl's eyes, Smoke shook his head and tipped his hat. He stared boldly at the curve of her bosom, then walked on, a picture of Ada Keller as she had appeared at the creek flashing through his mind.

The picture came alive. He was conscious of bumping

into someone as his eyes struggled to adjust to the gloom of Dulaney's place, and he backed outside again. Surprise held him speechless for a moment, then he smiled apologetically. It was not a daydream or mirage. It was Ada Keller, fully clothed and sparkling with pleasure. Her trim lavender dress was a splash of unexpected color against the sun-bleached buildings around her. She was on her way out of the store, a small package under her arm, when she collided with Smoke.

"Hello again," Ada said pleasantly. "Why aren't you out scouting the creeks today?"

Smoke laughed, feeling an intimacy with her in sharing the small joke. "That's what I was going to do tonight. I planned to ride over to Lost Horse Hollow to let you know I'm not going to let Nate dry up the creek down there."

The girl's long lashes lowered to mask her violet eyes. "It looks like you're too late. We were told the Wylie family might make trouble for us when we started inquiring about unsettled land, but I couldn't believe folks who have so much would care about so little. Some say your father's mean enough to kill us before he'd let us settle there."

Smoke disliked the sharpness of her tone, but the impulse to defend the family name subsided when she raised her glance to his face and asked meekly, "Do you think your plan is good enough to stop what your father's doing to us?"

"Maybe," Smoke said. "I'm going to take sides against him, and that might make him think twice before he gets too rough. He won't give up easy. Nate's used up a lot of his life building the Pitchfork, and he wouldn't have it if he'd given in to everybody who wanted a piece of the land. This time I want him to know how it feels to be the loser."

Her smile returned. She slipped her arm under his, hugging it to her while she pressed her body against his side. "You're doing this for me, aren't you?"

"And for me," he said. "I think Pa's big enough, maybe too big. He's so full of pride over what he owns that it doesn't leave room for any feelings about people. He ought to turn some graze over to Jerry Mead and Wade Stone and some of our other neighbors, but he figures he's the only one strong enough to hold it. He worries about the big syndicates that are trying to move in from the East. He's afraid anyone except him might sell out to them and the life we know would be gone forever. We need more people, but not their kind."

Her eyes met his in a lingering look. "It sound as though you don't like the Eastern companies any more than he does. Have they been after the Pitchfork?"

He laughed. "Yeah, and Nate really gets riled. He keeps getting mail from outfits with fancy names wanting to buy him out. They talk about setting up offices in town, bringing in new business, and building up Jackpine. He writes back that he'll personally shoot any of those lawyers and bankers who set foot on his range. I guess I would stand with him on that. We'd end up with a lot of money, but we'd be the only ones. With the Pitchfork as a base the syndicates would break the little ranchers. They'd be worse than Nate about throwing their power around."

Ada cocked her head and looked at him with a puzzled expression in her eyes. "You're a very strange man. One minute you're as protective about the Pitchfork as your father and brother, and the next minute you're talking about sharing the range with others. Won't Nate Wylie consider you a traitor if you side with us?"

"I don't care what he thinks," Smoke said. "I'll fight anyone who tries to do harm to the Pitchfork, but I won't push folks off land we don't use. That doesn't seem strange to me."

Ada Keller looked away, her tongue brushing along the edge of her lips. The set of his jaw and the sheen of Smoke's eyes seemed to unnerve her, and she appeared eager to be on her way. "It takes a lot of nerve to do what you're doing. I believe you really do want to help us."

"I usually keep my word," he said, and the softness of his voice betrayed his nervousness. "Maybe I can ride out to Lost Horse later and tell you more about it."

She leaned close to him, her voice husky, secretive. "You've been so good to me and I've done nothing for you. I'd like to make up for that. I could spend some time with you tonight if you want to come by the Pioneer House. My father thought I should move back to the hotel until he has a shelter built and we see if that dam is going to leave us any water. I'll try to make your visit something special."

He stood for a few seconds watching the swing of her hips as she walked away from him and went toward the hotel. He went into Dulaney's with a spray of sweat beginning to dampen his face, wondering for the first time about his motives. Was he doing this as a matter of principle, or was he doing it to please Ada?

Around him, the night was black enough to conceal his movements, but a nagging sense of guilt made Smoke feel like the whole world was watching him. A canopy of iron-gray clouds had slid in from the northwest before sundown, and the sky overhead pressed down on the stunted cedars which stood like spying sentinels on the cut-banks above him.

The nervous sweat which had broken out on him the minute he walked into Dulaney's store was still with him, and Smoke cursed the clumsiness of his hands. He tried to curb his haste; he wanted to do this job right and live to see the results. He had never handled so much dynamite before, but he assumed the task was the same as blasting out an ordinary water hole, which he and Nate had done together many times.

Waiting had built an almost unbearable tension in him. He had aroused no suspicion by making his purchase at Dulaney's because the proprietor disdained any interest in the affairs of the Pitchfork Ranch. Dulaney was aware of Nate Wylie's part ownership of Ed Jarvis's General Store and considered it unfair competition. It was only when Jarvis was unable to supply some item that the Pitchfork traded with Dulaney. He accepted this practice coolly, never engaging in idle conversation. Dulaney did not like Nate Wylie, and it was not likely he would mention Smoke's name except under unusual circumstances. He would not volunteer any information about Smoke's purchase of the dynamite.

It took Smoke half an hour to pick out the best places to plant the explosives and make the necessary connections along the face of the dam. Finished with that part of the job, he unwound the spool of fuse he had purchased along with the dynamite. He climbed up the side of a rocky wash and knelt behind a head-high mound of dirt and boulders. He scratched a match alight with his thumbnail. While the flame grew in his cupped hand he took a final look at the scene below.

Jerry Mead had followed Nate's orders well. He had chosen a narrow point on West Creek where two eroded hummocks pressed close together like half-open tongs. While he moved around the area to place the dynamite, Smoke had walked over the tracks of both men and horses. At the mouth of the wash he saw a massive iron scoop, rigged so it could be drawn by two horses, and this had hastened the building of the dam.

A row of giant boulders had been rolled into the creek to form the base of the dam. Dirt and gravel had been scraped off the cut-banks to the west and tamped behind the rocks to form a solid barrier which would back up the water and eventually turn it into an arroyo. The creek still trickled through the dirt in a few spots, but another day's work would complete the dam and there would be no way for the Kellers to survive in Lost Horse Hollow.

The match burned his finger and Smoke dropped it, grinding it into the dirt with his heel. It was a habit drilled into him by Nate Wylie as a precaution against wildfire on the prairie. He struck another match, touching it quickly to the fuse before he could change his mind.

The burning strand traced a sparkling path across the earth. The sizzling of it sounded loud in the stillness and the acrid odor of powder filled the night air. Fascinated, Smoke watched the blue-red sparks race toward the base of the dam. As the sparks neared the water he ducked behind the dirt pile and clamped his hands over his ears.

He was glad it was not a thunderous noise; it was more of a rumbling vibration than a booming explosion. The sound of falling rock and dirt was like a soft summer shower on the surrounding underbrush. Smoke remained doubled over in a crouch until the debris stopped falling. When it was quiet he rose slowly, planning to walk back to his horse without looking back at the damage he had done.

"That was a rotten thing to do!" a voice said at his back.

Chapter Sixteen

Smoke wheeled, the blood draining from his face. A clump of greasewood rustled nearby, and Hetty Mead stepped into view. She was dressed in her range clothes, Levi's and flannel shirt, and she was shaking her head in disbelief.

"Hetty!" Smoke's voice was a startled gasp. The girl did not move, and he strode quickly to her. He grasped her by the shoulders and shouted, "Why are you sneaking around in the dark to spy on me?"

Hetty looked stunned. Her voice was soft and emotionless as she said, "One of Wade Stone's boys has been sick and not able to eat much of anything. My mother thought he might like some canned peaches, so I took them over to them. I rode back this way to see how the dam was coming along. I wasn't spying on you. I thought you were miles from here—at the roundup camp. This is terrible! It—it's such a mean and sneaky trick. I wish I hadn't seen it."

She shoved his hands aside and tried to walk away, but Smoke moved ahead to block her path.

"Hold on a minute," he said. "I don't want you to tell anybody what you saw. Give me a little time and I'll tell Pa I blasted the dam, but I can't tell him now. You saw how mean he can be—how he threatened your own father. Somebody's got to show him he can't run over people, but I need to work out some things before I tell him I'm the one who stopped him."

Her gaze clung to his face and Smoke's nervousness began to subside. He smiled, remembering the many times she had forgiven him for his impulsive actions. He slipped his arms around her and pulled her close, saying, "I haven't had a chance to spend any time with you lately, but I'm going to make up for it."

He misread Hetty's silence as an indication she would yield to his embrace and continue to trust him, but when he bent to kiss her she shoved him away.

"You've picked the wrong time to try to sweet-talk me," she said, her voice quavering. "I'm fed up with your grudges and your dirty tricks. After what I saw from the hills the other day I'm fed up with chasing after you, too. From now on I'm going to worry about protecting the Circle M instead of you. You can bet I'll tell Nate who ruined the dam!"

Smoke's smile faded as Hetty continued to measure him with flashing eyes. His thoughts turned back to the day they quarreled at his roundup camp, and suddenly he remembered that part of the exchange which had seemed out of place—words which had escaped him, but now echoed clearly in his mind. At one point she had said, *". . . the next time I'll lower my sights."*

She had revived his memory just now when she said, *"After what I saw from the hills the other day . . ."*

Smoke felt a sinking sensation in his stomach. Before he met Ada Keller, he'd loved Hetty enough to think of marrying her, but at the moment he disliked her intensely. He said, "Good Lord! You're the one who tried to dry-gulch me! I was ready to blame Gil for that and— and it was you! You've been going back and forth to the Stone place a lot and you saw me in Lost Horse Hollow with Ada!"

She turned and stared at the muddy, frothing creek which gushed and gurgled nearby. After a moment she gave him a withering glance and said, "Sometimes I let my bad temper make a fool of me, but I'm not sorry about that shot. I ran into Gil that day when he was looking for you, and he told me about the blackleg scare in South Basin. You're right—I was on my way to visit the Stones, but I thought I could be of more help at South Basin. I went back home, got some cloths and liniment, then headed for the roundup camp. The shortest trail was across the hills, and that's when I saw you kissing that girl. A little later I saw you start a fight with Gil and I was furious, but I didn't try to kill you. I aimed five feet above your head. I just wanted to get you away from those people before anything else happened."

"Something else is going to happen if Nate hears I set off that dynamite," Smoke said uneasily. "In a few days I'll have enough land to start my own spread if Pa doesn't get too mad to keep an old promise. It's the only chance I'll ever have to live my own life. For God's sake, Hetty, don't turn against me when I need you!"

She walked toward the brush clump where she had left her horse. Her voice was still crisp with anger as she said, "I'm through making excuses for you—to myself or anyone else. Until you stop hurting the only people who care about you, you'll just have to face the consequences. When Nate finds out the dam has been ruined he's going to raise hob with Circle M for not having a guard up here. If he knows the truth about you, it'll get my father off the hook. Nate could ruin us."

The chill in her voice was an enemy Smoke could not fight. He felt trapped, helpless. He followed Hetty to her horse, making a last attempt to reason with her.

"I'm not trying to hurt your father," he said earnestly. "I'm trying to get back at Nate. I want him to know he's not in charge of this whole country—to worry about who's got the guts to buck him. While he's worrying I'll try to claim my share of the ranch. It shouldn't take more than a week—just time enough for Nate to approve my deed or go against it. Can't you do that much for me? I'll see that your father doesn't get blamed for this."

She went on, not answering, and Smoke's steps lagged. Hetty swung into the pinto's saddle and spurred away from West Creek. Smoke stood frozen in his tracks and watched her out of sight, hoping her anger would cool in a few hours and that she would not reveal his secret until he could decide on his plans for the future.

It was nearly ten o'clock when Smoke rode into the camp in South Basin. He had debated whether to return to the range or ride home, and the decision was made almost subconsciously when he turned his horse southward from the wrecked dam. He did not want to go to the Pitchfork until he knew what he would face when he got there.

He spotted the red coals of the campfire from atop one of the treeless hills, and slowed his horse to a walk as he rode toward it. When he was still a hundred feet away he saw a shadow stir in the blackness ahead, stretching presently into the gangling silhouette of Ed Slade.

As Smoke dismounted wearily Ed Slade relaxed, letting the rifle in the crook of his arm point at the ground.

"Oh," he grunted. "I wasn't expecting you."

Smoke was in a sour mood. "Why not? I'm your ramrod and we're on Pitchfork land. I was too tired to call out, but I didn't expect anybody to put a gun on me either."

He heard Slade's boots scrape across the grass, but he could not see the expression on his face. "I want to get along," Slade said. "Don't make it hard for me. Ike's got one of them jumpy spells on, says he's got a feeling something's going to happen. He told us to sleep with a gun close by. I guess I'm the only one who heard you coming."

His whisper could have been a precaution against disturbing Ike Yarby, whose bed was nearby, or it could have been Slade's way of warning Smoke not to push him too hard.

"I heard him," Ike Yarby mumbled without turning over. "I was just layin' low till I knowed what was up."

"I'm a little jumpy myself," Smoke said to Ed Slade. "Sorry I barked at you. Go back to sleep. You too, Ike."

The camp grew quiet. Smoke was so shocked and unnerved by Hetty's unexpected appearance at the dam that every thought of Ada Keller had disappeared from his mind. It was only when he stretched out on his blankets and tried to sleep that he remembered her invitation to visit her at the hotel. Her sultry tones and choice of words hinted that she expected him to make love to her in the privacy of her room, and at the time he had anticipated a night of sheer pleasure. Now, however, it seemed unimportant.

For the first time in days his thoughts dwelt more on Hetty Mead than on Ada Keller. Memories of the past flooded his mind and kept him from sleeping. He thought of the times he and Hetty had ridden the hills together, seeking out new places to watch an awesome western sunset; of the carefree Saturday night barn dances they had shared while growing up. He recalled their first kiss long ago when they both stopped laughing over some nonsense at the same instant and realized they were drawn together by feelings much deeper than a close friendship.

Those were good and happy days, but reflecting on them gave him no comfort. Shortly before daylight he fell into a sound sleep, thinking as he dozed off that if

Hetty failed to change her mind, he would lose much more than a chance to own his own spread.

An hour before sunrise Gil rode into the roundup camp and Smoke had his answer about Hetty's decision. Exhaustion had put him to sleep, but he awoke with a start when he heard the horse approaching. By the time Gil reined in beside the dead ashes of the campfire, Smoke was already pulling on his boots. Ed Slade and Paul Mabry were slower in realizing they had a visitor and did not rouse up immediately. Joe Santine and Ike Yarby, ever alert, tossed aside their blankets and sat up, trying not to show their curiosity over Gil's unscheduled arrival.

Nodding perfunctorily to the two cowboys, Gil kept his seat in the saddle and looked straight at Smoke.

"I do believe," he said quietly, "that you've gone plumb loco. Nobody in their right mind would do the things you do."

"Don't preach to me, Gil," Smoke growled. "I can get all I want of that from Pardee. I reckon Hetty and Jerry Mead paid a visit to the Pitchfork."

Gil's face was covered with a stubble of sandy beard, indicating he had been dispatched hurriedly on his mission. "They showed up in the middle of the night. We finished our gather on West Creek and was trailing cattle to the holding grounds. I was close enough to spend the night at home, but I didn't get much sleep. As soon as Jerry Mead told Nate what had happened to the dam I was sent for you. Pa wants you, and if you aim to start another fight let's get at it."

Raking his hair in place with his fingers, Smoke put on

his hat and reached for the saddle he had used as a pillow. "I feel like beating up on somebody, but it's not you. I owe you an apology for thinking you took a shot at me. It was Hetty. She saw me kissing Ada and had to blow off steam."

Gil Wylie was a cool-headed man, seldom permitting anything to rattle him. He had been offended by Smoke's earlier accusation, but he accepted the explanation of the rifle shot without so much as a flicker of his eyes. He nodded, shrugged, and put the subject aside. "I'm getting tired of running errands because of you, but this time you're going back with me. I just want to know if it's going to be easy or tough."

Hoisting the saddle to his shoulder, Smoke started toward the picket line where the horses had been held overnight. The other riders had risen now, but had drifted some distance away and were busy with the breakfast chores. Although they pretended to be unconcerned, Smoke knew they had heard most of the conversation, but at this point he did not care.

"You're not the one I want to fight," Smoke said. "I guess it's Pa."

"Don't ever try that either," Gil warned grimly. "You'll have to take on both of us if you do."

Smoke gave his brother a long look. "I'd probably do the same if you tried it, but that doesn't mean I have to like the way he runs over people. What's he going to do about the dam?"

Gil tilted his head, his eyes hard and challenging. "Are you man enough to find out?"

"I'm man enough," Smoke murmured. "It's like Nate

said—I've got no other choice."

On the ride to the ranch Smoke set the pace, keeping his bay gelding at a gallop. Dodging the brush and avoiding prairie-dog holes demanded his full attention on the trail and he had no time to think of anything else. He wanted it that way.

It was not until they reached a cleared area on the timbered ridge overlooking the Pitchfork ranch house that Gil tried to talk to him. As Smoke halted to let his horse catch its breath Gil pulled alongside, an uneasy expression on his face.

"I'm going to lag behind while you go ahead and have it out with Pa. I hope the war is over by the time I get to the house."

Smoke shrugged and said, "It'll be over. I'm going to force it to a quick finish. No matter how much hell Nate raises I'm pulling out for good this time."

"And then what happens?" Gil's voice sounded angry.

"Hard to tell," Smoke replied, shrugging. "My birthday has come and gone and I'm supposed to be able to claim West Creek. If Nate doesn't go back on his word I'll start me a spread there. If he does I'll do something else—maybe follow the Triangle T to Colorado."

Gil straightened in the saddle. "He set those deeds up so there wouldn't be any squabbles between us after he's gone. You can take that land, I guess, and he won't renege. Not Pa. It's going to hurt him, but I reckon that's what you want to do."

"It's back pay—a bonus for all Nate has taken out of my life," Smoke said.

Gil started to reply, but Smoke did not wait. He

snapped at the bay's reins and sent the horse plunging down the slope toward the ranch house. It was possible, he thought, that he was going there for the last time.

After it was over, Smoke could not remember everything that happened in the house that day in exact sequence and detail. He had only an album of fragmentary pictures in his mind—blue veins bulging out on Nate Wylie's thick neck . . . a saber-like cane slashing the air and tapping nervously at the silver pitchfork above the fireplace . . . his own voice choking out bitter epithets—bully, range hog, wife-hater, and others that were petty and mean.

He remembered clearly the shocked stillness which fell over the room when he told Nate Wylie he wanted to claim his heritage on West Creek. It was then that his father seemed to give up the fight, an attitude of futility that Smoke had never seen in him before.

The big-boned rancher slumped in his chair. His frame appeared to shrink to half its size and his sun-bronzed face paled to an ashen pallor. He clasped his hands on the desk and stared at them for several seconds.

"That ain't a good thing to do right now." Nate's voice was so meek it unnerved Smoke. "You're breakin' up a family and you're breakin' up a ranch. I've been rippin' you up good lately, but by damn, you've had it comin'. We can work things out, get on good terms again, you and me. You can square yourself right now if you'll go to Jerry Mead and tell him you'll help build the dam back and—"

"I'm going to West Creek," Smoke cut in, "unless you plan to hold out on me."

The color returned to Nate's face and fires of anger shone in his walnut-brown eyes. His chest swelled and he started to rise from his chair, then relaxed and stared stonily at Smoke.

"If that's what you want that's what you get," Nate said. "Maybe it's the best thing for you—get out on your own and burn your own brand. I did it, and if you're the man you think you are, you can do it. We'll see some day how much of your own land you'll want to give up to squatters."

Nate turned and looked out the window, knots of muscle jumping along his jaw. Smoke saw a hard swallow ripple his father's throat before the rancher faced him again.

"If you don't aim to stick by the family I don't want you in it," Nate continued. "To show you how much I don't want you in it, by damn, I'll send Charlie Ray into Jackpine with a message for John Bastrop. Your deed'll be filed before sundown and that's the last thing you'll ever get from the Pitchfork. I ought not do that much, but it's somethin' your mother wanted me to do and I can't go back on it. Now get out of my sight!"

Silence gripped the room as Nate's words died in a hoarse rumble. He swiveled his chair around, deliberately turning his back on Smoke as he studied the papers on his desk.

Smoke left the parlor quietly. He had a strange feeling that he should be going on his tiptoes. He felt no sense of victory. His stomach was queasy and his hands were slick with sweat.

Chapter Seventeen

His room was the last one along the hallway which ended at the back door to the house. Smoke spread a tarp on the bedroom floor and gathered up the things he would need, laying out blankets, clothing, and a few utensils so they would fit evenly into a canvas pack only slightly larger than an ordinary bedroll.

At one point he paused and swung his glance around the walls, which were decorated with strings of Indian beads, a variety of flint arrowheads, a broken set of Spanish rowels, and other mementos of his childhood. He switched his gaze quickly back to the task at hand, determined that he would not be swayed by nostalgia. Fifteen minutes later he walked into the ranch yard with a pair of loaded saddlebags over one arm and the bulging bedroll slung across his shoulder.

Gil was sitting on a battered chopping block, ten feet from Charlie Ray Jones's kitchen door, idly drawing lines in the dirt with a double-bitted axe. He looked up, his glance taking in the saddlebags and blanket roll. A look of sorrow settled on his face.

"You can go in now," Smoke said. "It's all settled and I'm moving to West Creek."

Gil cleared his throat and lifted one arm in an awkward wave. "I'll stick by you if you want to try to square things with Pa. We're a family with the devil's own temper. We have to let it out sometimes, but we ought to rein it in before we hurt each other."

Smoke forced a laugh. "Nobody can hurt Pa. He's

above all that. He doesn't give a damn about me, or you, or anybody else—and not much of anybody gives a damn about him."

Gil's fist knotted on the axe handle and coppery flecks sparkled in his eyes. "You stay on the prod so much you can't see it, but he cares about us. Pa's a hard man and he's always going to be that way. He had to be tough to survive when he started out and he doesn't know how to change. If it wasn't for people like him Texas wouldn't exist and folks in the East would still be hungry for beef. He won't beg to you, but he doesn't want you to leave. Don't you remember how he used to show us off to folks in town and boast that two strong sons were worth more than all the grass in Texas? He hasn't changed. You've changed. Breaking up the family like this could be the thing that kills him."

"Don't worry about it," Smoke said. He shifted the bedroll impatiently.

Gil chewed at the corner of his lower lip. "You think I'm trying to work on your sympathy, but Pa's not as fit as he looks. Sometimes at night I hear him groaning like he's in pain or having trouble getting his breath. It's either that or he's having nightmares about our mother."

"I hope the devil's chasing him through his dreams," Smoke said. His face darkened. "It would serve him right because of the way he treated her. I can remember him yelling and swearing at her in their bedroom. She couldn't stand it anymore so she left. He ran her off. There's not a woman alive who'd put up with Nate's mean and stubborn ways."

"Don't you think you're getting a little too old to be

whining about your mother all the time?" Gil asked angrily.

"Yes, I am," Smoke said flatly. "I'm old enough to get along without her now, but I keep thinking my life would've been better if she'd been around. I was always lonely and ignored when we were growing up, but she'd have listened to my worries and helped me understand things. Maybe I'd like Nate as much as you do if she'd stayed, so it's his fault that I don't. He forced her out and I can't forget that."

"You don't know what you're talking about," Gil said. "It wasn't the way you think it was."

"Quit making excuses for him," Smoke snapped. "I know what I heard the last night she was home. Nate was yelling and cussing at her for an hour, then I heard him tell her to get out of the house and never come back. Don't tell me I don't know."

Gil stared at the ground and said, "You didn't hear the end of it. You always got scared and dived under the covers so you couldn't hear the noise. A few minutes after Pa told her to get out he was begging her to stay, but you don't see her around here, do you? You've always blamed Nate, but you don't know why things were the way they were."

Dropping his gear to the ground, Smoke swung around to face his brother. His throat felt full of the tears he had swallowed back as a child and his voice trembled.

"You're right," he shouted. "I don't know anything because nobody would tell me anything. Except for Pa's yelling, I don't remember much about our mother. I have a dim picture in my mind of her telling me stories before I went to sleep. That's not much, but most of all I remember how I felt the day after she left. I knew she left because she couldn't go on being badgered by Nate. If you know something I don't, you'd better tell me now or shut up."

Gil stood up and started toward the house, then turned and gave Smoke a long stare. He glanced toward the horizon, avoiding Smoke's eyes as he spoke.

"I'm going to tell you all about our mother," he said finally. "You were five or six and I was almost nine when she left. That's when she left for good, I mean. She'd been gone before plenty of times, but Pa tried to keep us too busy to notice. She'd usually come back after three or four days. That's when you'd hear Pa yelling at her, but my room was closer and I heard everything. He was mad because she wouldn't tell him where she'd been and what she'd been doing. They used a lot of ugly words that only scared me then, but made me sick when I was old enough to know what they meant."

Gil paused and spat between his teeth, then repeated the gesture, as though his mouth would not come clean. "Her name was Cora and she was beautiful. I guess that was the trouble. Pa used to tell her that every time a man looked at her she wanted him to keep looking until he saw all of her. Every fight got louder and uglier, then they had the brawl that ended it all. Their yelling woke me up, but it was old stuff by then and I didn't get up until I heard Pa sobbing. He—"

"Pa was crying?" Smoke asked, surprised.

Gil nodded, facing Smoke at last. "He sounded like somebody going out of their mind. I looked into the parlor and saw him holding her hand and pleading with her. He kept telling her she ought to stay with him for the sake of her sons, but she wouldn't hear to it. She said she wasn't happy with Nate and never would be. She talked about a man she'd met who lived the way she wanted to live, somebody who'd make a lot of money and take her places she'd never been—New Orleans, New York, and maybe to Europe. Pa apologized for ordering her to leave, but the more he begged her to stay the more she talked about the good life she was going to have. I heard her packing things, then she left."

Smoke tried to cough away the hot lump which choked his windpipe. He wanted to accept Gil's words with an indifferent shrug, but he could not put up such a bluff. It took him a few seconds to digest the story, then he felt sick with guilt. Every critical word he had spoken about his father, every argument, and every defiant act had been unfair, and it was too late for him to do anything about it.

Anger pushed away the sadness in Smoke's lead-gray eyes as he glared at Gil. "You can blame yourself for letting me break up with Pa. Our mother deserted us, she was unfaithful to Nate, and you figured I didn't have a right to know. So did Nate. I ought to break your jaw, and Nate's too, for keeping family business a secret all my life. What gave you the right?"

Gil stared at his hands. "Pa doesn't know I saw it or can remember it. He never told you for the same reason I didn't. We were ashamed and hurt. You had a picture in your head of a pretty woman and a good mother. Nobody wanted to take that away from you. Pa'd rather have you hate him than know the truth, but I knew I'd tell you some day when the time was right."

"And that's now?" Smoke sneered.

Gil sighed. "I didn't tell you when you were younger because I didn't want you to feel the pain I felt. Later on you changed, turned into a loner and hardly ever talked to me. You didn't need a family. You didn't need anybody and you were ready to fight anyone who tried to change you. You were going to whip the world all by yourself and make Pa see things your way or drive him out of his head. For the past year I've been afraid to tell you anything—afraid of what you might do."

"You should have told me," Smoke said.

"I'm telling you now because you're pulling out," Gil said, "and it's a bad time for it. Ever since you killed Jesse Slater I've had a gut feeling we're in for some kind of bad trouble and we'll need you here. Pa won't ask you to stay because he figures you don't think much of him if you'll let a girl like Ada Keller break up the family."

Smoke picked up the axe from the ground where Gil had dropped it and sank the blade into the chopping block. "It's not her fault so leave her out of it."

Gil appeared unruffled by Smoke's anger. He said, "Those people don't sit right with me. Pa sent Charlie Ray to town for supplies, and he says folks in Jackpine are plumb curious about the Kellers. He found out that Ada's moved back to the hotel and the other woman— her mother, I guess—has been renting a rig at the livery almost every day and doing a lot of riding. Poor squatters can be bothersome, but those with money to spend are dangerous. It usually means they're not riding their own saddle."

"I'm riding mine," Smoke snapped. "Things have gone too far to change. After the spring roundup I don't want any Pitchfork cattle on the West Creek range. It's mine and I'm going to start my own herd on it."

Gil did not raise his voice, but there was a bitter edge to it. "I hope Pa's past letting you tear him up, but if he has a stroke after this quarrel I'll be looking to settle things with you—and I'm likely to forget you're my brother."

Grabbing his saddlebags and bedroll from the ground, Smoke started toward the corral. After a dozen steps he stopped and looked back at Gil. "You're not afraid of anything. I know that, but don't ever get crazy enough to pull a gun on me."

At the corral Smoke picked out the two horses which had always been considered his own—the bay gelding and the black mustang. As he stepped into the bay's saddle, he swung a final glance toward the house. A bulky shadow moved quickly away from a window and Smoke knew Nate had been watching him. He rode away thinking of the story Gil had told him about his mother's last night at home.

West Creek came out of the earth in a spoon-shaped gulch about a three-hour ride northwest of the Pitchfork headquarters. It started as a gushing, pebble-paved spring at the base of Deadline Ridge, and was an impressive symbol of the power Nate Wylie had wielded in this territory for more than a quarter of a century. It was almost within sight of the more arid sheeplands beyond the hills, and the spring was a temptation to those who were often without enough water to raise livestock. Still, as far as anyone knew, no sheepman had ever violated the boundary established by Nate Wylie.

The only memory Smoke attached to the place was one of boredom and hard work during the winter weeks he had spent in the weather-worn line shack which perched on high ground where the walls of the gulch flattened out and merged into the prairie. Now that he was sure the sheepmen had not been involved in the killing of the Pitchfork yearling he had no reason to suspect danger there. It was this sense of security which caused him to be completely unprepared when the man tried to kill him.

Deep in thought, Smoke dismounted in front of the cabin in late afternoon. The emotional impact of the split with his father was still having its effect on him, filling him with misgivings and indecision.

Only his pride kept him from going home and trying to make peace with his father—pride and a deep-seated anger toward Gil and Nate for not telling him the truth about his mother. Nate had wanted to hold together what was left of his family, but Smoke had refused to be a part of it. For the first time, he admitted to himself that he had been a fool, but he did not know any way to change things. He had chosen his own trail and he would have to ride it to its end.

The end was perilously close there at the mouth of the

rocky gulch, but Smoke did not know it until he entered the line shack. His arms loaded with the saddlebags and blanket roll, he left the horses standing and kicked the door of the shack open with the toe of his boot. He left the door ajar, knowing the place would need airing out after being closed since the last cold weather. He dropped his belongings to the floor near the door and stood blinking against the gloom. His nose first told him something was not right and his eyes picked up other clues.

The sparsely furnished room, with its two rough bunks, a square table, and an iron stove, was filled with a strange odor. It was not the fragrance from the cedar and pine logs, but a scent which did not belong there and was vaguely familiar. Frowning, he started across the room to open the shutter over the single window. He had taken only a step when he saw the tattered blanket on one of the bunks. He stopped, nerves taut. Aside from the stamping of the horses outside the cabin was quiet, but Smoke knew he was not alone.

At that moment he heard a sound, the very faintness of it making it eerie. His back was toward the entrance to the small lean-to which joined the cabin at the rear. When the whimpering cry he had heard a moment earlier came again, he wheeled in that direction.

"Whoa!" he yelled. "What the hell is going on in—"

There was not time to finish the question. The burlap sack which curtained the doorway swished outward and a tiny white lamb dashed into the room. The animal's blocky head was lowered and its sharp-pointed hoofs rattled against the earthen floor as it ran into a corner behind the stove, still bleating. Now Smoke knew the source of the odor he had smelled, and he knew something else—the lamb had not found its way to the cabin by itself.

The man who had been hiding in the lean-to must have guessed the lamb had given him away. He came out like a madman, tearing the sack from its nails with his charge. One of his arms was upraised, and Smoke caught the gleam of a butcher knife in the man's hand.

Before Smoke could recover from his surprise the man was tearing at him with the other hand. Instinctively, Smoke threw a forearm upward to block the wrist which controlled the knife. He got his fingers on the man's arm, but the momentum of the charge carried both of them to the floor. Smoke rolled as they landed, struggling to get away from the knife. He was not fast enough. A fiery pain shot through his left shoulder and he heard the ripping of his shirt as the knife tore into him.

The burning pain nauseated him and he wanted to give up and lie still. One thought hammered at his mind, however, and kept him alert. The man was not fighting to escape; he meant to kill Smoke if he could. But why?

Because he was moving the blade did not go deep, but Smoke could feel the warmth of blood as it ran down his chest. He rolled again, rising to one knee, hoping to get to his feet before the man could catch him. His attacker was already in mid-air, diving at him. Smoke caught only a part of the man's weight, but it was enough to knock him back to the floor. Then the man was on top of him again, the knife slashing at the dirt floor as Smoke twisted and dodged.

Drawing up his knees, Smoke finally got his boots against the man's waist. He pushed with all his strength and the man went sailing away.

This time Smoke sprang to his feet. He stood crouched, waiting for the next onslaught. The other man was just as quick. Less than five feet away he was also crouched low, his knife hand thrust forward, and Smoke got his first clear look at him.

He was about Smoke's age and was lean and sinewy. He wore a pair of patched and faded brown moleskin pants and his blue cotton shirt was threadbare. Under other circumstances his face might appear delicately handsome, but now it was covered with a day's growth of beard and his lips were curled back like those of a cornered animal.

Without the knife in his hand Smoke would have had no fear of him. He had whipped bigger men more than once, but he had faced few who showed such fear and desperation. It was a time for caution. Smoke circled warily to the man's left, trying to read his next move. Keeping the knife ready, the man turned with him, his chest heaving nervously.

Smoke took a darting step forward, then retreated. He expected the man to slash at him, and he meant to slam a blow at his face while the arm was in a downward sweep. The intruder had other plans. He lowered his head, lunged at Smoke's legs, and knocked him off his feet again.

It turned into a battle for the knife and Smoke was on the deadly end of it. The man's first charge had dislodged Smoke's gun from his holster and it lay halfway across the room, far beyond his reach. He made the mistake of trying to scoot toward it, and this gave his attacker time to throw a forearm under Smoke's chin and hold him down. He got a leg across Smoke's chest and the knife was poised only inches from his throat.

Grabbing the thin wrist, Smoke tried to match his strength against that of his attacker. The man's forearm across his throat was cutting off Smoke's breath, weakening him. The point of the knife started a slow descent toward his neck.

Smoke threshed and kicked, trying to throw the man off. The knife blade inched closer. There was a look of wildness in the narrow blue eyes which glared down at him. A chill of fear skipped along Smoke's spine and his mind groped for a way to gain an advantage.

Almost accidentally, Smoke found the answer in his hand. He had been favoring that arm because of the shoulder wound, using it sparingly beneath him for leverage. His fingers scraped across loose dirt which had been torn from the floor by the man's wild stabs. He managed to get a handful of the gritty soil. He brought the hand from beneath him and flung the dirt into the man's face.

Startled, the man gasped, sputtered, and dropped the knife to wipe his hands across his eyes. Smoke slipped sideways, drew up his knees, and kicked the man solidly in the chest with the soles of his boots. The man sprawled backwards toward the doorway.

After that, the odds were reversed. Smoke grabbed the knife and went after him. He piled on top of the half-blinded man and pinned him to the floor. His narrow escape from death gave him a maddening sense of power and he had to fight off the urge to kill the man.

"I don't know what you've got against me, mister," Smoke gasped, "but whatever it is goes double for me."

He drew the knife threateningly over the man's throat, watching fear twist at the man's face. "Maybe I'll let you talk me out of cutting you up and maybe I won't, but you can try. Tell me who you are and why you're hiding in my cabin."

The man cringed, but he did not try to get away. He ran the tip of his tongue across his dry lips, swallowing twice before he found his voice. "Name—name's Walt Sanger," he stammered. "You can go ahead and kill me without playing games. I know it's coming. Everybody knows what's likely to happen to a sheepherder caught on Nate Wylie's land. Before my old man passed on he told me a dozen times I'd get myself killed if I ever got caught on the wrong side of Deadline Ridge without good reason. I've got reason enough, but you probably won't buy it. If you're going to kill me, for God's sake make it quick!"

Chapter Eighteen

Walt Sanger closed his eyes, and his body stiffened. Smoke stared for a few seconds at the tanned face and saw the color fade from it as the man waited to die. Walt Sanger was not pretending, and he was not begging favors. He had accepted what he believed was fate—that a cattleman would kill a trespassing sheepman as quickly as he would kill a preying wolf. In many parts of the West such things had happened and would happen again, but Smoke would not kill an unarmed man.

His anger subsided and he released his grip on the man. He rose and motioned Sanger to get up. For a few moments, the sheepman stayed on the floor and eyed Smoke suspiciously, expecting a trick. When Smoke walked across the room to put the butcher knife on the side of the stove where it belonged, Walt Sanger got to his feet. He brushed at his moleskins and tucked his shirt inside the waistband.

"Are you saving me for old Nate to take care of?" Sanger asked nervously.

Smoke shook his head. He inspected the torn place in his shirt, pulling the blood-soaked flannel away from the wound. The glancing blade had gone just below the skin, leaving a shallow cut. There was a rusty stain the size of a man's hand on the side of his shirt. The wound was not serious, but it was painful enough, to make it difficult for Smoke to forgive Walt Sanger's unprovoked attack. Sanger had been driven by an ingrained fear of the Wylies, however, and this seemed as much of a crime.

"My pa and I have parted ways," Smoke told the man. "I'm going to ranch this place myself, but the rules set by Nate go for me too. I won't stand for any crowding by you folks from across Deadline Ridge. You'd be smart to get your lamb and head back that way."

Walt Sanger glanced at the lamb, which had curled up under a bunk and was looking out with an animal's curiosity. "That would suit me fine, feller, but I don't have anything to go back to. All the land beyond the ridge is being bought up by a big outfit from back East, and most of us had to drift. Me, I was coming over this way looking for work. I was going to camp here for just one night, then head on into Jackpine. When you showed up I figured I was a goner."

Sanger picked up the hats which had fallen to the floor during the fight. He put his own broken-brimmed Stetson on the back of his head and tossed the other one to Smoke.

"The lamb's sort of a pet," Sanger murmured, "so I kept it when I signed an agreement to sell out. I guess it was a mistake to bring it with me. That's sort of like waving a red flag at a bull around here, I reckon."

"Something like that," Smoke said. Most cattlemen hated men such as Walt Sanger, and the damage their smelly, sharp-hooved herds could do to cattle graze. He could understand the desperation which had driven Sanger to attack him, and he found himself feeling sorry for the man. It was obvious that Sanger had never had much of his own, and now he had nothing.

Smoke slapped his hat absently against his palm. "Why don't you head out to another range while you've still got the money from your place? I hear Montana is good sheep country. If you like sheep you ought to stick to them."

Sanger shrugged. "I was just getting started and I didn't want to sell, but everything around me was going, and I knew I'd get squeezed out. All I got was a hundred-dollar down payment, with the rest to come at the end of the year. It wasn't much money and I had debts.

The money's gone and all I've got left is a lamb."

"Nobody has a right to take what's yours," Smoke said. "Why didn't you stick it out?"

The sheepman's face turned grim. "The same reason the little ranchers over here don't talk back to the Pitchfork. A few weeks ago a sweet-talking woman showed up at the sheep settlement. First thing you know all the big sheepmen are talking turkey with her, and she bought up a lot of land for the Denver & Chicago Livestock Syndicate. She sent the rest of us word that we could sell at her price or we'd run into plenty of trouble. We don't know how to fight people like that, so we sold."

Smoke's breath quickened. "Was she a black-haired little firecracker with violet eyes and a walk that—"

Sanger's laugh stopped him. "She runs to the heavy side and is pushing fifty, but she still has a way with men. Those old geezers were shining up to her and giggling like bashful boys while they got cheated."

Smoke felt relieved. Recalling Gil's suspicions, he had immediately turned his thoughts to Ada Keller when the sheepman mentioned a woman. He felt guilty for having such suspicions, but for some reason he had been reminded of the Kellers from the moment he began talking with Sanger.

"Who is this woman?" Smoke persisted. "You must know her name if she was signing papers for your land."

"It didn't work that way," Sanger explained. "She had a bunch of forms which had been fixed up in Chicago and signed by somebody called J. Aubrey Wentworth who's the president of the syndicate. All she did was fill in the blanks left for a name and how much money the land was to bring. She had a bag full of money, and handed out the down payments in cash. She said names didn't matter, she was just a messenger, but if we wanted to call her something we could call her Dallas Rose. Me, I didn't call her nothing."

"Funny way to do business," Smoke said. He stared thoughtfully at Walt Sanger. "You need a job and I know some folks who need help. Maybe I can put you onto something that'll earn you some grub money for a while."

"I sure need it," Sanger said.

"There's a family trying to get a start in Lost Horse Hollow," Smoke said, "and they've got a hard row to hoe. They'll have to do a lot of chopping and grubbing before they can clear enough land for crops. I figure they'd be glad to take on a hired hand. You ought to ride down there and check with them. Tell Dewey Keller that Smoke Wylie sent you."

While Sanger rolled the blanket he had left on the bunk Smoke gave him directions. His suggestion to the sheepman was not completely unselfish. He was willing to help the man, but he was more interested in letting Ada know he was still an ally. He volunteered to lend Sanger the mustang to speed him on his way. Sanger had walked across Deadline Ridge, but if he had to travel afoot and lead the lamb on a rope, it would take the rest of the day and half the night for him to reach Lost Horse Hollow. The mustang would get him there in a few hours.

Sanger had little to say until he was mounted on the

black and ready to leave. Stroking the lamb's coat as he held it across his lap, he looked down at Smoke with a baffled expression on his face.

"It's strange how a man can spend a lifetime with his head full of wrong notions," he said. "I've always figured every cowman was out to do me dirt. When I saw you riding up a while ago I was sure one of us would have to die. A man oughtn't to think so much of his own hide, then he wouldn't go wrong so easy."

Smoke looked away, his face solemn. He thought of his father, of his own wrong notions, and of the trouble which had been between them so long.

"Yeah, strange," Smoke said. "You were mighty quick about jumping a stranger, though. I could have been just another wandering cowboy looking for a place to sleep."

"I knew better," Sanger said with a dry laugh. "I've been in Jackpine a few times when you was in town and folks pointed you out to me. You've got a rep as a real heller, so I wasn't taking no chances."

Sanger looked away, shrugging as though embarrassed. "I won't steal your horse. I'll get it back to you whether I land a job or not."

Later that day Smoke felt he was being rewarded for the good deed he did for Walt Sanger, especially the loan of the horse. He spent most of the afternoon cleaning the cabin, determined to make the place livable despite the pain which the exertion brought to the knife wound in his shoulder. Afterward, he put a clean bandage on the cut, and stretched out on one of the bunks to take a nap. He was asleep almost at once, the weariness left over from the night before claiming him despite the plans his mind wanted to make.

He awoke with a start, staring blankly at the ceiling for a few seconds with the bewildered sensation of a man who has slept in unfamiliar surroundings. He was even more uncertain of his whereabouts when he looked toward the doorway and saw the figure of a woman silhouetted against the purple gloom of dusk.

"Hello," Ada Keller said. "I brought your horse back."

Smoke smiled, surprised and pleased to see her. His eyes caressed the supple lines of her body. She presented a picture of tantalizing beauty in a snug blue riding skirt and a bright yellow shirt which was unbuttoned low enough to reveal the soft valley between her breasts.

Her smile grew slowly from the corners of her mouth, reminding Smoke of a shy young girl arriving at her first party. There was a daring swing to her hips as she pushed the door shut behind her and came toward the bunk.

Before Smoke could move she sat down beside him, her fingers sliding along his bare torso before they came to rest next to the bandage on his arm.

"I want to thank you for sending Walt Sanger down to help us," she said softly. "He told us there was a fight, but he didn't say you were hurt." Ada appeared worried and concerned. "Is this a gunshot wound?"

"He got me with a knife, but it's not bad," Smoke said. He felt his skin tingle under her gentle touch, and a fever which had nothing to do with his injury began to warm his brow. "Sanger had a notion that everyone named Wylie had blood in his eyes, so he thought he had to kill or be killed."

Her dark lashes concealed the expression in her eyes as she stroked his chest. "I'm glad it didn't work out that way. We hired Sanger, and we're glad you thought of us. You didn't come to the hotel, so I used the horse as an excuse to come to you. I'm going to repay you for the favors you've done. I'm not very experienced, but I'm going to make love to you like you've never known."

She leaned close and pressed her lips against his in a brief, fiery kiss, then straightened again. She left the next move to him. His hand was trembling with desire as he slid an arm around her and started to draw her down on the bunk beside him.

She pushed his arm away, whispering, "Wait."

Standing, smiling at him, she unfastened the buttons of her shirt and tugged it from the waistband of her skirt. She turned her back toward him as she removed the shirt and dropped it on a wooden stool beside the bunk. Just as swiftly, she unfastened the skirt, stepping out of it and turning to show Smoke she had worn nothing beneath it.

In the gloom of the cabin her full breasts and flaring hips took on the sheen of a marble statue. Smoke waited breathlessly, but again she was hesitant. He feared she was about to reconsider her promise when she turned to look cautiously behind her. He could not control his impatience any longer.

He reached up to pull her back to the bunk. Just as his fingertips touched the silky bare skin of her waist a commanding voice came at him from the darkness outside.

"Don't put your hands on her or I'll blow your brains out," a man shouted. "You've been too good, my friend, and I had a hunch you were laying a trap for Ada. Now I've caught you at it!"

Smoke jerked his head around, searching for a face behind the voice. Across the room he saw a rifle barrel poking through the window he had left unshuttered while he slept. The blood which had been racing hotly through his veins a moment before seemed frozen there. A long leg slipped across the window ledge, then Dewey Keller was standing in the room with the rifle's sight lined on Smoke's chest.

For a few seconds Ada Keller stood as if paralyzed. She put her hands to her face, gasped faintly, then grabbed her skirt from the floor and wound it hastily around her naked body. With her other hand she scooped up the yellow shirt, spread it across her breasts, and darted for the sanctuary of the lean-to.

Watching Smoke warily, Dewey Keller struck a match and lit the lamp on the table. Aside from his tight-lipped mouth and flashing black eyes, he looked little like the man Smoke had met in Lost Horse Hollow. A black frock coat and striped moleskin trousers had replaced the bibbed overalls, and as he came closer Smoke smelled the odor of perfumed soap.

"Nothing happened here," Smoke said lamely. "It might have, but you showed up before—"

"Oh, but something did happen. Something bad." Dewey Keller's voice was calm, businesslike. "At least that's the way I'll tell it to Nate Wylie, or to whatever authority is necessary. Any father who looks in on what I just saw can make a good case in court, or be justified in shooting somebody in the gut. Sanger told me you

222

were starting your own spread, and I thought we might work out an arrangement which would be mutually beneficial."

He paused, shifting the rifle in his hands while he took a cigar from his pocket and settled it between his teeth without lighting it. He rolled it around with his tongue and said, "I began to see the possibility of such a deal after Ada left with your horse, so I decided to join her. It occurred to me on the way that you must have been scheming to have your way with her all along. From what I've heard, the Wylies don't do favors for strangers without wanting something in return. Still, I was hoping to find the two of you chatting like good friends. Instead, I find you've stripped her naked and raped her. That's the way it happened, my friend."

Smoke felt his pulse pounding in his head. Surprise and shock tightened his chest muscles so quickly his breath came in short gasps. He knew at once that he had fallen into a trap—a trap which was not only a threat to himself, but to Nate Wylie and the Pitchfork Ranch. Dewey Keller was deadly serious and Smoke could think of nothing to do except stall for time.

Drawing a deep breath, he said, "We both know you're lying about what you saw, but Ada did her part so well you'll be able to make some people believe it. I guess I'll have to listen to that arrangement you were talking about."

Keller's cigar stopped its nervous dance between his teeth. Again he shifted the rifle, and his eyebrows lifted speculatively toward the narrow brim of his townsman's hat. His expression did not change as a sound came from the lean-to, but Smoke felt a surge of anger as Ada Keller stepped back into the room.

Smoke waited for another outburst of fury from Dewey Keller as Ada, fully-clothed now, stopped a few paces in front of her father. Keller ignored her and she hurried past him and went outside.

"I drew up a contract just in case I found what I thought I'd find," Keller said after the girl was gone. "It was done rather hastily, but I think it will suffice. During my ambitious young days I read law for six months in the office of one of the brightest attorneys in New Orleans. I think you'll find the contract simple and in good order."

He took a folded sheet of parchment from his pocket and tossed it on the table beside the lamp. "While I was preparing the contract I anticipated it would take a great deal of persuasion to convince you that you'd need our capital to make your venture here profitable. Read the contract, then we'll discuss the matter of my daughter's good name."

Smoke did not miss the meaning of the man's words. Keller was warning him, holding a weight over his head. The man's indignation had all been a sham, feigned to frighten Smoke. The whole affair had been carefully planned and timed perfectly. Ada's promise of surrender had been too impulsive, too eager. She had hesitated after undressing because she knew her father was waiting outside, and she was giving him time to make his appearance.

Silently cursing himself for being so gullible, Smoke moved over to the table and picked up the paper. His glance strayed to the wall where he had hung his holstered Colt on a peg above the bunk before he went to sleep. His sympathy for the Kellers was replaced by hate. He would settle this dispute with a gun if he could get to it. His hands shook as he unfolded Dewey Keller's document and ran his eyes over the neat script.

His voice barely above a whisper. Smoke read aloud, *"I hereby agree that all land owned by Zack Wylie, also known as Smoke Wylie, shall provide graze for any and all livestock furnished by Dewey Keller and his associates for a period of five years, with profits from the sale of said livestock to be divided equally among the parties whose signatures are affixed hereto."*

Smoke dropped the document on the table and looked at Dewey Keller, his pale eyes hard and unreadable. Keller had a confident smile on his face.

"You couldn't do better and still protect Nate Wylie's good name, my friend," Keller said. "I think he'd find a way to get you off the Pitchfork and out of the county rather than be known as the father of a rapist. He's too proud of his reputation to let you drag him down, but when you throw in with me you'll be able to play as big a game as Nate Wylie."

"That's big talk for a dirt-farming squatter," Smoke said. "Where do you figure to get enough cattle to stock my range and make us both so rich?"

Keller chuckled. "I'm afraid I've deceived you. I borrowed some suitable apparel early on to throw folks around here off the track, but I'm not a dirt-farmer. I've got connections in Denver and Chicago—important connections. I'll get the cattle."

The explanation was not necessary. Smoke had closed his mind against the suspicions expressed by Gil and Nate, but now they were becoming facts.

When he first met Keller in Lost Horse Hollow, Smoke thought it odd that a man drifting in search of land could afford expensive cigars. He should have paid more attention to other signs. Keller had been unfamiliar with the pockets of his overalls, an indication that they were not his usual dress. Smoke knew now why his meeting with Walt Sanger had reminded him of the Kellers. Sanger smelled of sheep, and the musky scent was the same Smoke had noticed in Keller's clothing that day—clothing borrowed from a sheepman.

Smoke picked up the contract and scanned it again. He threw it on the table with disgust. "Maybe I'll call your bluff. What happens if I don't sign this thing?"

The tone of Smoke's voice brought a scowl to Keller's face. He sensed a change in Smoke's manner, and saw anger driving away the panic he had seen in him earlier. He jammed the cigar back in his mouth, and lifted the rifle for a steadier bead on the belt of the Levi's which Smoke had worn while he slept.

"You'll sign," Keller said grimly. "You don't want to face your father after I tell him what I saw. He'll run you off this range. I've been told he won't stand for anyone mistreating a respectable woman. You've ruined my daughter, and Nate Wylie won't be able to live with that."

"You're crazy as hell," Smoke snapped. "Nate won't believe I raped Ada just because you say so."

"Oh, I think he will," Keller said confidently. "It'll be

two against one because Ada will swear you forced her into bed at the point of a gun. We know a lot about you and your reputation with women. Folks will believe us."

Smoke was surprised by Keller's knowledge of the Wylie family. He said, "You're bluffing again. You haven't been in these parts long enough to know anything about me, or my pa, or anybody else."

"You're wrong, friend." Keller smiled smugly. "We've known a lot about the Wylies for years, and lately we've learned more. A year or so ago we ran into a friend of the Wylie family over in Bonner Flats—a fat little preacher man named Eli Pardee. We've made it a point to follow him around his circuit since then. I've never seen a man who gets more pleasure out of passing along gossip. He's told us how Nate Wylie feels about women, and how you've caused him no end of trouble. Pardee predicted you'd eventually split up the family, and it looks like he's a good judge of character. Your father will believe my sad story because he knows you. When Ada breaks out crying over how she's been ruined for any other man, and will never find a decent husband, that'll cinch it."

"Ada won't go that far, even if she did help you set—"

Smoke's words were cut short.

"Yes, I will." Ada had been listening outside the door and her throaty voice was clearly audible through the weathered boards. "It happened just like my father said. I came here to return your horse and you pulled a gun on me and—and made me do it with you."

Chapter Nineteen

The voice outside the door crushed Smoke's faint hope that Ada might back down if she had to tell her lies in front of strangers. He was disappointed, but not surprised. He had been as wrong about the Kellers as he was about his father. For years he had tried to act as his mother's avenger—the man who would cut Nate Wylie down to size. Nate had fought him all the way, challenging him with reprimands and threats, but had stubbornly refused to destroy Smoke's image of his mother to gain his loyalty.

Smoke's lips were dry and rough as he ran his tongue across them. He tried to calm his nerves so his mind would be clear while he searched for a way out of his predicament, but he could not stifle the rage which burned inside him. He glanced again at the holstered gun on the wall peg, then shifted his glance to the boots he had left beside the bunk.

His only thoughts were of his hate for Dewey Keller—the man who had deceived and betrayed him. He wanted to 'hurt the man, punish him—perhaps even kill him. It would be the quickest way to end Keller's grip on him.

His voice low, Smoke said, "I need to get my boots," and walked toward the bunk.

Keller nodded assent, swinging the barrel of the rifle around to follow Smoke's steps.

Smoke sat down on the bunk and pulled on his left boot, fiddling with the rolled cuff of his Levi's while he reached for the other one. When he had a firm grip on it, he slung the boot at Dewey Keller.

It hit Keller on the second button of his frock coat. The hard leather heel echoed against the man's belly with a hollow thud. Keller dropped the rifle, gagging and weaving as the wind hissed out of him. Smoke rushed at him, his fist cocked to smash Keller's face. He had a grip on the man's shirt front, ready to throw the punch, when a gunshot crashed through the room.

Smoke jumped backward, shuddering as splinters spewed from one of the logs at the back of the room.

"Now stand back, handsome, before my little old pistol has to make a mess out of you."

The voice was small and calm, but the woman who owned it was big and purposeful. She had shoved the door open just as Smoke launched his attack. She came into the room with smoke curling up from the small blued-steel gun in her hand.

"You didn't think I'd forget to bring a witness, did you?" Keller gasped. "I wanted her here for the official signing of our contract, but she's also an excellent shot."

Some color returned to Keller's face, but he was still having trouble breathing. He left the rifle where it had fallen, feeling secure with the protection of the woman's gun.

"For the frame-up, you mean," Smoke growled. "It's taken me a while to put things together, but now it all fits. You folks made a stop at the sheep settlement before you came to Jackpine. This is the woman Walt Sanger told me about—the one who calls herself Dallas Rose. She's the one who bought up the sheep

229

outfits for the Denver & Chicago Syndicate."

With the woman's sudden appearance, the reasons for the trouble which had dogged Smoke for weeks and threatened the Pitchfork became clear. He took his eyes off the woman and glared at Dewey Keller. "You've been working on this for a long time. It was you who hired Jesse Slater to kill that Pitchfork steer and try to lay the blame on the sheepmen. I had to kill Slater because of you. I didn't want to do that, but I could kill you pretty easy for what you've done to me and my family."

Keller shrugged. "Oh, well," he said, "we can't be right all the time. My conscience is clear about Slater. He just thought he was better with a gun than he was. Since we're going to be partners I don't mind saying you've got things figured out right. I was watching from the hotel window the day you shot Slater. I figured he was the kind who'd want to get even, so I tracked him down and made a deal with him. He wanted money, and he wanted to get back at you. It wasn't the best idea in the world, but it was worth a try. We figured Nate Wylie's neighbors wouldn't want any part of a range war, and we could buy them out cheap. That would give us a ring around the Pitchfork—a chance to surround Nate with sheep until he got sick of them, maybe beat him down until we could buy him out, too. Then we'd go back to cattle, which is where the D. & C. expects to make big money."

Smoke stared at Keller, amazed by the workings of the man's mind. "You were sure betting a lot on mighty slim cards."

"Maybe, maybe not," Keller said evenly. "My plan might have worked if Slater hadn't been fool enough to leave some kind of sign that led you to him. It doesn't matter now. With you as our partner we've got West Creek, and we can pursue our plans to bring Nate Wylie to our way of thinking. We've got a lot of ammunition to pester him with."

"You're a fool," Smoke said. "Nate might believe your story about Ada—probably will. Something that happened to him a long time ago makes him get crazy-mad if he hears of some man messing up a woman's life. He might run me off, but that won't make him give up. He'll see you in hell before any Pitchfork land falls into the hands of—"

The woman made a shushing sound with her lips. Smoke broke off the sentence and looked closely at her for the first time.

She sat down in a chair at the end of the table, the seams of the doeskin riding skirt threatening to part with the flattening of her heavy hips. Her skin looked satiny despite the glare of the lamp, but the paint on her face stood out like a rash. Her small, straight nose and gently curved lips were strikingly perfect, but time and extra pounds had rounded her cheeks and given her a small extra chin. Smoke guessed that she must be in her fifties, but her eyes were bright, youthful, and only the excess weight detracted from what had once been a striking beauty.

Meeting Smoke's glance, the woman grew still, staring at him with a far-away look in her eyes. Her lips parted in what appeared to be a friendly smile, then she

231

sobered abruptly, shaking her head as if to clear it of distracting thoughts.

She gestured with the pistol and said, "Now, y'all might as well stop your infernal quibbling and try to get along." She nodded at the contract Smoke had left lying on the table, her free hand toying with the fringe on her buckskin vest while she talked. "I'll also swear before your pa and all his neighbors that I saw you attacking that poor girl, handsome, and they'll believe me. It won't be like a hysterical mother talking, either. Ada is Dewey's daughter by an old marriage, and nothing much to me. My friend Preacher Pardee has told me how Nate feels about a woman's honor. He'll run you off his ranch and out of the country, sonny. That way you lose everything. Sign Dewey's paper and you'll have a pretty good future."

"Like what?" Smoke asked bitterly.

"Like a big chunk of the Jackpine range," she said. "This creek has got four or five spreads watering off it after it passes Circle M and turns east toward the upper forks of the Brazos. Put sheep up here and cattle will turn up their noses for miles. That'll bother Nate a lot. It'll get worse when he sees what's happening to his neighbors. We're going to build a dam across West Creek and cut off the water for the small ranches until we buy them out. You can share in the results, run things for the Syndicate. The D. & C. has wanted to put together a big ranch in this country for a long time. They couldn't figure a way to get at Nate Wylie until I managed to meet the head man and convince him I had a surefire plan."

The woman's sudden laughter startled Smoke. She tossed her hair back and giggled like a schoolgirl. She had every right to be pleased by the apparent success of their scheme, but her joy sounded forced and artificial.

The Deep-South lilt in her voice was flattened by harshness when she spoke again. "No man has ever got the best of Dallas Rose, handsome, and I've never played for a bigger stake. Dewey and I have a deal with D. & C. which pays us a big commission if we lock in any part of the Pitchfork. I don't fancy walking away empty-handed when the payoff is this close. Sign the paper and you won't be nearly as sorry as you will if you don't."

His arms hanging limp at his sides, Smoke stared at the floor and considered his choices. He could sign Keller's paper, ride out of the country, and try to start a new life, leaving a blot on the family name which would tear at Nate's heart. That was a coward's way out, and Smoke would not take it. His other option was to sign the contract, stay here to share in the profits expected by the D. & C. Syndicate, and remain alienated from his family. Smoke did not like either choice.

Dewey Keller helped him make his decision. Smoke had been watching him from the corner of his eye. Keller shuffled his feet nervously. A fiery light danced in the man's eyes and Smoke sensed that Keller was running out of patience. His changing mood was more dangerous than Smoke expected. Keller suddenly scooped the rifle from the floor and stalked across the room. His hands were shaking and his body trembled. The muscles in his face twitched uncontrollably and his voice was unusually loud.

"I've been a gambler most of my life, but never won big or made a real stake out of anything. I've got a pat hand this time, and I'm not going to give it up, so you'd better listen good, Smoke Wylie."

Keller drew a ragged breath and wiped his left hand across his mouth. "I've got witnesses here to work in my favor. If you don't like our first version we can tell what happened another way, but you won't be around to hear it. We can say I came up here, found you in bed with my daughter, and lost my head. Before I knew what I was doing, I blew your brains out with this rifle. Dallas Rose was with me and saw the whole thing. I'll kill you before I'll leave without anything. Even with you dead, Nate Wylie would want to compensate me for the damage you've done to my daughter. He'd want to pay me off, and get me out of town."

The butt of the rifle tightened against Keller's shoulder and he screeched, "I'm not going to wait much longer before I pull this trigger!"

Keller edged closer, stopping with the bore of the rifle a foot from Smoke's chin. He had spilled out the truth about a life of failure and greed, and the fire in his eyes convinced Smoke the man was not bluffing.

Eyeing the man uneasily, Smoke sat down at the table and reached for the contract. Dallas Rose rummaged through her handbag, finally placing a quill pen and a small vial of ink in front of him. Smoke signed the contract, and afterward he felt sick at his stomach.

Keller snatched the document away from him and

retreated a few feet. He sighed like a man who had just finished a hard day's work.

He was immediately relaxed. "Now that our business is settled," he said, "we might as well be civilized. I'll want to stop by tomorrow on my way across Deadline Ridge to tell the herders they can drive some sheep down here. I need to outline the rest of our plans for you. After we have that straight, we'll get out of your hair. In a few days D. & C. will send down an executive to work with you. By that time Dallas Rose and I will be on our way to Chicago to collect our fee. What time do you want to talk?"

"Early," Smoke said tightly. "Make it sunup."

Keller nodded, smiling at Dallas Rose as she rose and moved toward the door. Before he went outside Keller turned and studied Smoke's face. His voice again assumed the oratorical tones which had impressed Smoke at their first meeting as he said, "It is indeed sad to leave a man of your stature with his vanity bruised and his ego crushed, so I'll pass on to you an ameliorating truth. Ada's on the verge of falling in love with you, and I fear she would've come to your bed quite willingly if I had not been around to insist that our business arrangement was the first priority."

Ignoring the man, Smoke dropped listlessly into a chair, barely aware of the sound the door made as it closed behind the Kellers. Somewhere outside an owl began its doleful night cry, and far back in the hills a coyote bayed. A field mouse crept out from the lean-to and stopped at the edge of the circular shadow cast by the lamplight. Smoke stared at its furtive eyes, thinking he must have resembled it while he stood gazing into the open bore of Dewey Keller's rifle.

Even as he obeyed Dewey Keller's demands, Smoke had silently made plans for the future. He would track down Dewey Keller, he decided, hold a gun on him, and tear up the contract he had signed. If Keller put up a fight Smoke would kill him.

Alone in the silent cabin, he discarded the plan as foolhardy. Ada and Dallas Rose would remain as witnesses against him, and Smoke was not cold-blooded enough to kill them all. His mind toyed with other notions. He could saddle the bay and start drifting, perhaps follow the Triangle T to Colorado, and let Nate settle things with Dewey Keller.

The idea of running away held momentary appeal for him, but in only a few seconds Smoke began to see himself as others would see him—a troublemaker and a coward, a man who had betrayed an innocent girl and his own father, and then run away while others fought his battles.

"I'll be damned if I'll do that," Smoke said fiercely. He did not realize he had spoken aloud until the field mouse scurried back into the lean-to, rattling the firewood stored there.

He got up after a while and retrieved the boot he had thrown at Dewey Keller. He stepped into it, stamped it firmly into place, and kept walking, pacing back and forth between the window and the bunk.

Smoke could swear to the empty cabin that Ada Keller was responsible for all his troubles, but he could not convince himself. It was difficult to feel hate for her, but he could hate himself for being weak enough to be swayed by the physical charms of a woman he hardly knew. A cautious, down-to-earth man like Gil would have spotted Ada for what she was—a scheming woman whose virtue held little value, even to her father.

Dewey Keller and Dallas Rose had struck their bargain with considerable ease. Only in recent years had the money men of the East—mostly bankers and railroad tycoons—realized that the ownership of cattle lands in the West could add to their fortunes. Numerous groups had pooled their resources to form syndicates, and many of them had eyed the Pitchfork as the key to taking over most of the hill country range. Smoke had been too concerned with his personal vendetta to pay much attention to Nate's indignant threats and curses when he received mail from them. Now Nate's concerns had become reality. With one of the Pitchfork creeks under its control, other territory would be easy prey for the Denver & Chicago Livestock Syndicate.

Smoke had unwittingly paved the way for them. His meeting with Ada Keller in Lost Horse Hollow had not been as much of an accident as it had seemed at the time. She could not have been sure she would meet him, but she had been in Lost Horse Hollow to attract the attention of one of the Wylies. Apparently Ada had spent enough time at the sheep settlement beyond Deadline Ridge to talk with some of the young women there, and Gil probably sounded attractive. It was clear to Smoke, however, that the information the Kellers had gleaned from Eli Pardee had set him up as the ideal target.

Smoke had reacted as they expected, risking the loss

of Hetty Mead's love in the process. The loneliness which gripped him as he thought of Hetty made him conscious of how much he regretted that loss.

Finally, Smoke stopped pacing long enough to put on his shirt. He winced as the sleeve dragged over the bandage on his shoulder. The wound was deeper than he had first thought, and he cursed the pain the pressure of the shirt aroused. It might have been better, he thought, if Walt Sanger's knife had found a vital spot. He had survived a sheepherder's crazed fear of a cattleman only to face a worse threat written in a few lines on a sheet of paper.

The words of the contract did not detail its true intent. Smoke was sure he would never share any profits from the agreement if he remained there as the syndicate's partner. It would be too risky to have him underfoot, and some kind of accident or an outright murder would be arranged. That would leave the D. & C. a free hand. He ran over the words of the contract in his mind. It was difficult to believe a document so brief could tie his hands completely.

Swearing under his breath, Smoke strode across the room and lifted his gun from the wall peg. He strapped it on and headed for the door, his heart racing with apprehension. He had searched his mind for answers to his troubles and he had found none. He had prided himself as a loner, a man who tackled the world head-on, did as he pleased and refused to answer to anyone, but he could not win alone against Dewey Keller.

Smoke needed help and he could think of only one place to find it. He could not remember the last time he had asked for his father's help, but he needed to talk with Nate Wylie. He needed to admit he had been a fool for allowing Dewey Keller and Dallas Rose to capitalize on his weaknesses, but he also needed to tell Nate that some of his old weaknesses had turned to strength—that he had not realized how important the Pitchfork and his family were to him until both were threatened.

One way or another, this had to be a Pitchfork fight. Smoke could not live with the possibility that his friends and neighbors would be drawn into a live-or-die range war because of him. It would not be hard for him to say such things to Nate—but would Nate listen?

A dozen feet from the cabin door Smoke found the black mustang Ada had returned, its reins trailing. He led it to the pole corral behind the cabin and roped out the bay gelding.

He swung into the bay's saddle, pointed its head toward the Pitchfork, and put the horse into a gallop. Before daylight he would be back at the line shack— either alone or with Nate and Gil at his side. He was not sure which way it would be, but Dewey Keller was in for a fight.

Chapter Twenty

Nate Wylie's hulking frame made the small line shack look crowded, even though his two sons were the only other persons present. The rancher sat on a wooden stool in the center of the floor, his face creased in a frown, his best black Stetson pulled down close to his shaggy eyebrows. Gil Wylie lounged on the bunk a few feet to his

father's left, one leg propped on a chair while he whit-
tled methodically on a cottonwood stick. Smoke stood
to the right, his eyes squinted as he peered through a
crack in the shuttered window.

"Here they come," Smoke said presently. He shaded
his eyes with one hand as the sun's first rays struck the
shack. "Right on time."

"Who's going to talk for us?" Nate asked quietly.

Gil stopped whittling and shoved his knife into the top
of his right boot. "I'm just here to watch—and wait until
I'm needed."

"You do the talking, Pa," Smoke said. Nate squared
his shoulders, pleased at Smoke's show of respect.

There was no further planning to do. A knock sounded
at the door, and Smoke moved back to stand across the
room from Gil, their father between them.

Smoke said loudly, "The door's open," and Dallas
Rose came inside, bringing a scented wave of perfume
with her. She wore a green wool riding skirt, topped by
a tan satin blouse which glistened across the bulge of her
heavy bosom. Her dimpled hands clutched a leather
handbag, which she almost dropped when she saw
Smoke was not alone in the cabin.

Dewey Keller, his cigar trailing a thin plume of
smoke, was a step behind her. Dallas Rose stopped so
abruptly that Keller bumped into her, almost causing her
to lose her balance. She seemed unaware that he had jos-
tled her or of Keller's instinctive apology. She was too
busy staring at Nate Wylie, her mouth open, the color
fading from her face.

Nate Wylie broke the silence. He rose slowly, pushing

his six-foot-three frame to its full height. His voice was a hoarse rumble when he said, "Howdy, Cora. It sort of knocks the wind out of a woman when she sees her husband for the first time in seventeen-eighteen years, don't it?"

"I—I sure enough didn't fancy seeing you here," she stammered. "I thought Smoke would be too scared of your awful temper to bring you into this until it was all finished and I—I was out of the county."

"Well, you never did understand the Wylies, Cora," Nate said. "Of course the boys were too little for you to know how they'd turn out, but we hang together in a tight fix. When Smoke rode in last night to tell me about the mess he was in—how the woman in the deal knowed about the ranches which feed off of West Creek, where it went and where it emptied into the Brazos, I figured it was somebody who knowed a lot about the Pitchfork. Then he told me that paper he signed included his real name, Zack, and that was a dead giveaway. We've been callin' him Smoke since he was a splinter, and hardly anybody hereabouts knows his borned name. Puttin' everything together, I wasn't fooled none by that name you're usin'. I didn't want to say anything to Smoke until I was sure, but I had a hunch I'd find you here today."

The muscles in Smoke's legs felt limp, and he wanted to sit down. He watched Nate Wylie chew at the uneven strands of his mustache, heard the woman's stunned gasp, and he began to remember things which had been of no interest to him earlier.

Keller had told him the woman was ill, confined to her

room at the hotel. One of the Pitchfork riders had told Gil later that she slipped out of town occasionally for long buggy rides. Those rides were along the wagon road which led to the sheep settlement, Smoke guessed, where she continued to make deals for more land. But she had not mingled with the residents of Jackpine, afraid Ben Toler or some other old acquaintance would recognize her.

"Good Lord," Smoke mumbled. "This woman's been calling herself Dallas Rose, so I never would've made any connection—"

"She's had a lot of names over the years," Nate said. "Fancied herself as one of them show people, always changin' names. She was singin' in an Abilene saloon under the handle of Rebel May Rainey when I met her. Out of a Memphis family, she told me. Maybe I was fooled by her just like you was by that Ada filly. I was too taken by what I saw on the outside and didn't look hard enough at the kind of woman she was inside."

For a dozen long breaths, Dallas Rose said nothing. She swayed slightly, as though she might faint, and seemed to want to do something with the heavy handbag in her hands. She recovered her composure quickly.

"I never guessed you'd get so almighty rich, Nate," she said, "or I might have stuck it out. You just don't understand women like me. I wanted to be needed, to be some man's partner and work along with him. I wanted to learn to ride broncs, to rope a calf or doctor sick cows—be a real ranch wife. You just had me for decoration, like a pretty picture on the wall. All you did was hover over me like an old mother hen, loving me to death and doing anything I asked. What I needed was a man to shove me around some, make me do things that would keep my mind alive. I hated to leave my boys, but you were tiresome company, Nate. You were too jealous to let me out of your sight. I was dying. . . ."

A wan smile passed over her face and she toyed with the handbag. "A few years after I left, after I gave Ben Toler the dodge, I began hearing tales about how the Pitchfork was an empire. I started grieving over things I could have had—good clothes, jewelry, a big fine house, and money to spend. You were mostly just paying debts when I was around."

"I know," Nate said. "I wanted to make up for that. That's why I had Ben Toler and other people tryin' to get a line on you."

"So I heard." She lifted her hands and shrugged. "That fool Preacher Pardee has been looking me in the face off and on for two years, asking me to help him find a woman named Cora Wylie. I wanted something from Pitchfork, Nate, but I didn't want you hounding me. My little old brain kept searching for a way for me to get my hands into your pocketbook without having to take you with it."

"You sure ain't one to build a man up much," Nate growled.

"I really don't like you much, Nate," she said. "I'm sorry I hurt you, but I was scared when I learned how hard you were trying to find me. I thought you might have me killed for running out on you, but I kept looking for a way to get my hands on some money. The answer finally came to me. I remembered what a fool you were

243

over the boys, how you'd put the land around the creeks in trust for them. After that I just waited until they were old enough to claim their deeds, and then started making proposals to the syndicates. The Denver & Chicago crowd took me up, so Dewey and I started praying that one of the boys had turned out a little wild, and would do most anything to get his hands on a woman with the kind of face and body that Ada has. Eli Pardee told us enough about Smoke to let us know he was the one to work on."

"You had Smoke so scared of me it almost worked," Nate said. "He didn't know I'd never believe a word of your tale, mainly because Smoke don't have to force any woman to go to bed with him. Most of 'em would chase him down for the chance."

"It did work," Dallas Rose corrected. "We've got ourselves a sweet little contract and I don't think even the mighty Nate Wylie will want to stand up in court and fight it. Not with what we can say about Smoke."

Dewey Keller had remained in the background, his eyes shifting from one face to another while he tried to judge the significance of Nate Wylie's presence. He stepped forward now, holding the folded contract upraised in one hand like a victory flag.

The thin smile which pulled at Nate's mustache was one of defiance. "I reckon that's the paper which says you can graze stock on any land Smoke owns or controls."

"That's right, Mr. Wylie," Keller said triumphantly, "and it's as legal as money."

"Sure it is," Nate said. "Only trouble is, Smoke ain't

got no land. He sold it back to me."

The rancher pulled a soiled tally book from his back pocket and slapped it against his thigh. "This don't look so official, but there's a piece of writin' in here signed by Smoke and witnessed by two of my cowhands. It says he's transferred West Creek back to me for one dollar, paid in hand. Now, where do you aim to graze them sheep?"

"It's still a contract on West Creek," Keller snarled. "You'll have to honor it just as he would."

"You're bad wrong, Keller," Nate growled. "You left somethin' out of your paper. When I was puttin' the Pitchfork together, I had to have about a dozen deeds written from folks who had give up their land and pulled out. I learned there's somethin' all good lawyers write in deeds. It has to do with what they call 'heirs and assigns,' meanin' deals have to stick when land changes hands. You left out that part when you wrote your contract. This is my land and, by damn, I'll kill you if one woolly hoof ever touches it."

"Stupid!" Dallas Rose's voice was choked with fury. "You're so slick and educated, Dewey—so smart you think you can outwit everybody, but you always fall flat on your face. Why in the world did I ever believe your big talk about the great life you could give me?"

Nate took his seat on the stool again. He picked up his cane, pointed it first at Dewey Keller, then at Dallas Rose, and told them to get out of his sight, off his range.

"One thing you'll learn when you're as old as I am," he stormed. "Don't try to brand a calf if you don't

245

know how to hold the iron or you'll get your hands burned."

Dewey Keller's astonished breath sounded like a death rattle in the stillness of the room. He let his hands drop to his sides and turned a forlorn look toward Dallas Rose.

"Looks like he's got us with that loophole," he said. "Maybe we'd better get out while we can, Rose. I wouldn't be surprised if he has a band of armed cowhands standing by to lynch us. He could claim we're trespassing."

The woman's movements were jerky. She appeared to agree, half-turning toward the door. It was a deceptive gesture. The leather bag in her hand flipped open and Dallas Rose whirled with surprising swiftness. She had the blued-steel pistol in her hand, the sight lined on Nate Wylie's head.

"Don't either of you big hellions move," she warned, shifting her eyes between Gil and Smoke, "or you'll just rush the funeral."

Her bosom rose and fell with her heavy breathing, and the gun began to shake in her hand. "This was the only big money I've ever had a chance at, Nate, and you've taken it away from me. The syndicate was going to pay us ten thousand dollars—enough for us to live good for a long time. We've spent all their expense money, and we're flat broke."

As she continued, her words came faster, distorted by tears. She shouted a curse at the man who once had been her husband. "I'm going to kill you, Nate. It's the only thing that'll make me feel good. Everything's all messed up, but I'm going to kill you, and get all the regrets out of my mind."

She meant it. Since leaving Nate Wylie she had heard much about his wealth and power while her own dreams of adventure and excitement with Dewey Keller had ended in failure. Her hate was fueled by the knowledge that she could have shared in the wealth and prestige of the Pitchfork had she remained faithful. Frustration and failed hopes had twisted her mind, and killing Nate Wylie to make sure he would not enjoy the success she had abandoned was the only answer she could find for her own misery.

The rancher could read these thoughts in her face, but he made no move to stop her as she moved toward him in slow, menacing steps. He stared at the gun, a film of sweat spreading across his forehead. Once he shook his head sadly from side to side, but otherwise he was motionless.

When Dallas Rose was less than five feet from Nate Wylie Smoke cast a hurried glance at Gil, wondering desperately what they could do. Gil was on his feet, crouching with a hand spread above his gun butt. Smoke could understand why Gil was frozen in indecision, because their thoughts had to be the same: Their father was about to die, and although she was a stranger to them, they could not escape the thought that the woman threatening to kill him was their mother.

Even to protect his father, Smoke found it hard to consider drawing his Colt and shooting her before she could fire the pistol. It was a trait of human nature, and he hoped it ran as deeply with her as it did him.

Smoke made a gamble of it, calling frantically, "Ma, you'll have to shoot through me if you want to put a bullet in Pa."

The interruption stopped her. Her eyes were fixed in a vacant stare and she appeared to be listening to far-off voices. Her hesitation gave Smoke time to reach his father's side, then step around in front of him. Dallas Rose looked confused, but she kept a firm grasp on the gun, its sight now lined on Smoke's chest. Her finger tightened on the trigger, but Smoke never knew whether or not she would have shot him.

While she was distracted Gil moved away from the bunk. Before she had time to react he grabbed her wrist and shoved her gun hand toward the roof.

Despite her size, she was not clumsy, and she was strong enough to put up a struggle. She fought Gil for control of the pistol, and when she saw she was losing the battle she screeched, "Don't just stand there like a fool, Dewey. Use that gun!"

Smoke had almost forgotten the dark-eyed gambler. Keller had not carried his rifle on this trip, and Smoke assumed the man was unarmed, but Keller was only waiting for Dallas Rose to play out her hand.

Wheeling away from the grappling couple, Smoke turned his glance in time to see Dewey Keller's right hand dart into the side pocket of his frock coat. Keller had a head start on him, and his hands were quick. Smoke heard the thunder of exploding gunpowder in his ears, saw smoke and flame bursting around Keller's short-barreled derringer. An instant later Keller was on the floor, clutching his right shoulder with a bloody hand.

Smoke took a step toward the man, his heart pounding. His own gun was in his hand, and the room echoed with the roar of an exploding shell. With hardly a conscious effort he had drawn and fired, and his slug had found its mark. A chill shook him as he swung his eyes around and saw the bullet hole in the wall behind him. It seemed impossible that he was still alive, and that the cabin was so quiet in the wake of so much noise. Nate Wylie had remained on the stool, but Gil stood beside him now, a leveled gun in his hand. In front of them was Dallas Rose, her head bowed on her breast, her shoulders shaking with dry sobs.

"Get some kind of bandage on Keller to stop the bleedin', Smoke," Nate Wylie instructed calmly. "I want him and this good partner of his to be ridin' as soon as that's done."

Dewey Keller squirmed to a sitting position, the shock of the bullet which had torn across his shoulder showing in his ashen face. He said shakily, "I thought things went too easy, and I was afraid we'd be challenged in some way, but Rose was dead certain Smoke wouldn't dare tell his old man he was in trouble over a woman. I've still got a hole card—one that'll win this hand. If you'll take a look outside, gentlemen, you'll see I've got a man with a rifle covering this room."

Keller's voice grew stronger as he shouted, "Give them one minute to throw down their guns, Sanger, and about ten seconds for the old man to tear up that tally book. If they don't move fast enough, I want you to kill the first man I point my finger at. We're going to collect that ten thousand dollars one way or another!"

Smoke drew a deep breath and exchanged glances with Gil and Nate. He nodded, indicating that Keller was probably telling the truth. If Walt Sanger had been keeping under cover nearby, awaiting a signal from his new boss, the sound of gunfire would have drawn him to the cabin. The grim expressions in the eyes of Nate and Gil told Smoke they were going to fight it out, but their chances were not good.

Fear crinkled the hairs along the back of Smoke's neck. A hidden man who knew how to trigger a rifle with accuracy could kill them before they got a clear shot at him. Dewey Keller could still deliver the grazing agreement to the D. & C. Syndicate if there were no witnesses left to dispute it.

Walt Sanger made his presence known almost immediately. Before he came inside, however, he shouted, "I ain't got no gun, folks. I left Keller's rifle back a ways with the horse he loaned me."

The sheepman stepped through the doorway and stopped with his hands dangling at his sides. An uneasy grin spread across his lips. "I need work bad, and I'm a fair shot with a rifle, but nobody can hire me to do their killing. I didn't aim to work long for these folks anyway. When I got to Lost Horse Hollow I found the woman who'd been buying up our land. Right then I decided I'd play along for a while and see what I could do to throw a hitch in their scheme. She didn't even remember my face. She looked at me like I was dirt, and started giving me orders. I could tell from what I heard through the door that something shady was afoot here, and I don't aim to help them pull no deals like they pulled on me. After this I'll probably never be able to make a living around here, but—"

"You'll make a livin', mister," Nate Wylie cut in. "Once the syndicate finds out Keller and Cora spent a lot of money and didn't even get a little slice of the Pitchfork, I figure they won't care much for that land across Deadline Ridge. They'll want you to take your sheep land back before they have to pay you for it. In the meantime, I'll see you get along. Head out for the Pitchfork and wait for me there."

Sanger hesitated only long enough to make sure Nate Wylie was sincere. Smoke told him he could ride the mustang back to the ranch, and Sanger left without looking at Dewey Keller's bewildered face.

After the sheepman was gone, Nate Wylie walked to the window, opened the shutter, and looked out over the sunlit prairie. He had his back to Dallas Rose, and Smoke knew he would remain that way until she was gone.

Smoke did what he could to hasten her departure. He found a clean cloth on a shelf above the stove and tossed it to Dewey Keller so he could attend to the gunshot wound himself. Afterward, he emptied the shells from the woman's pistol and Keller's derringer, handed the weapons to them, and went to stand beside Gil while the couple walked out of the cabin.

As the sound of creaking saddle leather drifted inside, Nate Wylie turned away from the window, and Smoke felt a lump in his throat. Nate's eyes were moist and a tear slid down the rancher's left cheek.

Half an hour later, Nate Wylie and his sons saddled their horses and rode toward the Pitchfork. The affair at the cabin was a matter not easily discussed—an experience which had cut deeply at Nate Wylie's emotions and left Smoke and Gil with an unexpected sadness. They rode in silence until some of the tension had worn off.

After a while, Nate drew his horse to a halt and his sons pulled alongside. The rancher took the tally book from his pocket and ripped out the page which had been used to record his agreement with Smoke.

"I'll give you this back if you'll give my dollar back," Nate said. "Our deal's off."

Reaching across his saddle, Smoke took the paper and dropped a silver dollar in Nate's palm.

As far as I'm concerned it's still up to you to say what happens to West Creek," Smoke said.

"Not anymore," Nate replied. "You've earned your right to it. I never could get close to you, never could figure what was goin' on in your head. Last night I learned something. In spite of your ornery ways you believe in your pa, and I still believe in you. That's all I need to know. I figure I won't have to worry about somebody tryin' to get the upper hand on us again."

Smoke shifted his weight in the saddle and tugged at his hat brim while he struggled with his pride again. After a moment he said, "If it's all right with you I'd like to go on back home, and leave West Creek as it is for a while. There's some things I need to do before I set out on my own. I was thinking about taking the day off to handle some personal business."

From the corner of his eye, he saw Nate's back stiffen. The rancher's cheeks reddened and his breath came out in an impatient hiss.

"Stayin' on at the Pitchfork suits me fine," he said, "if you're willin' to act right. It looks like you're already headin' back to your old ways. By damn, I've got no more secrets to hide, and if you live on the Pitchfork you won't be spendin' time in Jackpine with them saloon girls or drinkin' and fightin' and throwin' your gun around. If you think you're gettin' the day off so you can celebrate gettin' out of that scrape with the Kellers, then by damn, you can—"

"Whoa, Pa, whoa!" Gil interrupted. "Give him a chance to tell us about this personal business before you take his hide off."

Smoke looked at Gil and heaved a sigh of relief. He turned toward his father, a sheepish grin on his face. "What I wanted to do was to ride over to the Circle M and have a long talk with Hetty Mead. When she gets over her mad spell I'm going to ask her to marry me. I've always loved her, and I'll need her with me when the time comes for me to move to West Creek. She'll see that I do what I'm supposed to do."

Nate Wylie relaxed. He stared at Smoke a moment, then swung his glance briefly toward the trail Dewey Keller and Dallas Rose had taken when they rode away.

"You're gettin' plumb smart today, son," he said. "I need to do some fence-mendin' myself. I need to get down to Jackpine pretty soon and have a talk with Ben

Toler, let him out of an old promise he made to me."

He shook his head sadly. "I'm real glad I saw Cora again before I cash in my chips—glad I finally learned how she feels. I can put her out of my mind, and change my will. I was savin' Middle Creek for her. I thought it might bring the three of you together again when I was gone, but she'll never come back. She's got what she bargained for."

"And you?" Smoke asked softly.

Nate squared his shoulders and thrust out his chin. "Me? I've got my land—got my sons. Maybe some day I'll have grandchildren, and then I'll know what to do with Middle Creek."

Smoke chuckled, feeling at ease with his father for the first time in years. He said, "I'll just swing south from here and head for the Mead place."

Nate's voice stopped him. "Not so fast. In my time we did our work by day and our courtin' at night. You can go to the Circle M when the day's over if you want to, but right now we've got a roundup to worry about."

Gil laughed out loud. "You should have known better."

"Ain't that the truth!" Smoke said, and the three of them started their horses moving toward the Pitchfork.

Center Point Publishing
600 Brooks Road ● PO Box 1
Thorndike ME 04986-0001 USA

(207) 568-3717

US & Canada:
1 800 929-9108